I Shall Not Want

Also by the Author

The Lord Is My Shepherd, Book One in The Psalm 23 Mysteries

I SHALL NOT WANT

The Psalm 23 Mysteries

Debbie Viguié

Abingdon Press fiction
a novel approach to faith
Nashville, Tennessee

I Shall Not Want

*To Peggy Hanley for all her support
and encouragement*

Acknowledgments

As always there are so many people I need to thank.

Thank you to Barbara Scott,
a fantastic editor and cheerleader.

Thank you to Donna Lewis and everyone
at Alive Communications.

Thank you as well to Michael Mueller, Amanda Goodsell,
Delia Valentin, and Laurie Aguayo, who have cheerfully
read my books and been there for me.

Finally, my most fervent thanks to Calliope Collacott
for all your help in the eleventh hour.

1

Cindy Preston loved Fridays. Anything-can-happen Fridays was how she liked to think of them. As they neared the holidays and First Shepherd church became a center of activity, Fridays became even more deserving of their name. Being a secretary at a church was a far more chaotic job than most people imagined.

For Cindy, the job had turned even more exciting several months earlier when she had stumbled across a dead body in the church sanctuary. The week that followed had seen many people murdered by a serial killer, one whom Cindy had helped stop.

For a couple of months afterward, the church had seen a large swell in attendance as people wanted to come gawk at the woman who had survived attack by the Passion Week killer and had helped the police turn the tables on him.

Their interest had gradually waned, and aside from three new members who had actually joined the church, things had pretty much returned to normal.

The one unfortunate thing was that her friendship forged in shared danger with Jeremiah, the rabbi at the synagogue next door, slowly faded as well. They still exchanged pleasantries over the shrub hedge that separated the parking lots of the church and the synagogue, but not much else. It made sense, really. They had nothing in common.

At first the return to normalcy had been a relief, a sanctuary from the days of terror she had lived through. Lately, though, she had felt a growing restlessness. In a fit of what could only have been insanity she had actually decided to do something daring with her weekend.

Of course, as daring went, participating in a speed-dating event would rank low on most people's scales. To Cindy, though, it seemed bold and risky. She was always so selective about who she dated, thoroughly getting to know a guy before even considering spending time alone with him. Many people had told her she was paranoid, but it wasn't like she didn't have a reason. After all, the last man she ate dinner alone with turned out to be the very same one who killed the man whose body she found. A girl didn't get over that quickly.

No, anything-can-happen Fridays constituted her idea of big excitement. The most risk she normally wanted to take was showing up for work that day.

It was the week before Thanksgiving, and people were starting to get that crazed look in their eyes that said Christmas was coming.

Poor Thanksgiving had been relegated to the position as herald of Christmas—not even allowed to stand on its own as a holiday. What a shame. It was such an American custom, and in a world that seemed on the verge of constant chaos, people needed that oasis of time to contemplate what had gone before and to be grateful for having survived it one more year.

Geanie, the church's graphic artist, flopped down in the chair next to Cindy's desk. Her red leather mini-skirt and black silk blouse might have looked odd on someone else, but on Geanie the look was almost elegant. By contrast, dressed in a long black skirt, white sweater, and sensible shoes, Cindy felt boring.

The front door to the church opened, and Joseph, one of the church's most prominent members and Pine Spring's most eligible bachelors, walked in. Clarice, a large white poodle, paced beside him. Joseph walked right up to her desk without hesitation and sank into the chair across from her. The dog lay down next to her master.

"How's it going?" Cindy asked.

Joseph looked bone-tired but smiled in that way people did when the answer was "crappy" but they were too polite to say so.

"Fine."

"Are you all set for the big event?"

He nodded and closed his eyes. "You're still coming tonight, right?"

"I wouldn't miss it," Cindy said. "This is huge, and I want to support it."

"I knew you wouldn't let me down."

In addition to all of his church activities and owning his own media empire, Joseph kept himself busy with charity work. His latest project, targeted at helping the homeless improve their lives and find the inspiration and help to get back on their feet, was ambitious. Many critics said he was crazy, but Cindy believed in his idea. The church, along with all the others in the area, supported a local homeless shelter, and Cindy had frequent dealings with several of its regulars. After weeks of preparation, the program would be launched that evening on the lawn outside of Joseph's family mansion.

"How's it going, Clarice?" Cindy said to the poodle. "I haven't seen you since you had your puppies."

Clarice looked at her and gave a slight shake of the head, rattling her dog tags.

"She needed a break, so I brought her with me. Seven poodle puppies are enough to drive anyone insane. They're fast and clever. She and I have been chasing them all over the house this morning trying to corral them into one room."

Cindy bit her lip to keep from laughing out loud at the image. Instead she changed the subject back to the event. "Six o'clock, right?"

"It starts at six. Please tell me you'll be there before that."

"I'll head straight to your house from work. It should only take me about ten minutes."

"You're an angel," Joseph said.

"Do you need me to bring anything?"

"A sense of humor. Somebody needs one tonight, or this could get depressing really fast."

She couldn't help but laugh. "I'll do my best."

He stood abruptly. "That's all anyone can ask. Thanks, Cindy."

"You're welcome."

He waved to Geanie and then left the office.

"You should totally go out with him," Geanie said.

"Not my type."

"Yes, because tall, dark, and rich are sooo unattractive."

"Why don't you go out with him? You're not seeing anyone, right?"

Geanie made a face, and Cindy bit her lip. The younger woman was once again between boyfriends and didn't like it one bit.

⚬──✦──⚬

When five o'clock rolled around, Cindy chased everyone out of the office, locked the door, and headed for her car. Ten minutes later she was driving up the hill to Joseph's house.

She rounded a curve and was surprised to see a dozen people lined up on either side of the road holding up signs.

PETS DESERVE SAFE HOMES.
KEEP DOGS SAFE.
DON'T JEOPARDIZE LIVES FOR YOUR EGO.
STOP BEING PART OF THE PROBLEM.
BORN FREE, LIVE FREE.
COLLARS ARE CRUEL.
FREE ALL CAPTIVE ANIMALS!

A homeless man who wore a ripped coat and sported dreadlocks jumped in front of her car waving a sign that read FOOD, NOT FRIVOLITY! Cindy slammed on her brakes. He pounded on the hood of her car before a private security officer dragged him away.

Shaken, Cindy cautiously edged the car forward, eyes darting right and left and wondering who else would try and stop her. If the road had been wide enough, she would have turned around and fled. It wasn't, though, so she kept inching forward until she made it to the designated parking lot. She wedged her car in between a Humane Society vehicle and a news van, and turned off the ignition.

Odds were good that once the event ended, the protestors would leave. After they left, she'd leave. Until then she was sure Joseph would need a hand cleaning up his mansion.

Reluctantly, she slid out of her car. She spotted more people milling about, but none of them held up signs, although quite a few of them appeared homeless. Half a dozen large tents, illuminated by outdoor lights, had been erected on the lawn. Several small paddocks, surrounded by portable wire fences, held a variety of dogs that napped, ate, or played with each other.

Joseph stood on the lawn with Clarice beside him. Cindy walked up and tried not to interrupt as he issued orders to a caterer. After the woman hurried off, Cindy asked, "How are you holding up?"

Joseph turned and hugged her impulsively. Surprised, Cindy hugged him back but pulled away when she saw a flash from someone's digital camera.

"What do you need?" she asked. "I'm your go-to girl just so long as it has nothing to do with protestors."

"Agreed. Actually, if you could go inside and tell my assistant, Derek, to bring out Buford Augustus Reginald the III, that would be great."

"Who?" Cindy asked.

"It's a puppy."

"Oh. Buford . . . August—"

Joseph stopped her with a raised hand. "Just ask him to bring out Buff."

"Okay, I think I can handle that," Cindy said. "Any idea where I can find Derek?"

"No, I've called his cell twice, but he's not picking up. His car's here, though, and he's not outside, so he must be in the house. Try my office—second floor, third door on the right."

"Got it." Cindy headed for the house.

She knew the massive mansion had been built by Joseph's grandparents. She had been in it twice before for church functions. The foyer was empty.

"Derek?" Cindy called. It wasn't dignified, but it would be a lot faster than searching the house. She headed up the stairs, listening.

"Derek!" she called again as she reached the landing.

Suddenly, she heard the sound of smashing glass, like somebody had dropped a water goblet. It came from the right side of the hallway. She walked down its long length, hoping she hadn't startled Derek into dropping something.

The third door on the right stood ajar.

"Sorry to startle you," she said, swinging the door open. The room was empty. "Derek!"

Then she saw a cell phone on the desk and wondered if it was the assistant's. Joseph had worn his on his belt, and he had said he'd been trying to call Derek. She moved toward the desk to grab the phone and then turned. Her shoe crunched on broken glass that had been scattered to the left of the desk. Some shards had landed several feet in all directions.

Behind the desk that stood in front of a balcony, the sheers fluttered in the breeze. Cindy walked around to the right of the desk and sucked in her breath.

Derek. He was lying on his back, a pool of blood beneath his head, and his eyes fixed at the ceiling in a death stare. In his fist he clutched a dog's leash.

Cindy screamed and leaped backward. She dropped the cell phone on the floor, dug through her purse, and hit the speed dial button on her own cell that still had Detective Mark Walters's phone number programmed into it.

"It's Cindy Preston," she said as he answered the phone.

"Cindy? What's up?"

"I'm at Joseph's house. Remember? The guy who lives on the hill who loves dogs? Someone's been murdered."

"I'm on my way. I'll call it in. Make sure nobody touches anything."

"I will."

She heard footsteps racing up the stairs and down the hall. "Are you okay?" a familiar voice asked behind her. She spun around and stared at Jeremiah in shock. "What are you doing here?"

"The charity event. The synagogue is supporting it. What are you doing here?"

"So is First Shepherd. Joseph asked me to come."

15

Jeremiah moved slowly into the room, his eyes roving over the scene. "Did you scream?"

"Yes," she said, coming to her senses after the surprise of seeing him there.

"What happened?"

"Well, it seems you've come to my rescue again," she said, her voice starting to quiver.

"I don't follow."

She nodded to the floor behind the desk, and he moved closer. He stopped and she watched him as he looked the body over. At last he turned his eyes back to her. "You just found him?"

She nodded.

"You've got to be kidding me."

She shrugged her shoulders as tears spilled down her cheeks. "It's anything-can-happen Friday."

⊷────✦────⊶

Jeremiah stared at her and fought the urge to laugh. It wasn't funny—none of it. Not the dead body, not Cindy's tears, not the fact that the police would be there any minute. So much for keeping a low profile. He'd worked hard to not draw too much attention to himself during the whole Passion Week killer fiasco.

"Have you called the police?" he asked.

"Yes. I called Mark."

Great. He moved toward her as he thought about how much better she was handling the situation compared to the last time she found a body.

He got a good look at the corpse: late twenties, blonde with a goatee, blue eyes. Broken glass mixed with the blood that pooled around his head.

Glass and blood sprayed out for a couple of feet. A cell phone lay on the floor next to the man's foot. In his hand he held a red leash, but there was no sign of a dog or a collar.

Jeremiah's eyes were drawn to the balcony.

"I heard the glass breaking when I was in the hall," Cindy said.

"And no one ran past you?"

"No."

Jeremiah approached the balcony, crouching down slightly. The sheers were moving gently, and he could feel a breeze. *Wait for the police*, he urged himself. But he knew there might not be time for that.

He pushed aside the flimsy material and saw a large, half-circle balcony that held a small wrought-iron chair and table. He stepped outside and looked around, and then he walked to the edge and looked down. It was about a ten-foot drop to the lawn on the side of the building facing away from the area where the festivities would be held.

He turned back and saw Cindy staring at him with wide eyes. "Is it possible it was an accident?" she asked.

"Not likely since those aren't mine," he said, directing her eyes down to the bloody footsteps on the balcony.

She sucked in her breath.

Jeremiah took one last look at the balcony and also turned to look at the face of the building to make sure there wasn't a window the killer could have reached. Convinced that the killer had jumped, he turned and walked back inside, careful not to step in the blood.

He crouched down and stared intently at the body. "Do you know who he is?"

"Derek Anderson. He's Joseph's personal assistant."

Jeremiah heard footsteps in the hall. He stood and took a step back.

"You've got to be kidding me," a familiar voice groaned.

Jeremiah turned and saw Mark standing in the doorway. The detective stared from him to Cindy and back again.

"Detective," Jeremiah acknowledged him.

"Samaritan," Mark baited him.

Jeremiah refused to let the man get to him. He had been referencing Jeremiah as a good Samaritan since their first meeting, despite Jeremiah's protests and despite the fact that he was Jewish.

Mark's partner, Paul, followed him into the room and behind him was Joseph, worry filling his eyes.

"What is going on here?" Joseph said.

"He's over here," Cindy said, gesturing to Mark.

The three men moved closer, and Jeremiah stepped back to give them room.

"Would someone please tell me what this is all—" Joseph stopped in mid-sentence. He gasped and swayed for a moment, grabbing the edge of the desk for support.

"I'm sorry, Joseph, I should have called you right after I called the police," Cindy said, flushing. "I found Derek." She took a deep breath. "Someone killed him."

"Why?" Joseph asked.

⌐══✦══⌐

Cindy's heart ached for Joseph as he turned his pain-filled eyes on her. She wished she knew what to say. She reached out and took his hand and gave it a squeeze.

"That's what the police are going to figure out," she said.

Mark cleared his throat. "I need you to all move away from the crime scene. Is there a room nearby where we can talk?"

Joseph nodded woodenly. "Across the hall is a guest room."

He turned to lead the way, then stopped and twisted back, eyes locking on the body. "Where's Buff?"

"Who?" Mark asked.

"A puppy," Cindy said. "I came up here to tell Derek to bring him outside. I haven't seen him. There was no puppy in the room when I came in."

"That's his leash," Joseph said.

"Don't you have several dogs?" Mark asked.

Joseph nodded.

"Then how can you tell whose leash that is?"

"It was specially made for him—for today," Joseph said, his voice catching. "See the white lettering?"

Cindy and the others looked more closely. There on the leash, just above Derek's hand, white letters spelled out HOPE.

"Hope?" Jeremiah asked.

Joseph nodded. "That's what he's supposed to represent."

"Okay, we'll look for the puppy too," Mark said. "Now let's get you out of this room."

Cindy found herself in the next room a minute later, seated in a chair between Joseph and Jeremiah. Mark pulled up a chair across from them as more officers arrived and his partner took charge of the crime scene.

As guest rooms went it was huge. It felt bigger than her whole house. It probably wasn't, but it was impressive. A huge canopy bed stood against the far wall. They were clustered around a mahogany table that could easily sit six.

Being a guest in Joseph's castle had to be a lot better than being king of your own. His family was old money, and despite the fact that he was her age, he didn't need to work. His two dominating passions, which took up much of his time, were dogs and charity work. She knew how special the day was for him because it would be the first time he could really combine his two loves.

Mark flipped open a notepad and jotted a couple of things in silence. It was funny. She hadn't seen or talked to Mark once since the events of Easter. Half a dozen times she had meant to take his cell phone out of her speed dial, but each time she didn't really have anyone she wanted to replace him with.

Cindy looked at Joseph, who shook slightly. Tears shimmered in his eyes. She glanced at Jeremiah, who sat still, quietly observing everyone with guarded eyes.

She reached into her purse and grabbed a deck of cards that she shuffled one-handed as she waited. It was a habit that always calmed her nerves.

Finally, Mark seemed ready to talk. "There's a big event here today, it looks like."

"It's a charity event," Joseph said.

"And you're here . . . ?" Mark asked Cindy.

"As a friend and a representative of First Shepherd."

"And you're here . . . ?" he asked Jeremiah.

"As a representative of the synagogue."

"Of course. Okay, Cindy, you found the body?"

"Yes."

"Joseph, fill me in on what happened earlier today."

After half an hour Mark seemed satisfied and snapped his notepad shut; he stood up as his partner, Paul, walked in.

"We need to break up the party on the lawn. People are getting restless."

"No," Joseph pleaded. "We've spent months working on this, and we've got to continue. We owe it to the people who came here today."

"Are you sure?" Cindy asked him. "I can always tell people there's been a tragedy and that we're rescheduling the event."

She snapped her mouth shut as she realized that she had just volunteered herself for public speaking.

"Thanks, but I have to do this," Joseph said with a shuddering sigh.

"I've got a question," Paul said.

"Yes?" Joseph said.

"Did Buff have a dog tag on his collar?"

"Yes. All my dogs have tags with their name and address. Did you find him?"

The detective shook his head. "We've found a dozen dogs here, not counting what the Humane Society brought, and none of them are Buff."

"What are you saying?" Joseph asked.

"I'm saying that the dog is gone. It's possible that he ran off or is hiding somewhere."

Cindy thought of the dog leash clutched in the dead man's hand. "I think there's another possibility we have to consider."

"And that would be?" Mark asked.

"What if whoever killed Derek also stole the dog?"

Next to her Joseph covered his eyes with his hand.

"Is he valuable? I mean, more than just to you?" Mark asked.

Joseph nodded. "Buff comes from championship lines. Of all the puppies in Clarice's latest litter, he's the best—nearly perfect in every way. He's easily worth twenty thousand. Of course, there are others in the circuit who would pay more to get their hands on one of my puppies."

Mark shook his head grimly. "Maybe one of them did."

2

MARK WALTERS FELT AS THOUGH HE WAS HAVING A BAD CASE OF DÉJÀ VU. Cindy, Jeremiah, and Joseph all belonged to one of his closed-case files, and he would have desperately liked to leave them there.

He took a deep breath. The odds that they were dealing with a serial killer again were a thousand to one, maybe higher. No, this was a simple murder, possibly linked to a theft. The fact that these three were involved was just unfortunate.

"Who had access to the house this afternoon?" Mark asked.

Joseph shook his head. "Today, the whole world, or at least it seemed like it. There were caterers, volunteers, Humane Society personnel, press, probably even some of the homeless who have come forward to be part of the first stage of the program."

Mark swore and didn't bother to censor himself. Cindy colored slightly, and Joseph looked away. He could have sworn, though, that he caught Jeremiah hiding a smile behind his hand.

He signaled to his partner, and Paul came over. "We need to close down the perimeter. No one in or out until we can search the grounds and question everyone."

"We'll need a lot more officers."

"Call them in."

Paul moved off, and Mark turned back toward his audience. "I'll need to question each of you in detail. Joseph, I'll also need a detailed description of that missing puppy."

"Of course. Also, I'd like to proceed with the event we're all here for."

"Don't you care that your personal assistant was just murdered?" Mark snapped.

"Of course, but my mourning him and losing sight of the thing we have been working so hard for all these months will not help anyone else, particularly those we have gathered here today."

Mark wasn't sure whether to support Joseph or to arrest him on principle. He had been a detective long enough to know that everyone dealt with death in their own way and in their own time. All things considered, busying himself with concern for the welfare of others was not a bad way to grieve.

"Agreed. As soon as we're done here, you can continue with the preparations. Joseph, can you step over here for a minute?" Mark asked as he steered him away from the others.

❦

Jeremiah deeply regretted his decision to attend the charity event instead of sending someone in his place. He didn't relish sitting in the guest room waiting for his turn to be questioned by the detective. He glanced over at Cindy, who looked as miserable as he felt.

"Long day?" he asked.

She turned to look at him, and he wasn't sure if she was on the verge of laughing or crying. If she went hysterical, she wouldn't be much good to anyone.

"You could say that."

"You know, we really do have to stop meeting like this," he joked.

"Over dead bodies? Yeah, it's not doing anything for our reputations."

"Well, maybe not for *yours*."

She laughed and he relaxed, relieved that he had been able to tip the scales.

"So how have you been?" she asked after a minute.

"Bored," he said, surprising himself with his own honesty.

"Me too."

"What, the glamorous, hectic life of a church secretary not enough for you?"

"Some days I wonder."

He nodded, then before she could ask him a question, he changed the subject. "Did you know Joseph's assistant?"

"Derek? I'd met him a couple of times. I can't say I actually knew him. I think he'd been working with Joseph for about six months."

"What happened to his last assistant?"

"She got married and moved out of town."

As they continued to talk, Jeremiah watched Mark interviewed Joseph. Joseph didn't strike him as someone who could hurt a fly, let alone kill someone. He could tell from Mark's body language that the detective didn't consider him as a suspect, either. Still, there were many things that could turn a gentle person into a killer; you never knew what might set someone off.

He looked back at Cindy. She looked good—stronger somehow. Their first adventure together had been good for her, given her more confidence. Looking at her innocent face, he couldn't help but wonder what it would take to turn her into a killer.

"What is it?" she asked him.

He shook his head and forced a smile. He would do well to remember that she had a card player's eye for reading facial expressions. She still shuffled a deck of cards absentmindedly, and he wondered if she was even aware that she still held them.

He heard movement and glanced over to see Mark walking toward him, notebook at the ready. "Who's next?" the detective asked.

"You can interview us together," Cindy said.

"Just like old times," the detective said, unable to keep the sarcasm out of his voice.

"I arrived a little after five," Cindy began. "I saw Joseph outside. He asked me to go find Derek in the house and have him bring out Buff. He said he'd been calling Derek's cell phone, but there was no answer. Joseph said I could try the upstairs office. I entered the house and didn't see anyone. I called out, but no one answered. When I climbed the stairs to the second floor, I heard glass breaking. I entered the office, but it was empty. Then I saw a cell phone on the desk and walked over to pick it up, wondering if it was Derek's. I dropped it after I saw the body."

"So we'll expect your fingerprints on it," Mark said.

She nodded. "When I got the phone, I noticed there was glass on the floor. I wondered if someone was out on the balcony, so I moved toward it, and then I found Derek." She took a deep breath. "I screamed, dropped his phone, pulled mine out of my purse, called you, and then Jeremiah came to my rescue. Again." She smiled at the rabbi.

"And you just happened to be lurking around?"

"The synagogue is supporting this charity endeavor, and I'm here as the representative. I was standing outside, underneath the balcony, when I heard a woman scream. I ran inside, up the stairs, into the room, and found Cindy. Again."

"Of course," Mark said with a sigh. "Here we all are—again."

An hour later Cindy stood on the lawn. Large floodlights had been brought in at the last minute to illuminate the scene, both to help the investigation and to allow the event to continue. She watched Joseph as he strode to the podium. His smile was firmly in place, but his hands were shaking.

The police still hadn't found the murderer or the missing puppy. The longer it took, the more she was convinced the two were together somewhere far away.

"Thank you all for coming," Joseph said. "We've gathered here together to fulfill a dream and to restore the hopes and dreams of others. We're here to launch the new Animals to the Rescue program. For our initial launch we are pairing up twenty puppies and dogs with owners who are homeless. Each person who receives an animal also receives an ID card, which entitles their dog to free food and health care for life at any veterinary office in Pine Springs. The charitable contributions of many churches and businesses are supporting this program with the hopes that the animals and the owners will help and inspire each other to strive to fulfill their dreams and achieve a better life."

The enthusiastic round of applause seemed only slightly strained for the tragedy that had unfolded just steps away.

"Representatives from each of the organizations who have contributed to this cause are here, so please wave your hands."

Cindy and Jeremiah both waved, though she noticed he did so much less enthusiastically than she and most of the others. As cameras went off, she noticed that he moved behind her, partially obscured. She tried to shift to the side, but he seemed insistent on hiding.

"And now, I would like to match the first pet with its new owner," Joseph said. He held aloft a poodle puppy that looked a lot like Clarice. Cindy knew he had meant to give Buff away, but when the puppy couldn't be found, he had selected one of his sisters instead. "This is Duchess, the daughter of my own beloved dog. And today Duchess will find a new home with an owner who will love her. Duchess is going to live with Randy Garcia."

Applause sounded again as a man in his forties stepped forward. Cindy had seen him before at the homeless shelter that First Shepherd supported. Usually he had long, unkempt black hair and filthy clothes. He had dressed up for the occasion, though, and wore clean clothes and had his hair tied back in a ponytail. When he took Duchess out of Joseph's hands, she could see the tears shimmering in Randy's eyes.

"Thank you," she heard Randy choke out.

"You are very welcome," Joseph said, leaning close so that he wasn't speaking into the microphone but directly to Randy. "She's a good girl."

"I'll take real good care of her," Randy promised, before turning and walking away.

Cindy felt a lump in her own throat. Animals brought millions of people comfort by their presence. Could it be that those most in need of comfort had been too long deprived of the creatures that could most help them? She prayed that Joseph's charity would work, that the animals would be safe, and that the people would find the love and strength to change their lives because of their dogs.

Joseph cleared his throat and then lifted his hand and pointed toward the enclosures with the dogs that she had walked by when she first arrived. "And now, there are some other very lonely dogs and puppies who have just been waiting at the animal shelters for good homes. I think it's time to make sure they get the loving owners they deserve."

Cindy watched as men and women of different ages, ethnicities, and abilities made their way over to the enclosures to meet and select their new pets. Among them she saw Harry, whom she had more than once caught sleeping in the church sanctuary, now joyously hugging a Labrador-mix puppy who licked his face in ecstasy.

Tears streamed unchecked down her face. She realized that after a minute Joseph moved to her side and that he, too, was crying. She watched as people from the animal shelter helped the homeless fill out forms.

"What are they doing?" she asked.

"All of the dogs are chipped. They'll match the name and any other contact information of each person with the code for their dog's chip and enter it into the database. That way if any of the dogs is lost, a scan by a veterinarian or shelter will let them know who the dog belongs to. Some of these people have been off the grid for years, so it's a big step for them. It also assures them that they can find their dogs if they're lost."

"I hope this works," Cindy said.

"Me too. Pine Springs doesn't have a huge homeless population, but I wanted to start here and help those in my own backyard. If it works, we'll be taking the program into some of the cities next."

Mark walked up to them and she could swear that even he looked affected by the touching scene. He stared hard at Joseph, though. "We're almost done talking with the crowd. We need another half hour before we can start letting people leave."

Joseph nodded and moved back to the microphone. "We're going to have photograph opportunities for the next half hour. During that time, please make sure to enjoy the refreshments in the tent to my right. After that I'll be back with you for a few brief closing remarks and then we can wrap up this evening."

Cindy walked around. The shelter had brought more dogs than there were homeless so that every person got some choice in the dog they received. It was nice for the people, but Cindy felt sorry for the dogs, who had come so far only to not be adopted. After the last homeless woman had chosen her dog, there was a surge toward the pen by some of the other guests, and Cindy realized she wasn't the only one feeling sorry for the unwanted animals.

She saw half a dozen people filling out forms and realized that several dogs were finding homes among some of the donors and members of the press who had turned out for the event. She even thought she saw Mark hovering around the pens for a moment, staring at a cute little beagle who jumped up and down to get peoples' attention.

Half an hour later the evening came to a close. Cindy lingered behind, waiting for the crowd to thin out so she wouldn't have to sit in the traffic jam. She regretted her decision when a few minutes later she saw the coroner bring the body bag out of the house.

A hand settled on her shoulder, and she jumped. She turned and gave Jeremiah a wan smile.

"Are you okay?" he asked.

"I think so. I mean, it was terrible, but it had nothing to do with me, not really. Had I not showed up when I did, Joseph would have probably gone inside and found the body."

"Or sent some poor caterer."

Cindy nodded. "I'm a bit shaky, and I'll feel a lot better once they catch the killer and find Buff, but I think I'll be fine."

"Good. I wanted to make sure before I left tonight."

"I release you. Go home and don't worry about me anymore tonight."

He nodded and left. She hugged herself tight and made her way toward her own car.

When she finally got home, Cindy flipped on the television, but news of the murder dominated every station so she turned it off. She could still see Derek's lifeless eyes staring heavenward.

Why do the eyes always have to look like that? She shivered and wondered if she was truly okay as she had tried to convince Jeremiah. Finally, she sighed and decided to go to bed and get some sleep, but first she double-checked the locks on all the windows and doors.

When the phone rang, Cindy sat up in bed. She glanced at the alarm clock. Three minutes after five. She checked caller ID. Her mother. Not a surprise.

"Hi, Mom."

"When were you planning on telling me?"

"Telling you what?"

"About you at that charity event. Don't try to hide it; I've seen the article *and* the picture."

"I'm not trying to hide anything, Mom," Cindy said. She suppressed a yawn as she rolled out of bed. "I got home really late, too late to call." She knew from experience that it would be pointless to remind her mom that five o'clock in the morning was too early to call on a weekday, let alone a Saturday.

"Am I supposed to believe this just happened? You woke up yesterday, and it was a surprise?"

Cindy walked into the bathroom, squinting as she flipped on the light. She looked at herself in the mirror. Huge dark circles shadowed the skin under her eyes, and she had that vacant stare she got when she hadn't had enough sleep. "Yeah, Mom. Generally, I've found that murder is a surprise."

"What on earth are you talking about?"

"The charity event last night, the dead body I found . . . again." Cindy paused. "What are you talking about?"

"Your boyfriend."

"My what? I don't have a boyfriend." Cindy leaned against the wall and wished she was still snuggled under her comforter.

"That's not what the papers say."

"What are you talking about, Mom?"

"The newspapers all show pictures of the event, and each one of them has a picture of you hugging a man named Joseph. They say you're his girlfriend."

"Are you kidding me?"

"No, but I want to know who this boyfriend is you're telling me you don't have."

"He's just a guy from church." Cindy headed for her computer. "Mom, where did you see this picture?"

"The Internet. It's in the *Pine Springs Gazette* and the *L.A. Times.* Right there for the whole world to see."

Cindy dropped into her desk chair and clicked on her desktop icon for the *Pine Springs Gazette.* There on the front page was the picture: Joseph with his arms around her and the headline CHARITY IS MURDER. Beneath the picture was the caption JOSEPH COULTER WITH GIRLFRIEND CINDY PRESTON.

She skimmed the article about the event, the murdered Derek, and two more references to her, one identifying her as the person who found the victim and the other giving her background from church secretary to the confrontation with the Passion Week killer to the fact that her brother was a travel show host for the Escape channel.

Her eyes flickered back to the photo. Joseph was hugging her tight. She remembered the hug when she had arrived at his mansion.

"It's not true. He's just a friend," she heard herself saying even as she continued to stare at the photo.

"Are you sure?"

"Yes. How did you even find this?" Cindy asked.

"I have a Google alert set up."

"For me?"

"No, for your brother. It's the only way I can keep up with all the articles about him."

Of course. Her mother adored Kyle and never let one of his achievements go by unannounced. "How *is* Kyle?" Cindy asked, knowing her mom would volunteer the information, anyway.

"He's doing so well. His shows are on television all the time these days. I can't turn on the television without seeing him, it seems."

"Maybe if you changed the channel once in a while."

Her mom ignored the sarcasm and kept talking. Cindy got up and wandered back into her bedroom. She closed the door, and there, in its customary place, was the dartboard with her brother's face on it. She pulled the handful of darts out and sat on the bed.

"He's coming for Thanksgiving."

"Oh, that's . . . nice," Cindy said, tossing the first dart.

"He's been seeing a new woman. He's bringing her home for Thanksgiving."

"Kyle's bringing his girlfriend to Thanksgiving? Wow, that's a big step." Cindy threw the second dart.

"I have high hopes. After all, someone has to give me grandchildren."

Cindy gritted her teeth and threw another dart at Kyle's head. "I'm sure Kyle and what's her name will have beautiful children."

"Are you coming home for Thanksgiving?"

"No, Mom. I'm busy."

"If you change your mind, let me know. I can always set the table for one more. And then you could meet Kyle's girlfriend."

When she finally hung up the phone, it took all of Cindy's restraint not to throw it against the wall. She had lied to her mom about being busy because she didn't want to be pressured. She hadn't gone home for four years, and she didn't want to.

She sighed as she wondered what she would do for Thanksgiving. She was getting nervous. Less than a week before the big day, and she hadn't had any invites yet. Normally, she found her way to the home of someone who took in stragglers for the holiday.

She thought about going back to sleep but realized it was useless. She had too much on her mind, from Derek to Thanksgiving to wondering how many people would believe she and Joseph were dating to worrying about actual dating. She took a deep breath. It was Saturday, the day she had promised herself she would do something risky. She wondered if it was too late to change her mind.

3

JEREMIAH WOKE EARLY, PREPARED FOR MORNING SERVICES, AND THEN grabbed the paper to peruse over breakfast. The charity event and the murder took up the majority of the front page. His eyes gravitated to a picture of Cindy hugging Joseph. He glanced at the caption and choked on his coffee. *Girlfriend?*

His initial reaction was skepticism, but then he thought about it. Joseph and Cindy went to the same church, and he and Cindy had barely spoken in months. He would be the last person to know if she had a boyfriend.

He reached for the phone and called her.

"Jeremiah, what's up?"

"I was just wondering how long you've been cheating on me with Joseph."

"What do you mean?" she blurted out.

"I mean, we've been married more than six months, and now I find out Joseph's your boyfriend."

He was teasing her. Over Easter when she'd been taken to the emergency room, he'd had to lie and claim to be her husband so he could gain access and protect her from the serial killer.

"Oh, my gosh! He is not my boyfriend!"

"Ah, but you admit I'm your husband?"

He could hear her spluttering on the phone. "You're impossible."

"So, seriously, you're not dating Joseph? I was calling to congratulate you."

"No. Unfortunately, the *Gazette* isn't the only one that's got that picture and caption. The *L.A. Times* has it too."

"Ouch."

"Tell me about it. My mom called this morning and wanted to know why I hadn't told her."

"Good luck dealing with that."

"Thanks. You okay?"

"I'm fine," he said. "Just getting ready for services."

"That's right. Good luck to you too."

"Why, do you know something I don't?"

"If I did, you'd be the first to know."

"Thanks, that's very comforting," he said.

⚯

Jeremiah made it through services and realized he wasn't in the mood to go home. He drove to the park, not bothering to change his clothes. Instead of taking his usual run, he decided to just walk, breathe in deeply, and try to find some peace after the events of the day before.

The air was crisp and clean, and he was able to focus on the environment around him and the physical sensations of the ground beneath his feet, the wind against his face, and the smell of the earth and the trees.

He saw a couple of people from his synagogue, and he smiled as he walked past. He turned inward toward a part of the park with denser trees and fewer people enjoying the space. He saw a man sitting on a bench, rocking back and forth with his head in his hands. His clothes were tattered, his hair unkempt, and at his feet sat a German shepherd who looked at him adoringly.

For a split second Jeremiah thought it was one of the homeless people participating in the program, and then he realized he had not seen the dog the night before. Suddenly, the man lifted his head and stared right at Jeremiah. The hair on the back of Jeremiah's neck stood on end as he realized there was something hauntingly familiar about the eyes that looked back at him, that widened in recognition. He was looking at a ghost. The ghost leaped to his feet, took a step forward like he meant to address him, and then turned and ran.

Jeremiah jumped forward, intent on pursuit so that he could get a better look at the phantom. After a half dozen steps he forced himself to stop. He stood, hands clenched into fists at his side, his entire body strung so tightly the muscles quivered. The dog had leaped up and followed after his master.

Jeremiah watched them go and wondered if his eyes had deceived him or if he knew that man from another time and place. Either way, it wasn't good.

⚬══✦══⚬

Mark hated working on Saturdays. His wife wasn't too pleased about it, either. She had already called twice to inform him that if he was late for dinner there would be trouble. He couldn't blame her; it wasn't easy being the wife of a detective. Sometimes his job was all-consuming as he strove to put killers behind bars. She was left home alone waiting for him.

They had talked about having kids, but they weren't ready. Still, she needed someone to keep her company when he wasn't there. He had been thinking for a while about getting her a dog. She had grown up with dogs, but the two of them had never had one. Watching the dogs being adopted the night before had pushed the idea to the forefront of his mind and all but convinced him it was the right decision.

He glanced at his watch. He needed to get going. He stood up from his desk, put on his jacket, and started walking toward the door. Out of the corner of his eye he saw Paul leap to his feet and head in his direction, a piece of paper clutched in his hand.

"Am I going to like this?" Mark asked.

"No. Neither is your wife. If you want, I'll call and tell her you'll be home late."

"Please tell me we at least got a break in the case."

"I wouldn't exactly call it a break."

⚬══╪══⚬

Cindy cursed the need to take a risk that had driven her to stand in the cold on a Saturday night outside a hotel ballroom. She sucked in her breath. The doors to the ballroom opened toward the parking lot, so she hadn't had to walk through the lobby enduring the stares of others.

Half a dozen people walked past her. A couple turned to stare at her as she shifted her weight nervously from one foot to another. She wore an emerald green dress and a pair of matching pumps. The shoes had been a mistake. They pinched her toes horribly, and sooner or later she would need to sit down either by going back to her car or by proceeding inside.

She thought of half a dozen excuses why she shouldn't go in, shouldn't take part, shouldn't take a risk. *Come on, just make a decision.*

She turned, deciding to go home instead. She paused, though, as a man she knew walked up to her, a look of surprise on his face.

"Joseph!" she blurted out.

He smiled. "What are you doing here?"

"Taking a risk," she said, without thinking. "Why are you here? Shouldn't you be, I don't know . . ."

"Home doing serious things instead of out participating in speed dating?"

"Yeah." She colored in embarrassment. It was bad enough she had signed up for speed dating, but she hadn't wanted anyone else to know.

"It can be difficult to find women who like me for me and not for my bank account. It was Derek's suggestion that I try speed dating so that, you know, it would be nice and anonymous during the whole first-impression stage. He set it up and was insistent that I go. I figured coming here and doing this was better than sitting at home watching the cleaners try and remove all the blood from the office."

"I'm sorry." Her stomach twisted as she remembered what that blood had looked like.

He shrugged.

"At least the event seemed to go okay yesterday . . . despite everything."

"I am grateful for that," he said.

"Yeah."

"So why are you standing out here?"

"Chicken to go in," she admitted.

"I sat in the car for ten minutes," he said with a grin. "I hate dating."

"So do I."

"Well, then, let's go in together for moral support."

"Works for me," she said. "Although it might be a little odd given that we're supposed to be a couple."

"Oh, you saw that, huh? I'm sorry. I already called both papers and tried to set them straight." He turned bright red.

"It's okay, although my mother called at five a.m. to ask me about it."

"You want me to call her too?"

"No! I think that would just end up making it worse."

They ended up being the last two to sign in. Small tables were arranged in a circle with two chairs at each table that faced each other. Cindy was given a pen, a notepad, and a nametag with the number *20* on it. The men were assigned letters, and Joseph ended up with *T.* She took her seat at one of the tables in the interior ring, her back toward all the other women.

The men all started at a table and after five minutes would rotate clockwise until they had gone all the way around the room. Each pairing had just five minutes to talk and impress each other. At the end of the evening, everyone would turn in their notepad, identifying the numbers or letters of the people they were interested in. The organizers would then go through and see if there were any matches. If Cindy and a man both were interested in each other, they would be given contact information and encouraged to go out on a real date.

Cindy clutched her pen, her heart pounding. She was crazy for doing this.

Joseph sat down at her table and gave her a tentative smile. "This way we can ease into this," he said.

The bell rang to start the session, and he leaned forward. "I enjoy travel, and my dream destination is Ireland. I also love dogs. I breed and show poodles. I own my own company. I'm involved in charity work."

Cindy couldn't help it. She started laughing so loud that she drew stares from the woman sitting to her right.

"What?"

"If you don't want women to be attracted to your bank account, you might not want to mention companies, charity work, and dog breeding."

"Oh," he said, looking crestfallen. "I love movies, particularly romantic comedies."

"Better," she said with a smile.

"Okay, how about you?"

"Me?"

"Yeah, your turn to introduce yourself."

"Um, I'm a church secretary. I find this whole thing a huge risk, and I don't know why I'm here. I moved to Southern California for college."

"Bor-ing," Joseph said, pretending to fall asleep.

"Hey!"

"Well . . ."

"Okay, I play a mean hand of poker, I'm great at darts, and I like Chuck Norris movies."

"What kind of guy are you trying to attract?"

She hit him in the arm. The bell rang, and she shared a dismayed look with Joseph as he got up and moved.

Guy S took his place, giving her a smile that was somewhere between cheesy and slimy. "I like long walks on the beach, candlelight dinners, and curling up in front of the fireplace with a nice bottle of wine."

"I like playing poker and watching Chuck Norris movies," she said.

He looked startled and then changed his tune. "That's cool, you like to do more guy stuff. Clearly I'm a guy, and I like to do . . . stuff."

When the bell rang and Guy R sat down, she almost gasped with relief. "I'm a computer programmer, I don't have time to date, but that doesn't mean I don't want to. I like going to the theater and traveling when I have the time. I need more excitement in my life, but I don't have the first clue how to make that happen."

"Wow, that's honest," she said. "I'm a church secretary. I also like theater. I'd like to travel but I'm scared of taking risks, even though I also need something more in my life, excitement probably, but that's hard to admit."

He smiled at her, a tired, weary smile. "Cool. I've been to three of these things, and that's the best intro a woman's ever given herself."

She was a little disappointed when the bell rang and Guy Q sat down. He was blond, buff, and full of himself. "I like to travel, and I'm into extreme sports. I don't like to brag, but you'll probably never meet a bigger daredevil than me."

"My brother is Kyle Preston," she said stonily.

His eyes opened wide. "Dude, really?"

She nodded. "Really."

"Can you get me his autograph?"

"No. I think we're done here."

They spent their remaining four minutes in silence.

The next eleven guys were remarkable in that they all seemed to blend into each other and become one indistinguishable ball of bland.

Guy E was a police officer whom she thought she remembered seeing the night before. He seemed to recognize her too. Ultimately, she decided that it might be too weird. Mr. D was a lawyer with a warm smile and friendly manner that put her at ease. C and B both looked as tired as she felt by the time they reached her but seemed like good guys.

She flashed Guy A a big smile, relieved that she was five minutes to freedom and then recoiled as he burst into tears.

"My girlfriend left me, and my buddy made me come here. Said I had to get out and meet people."

"I'm sorry, when did she leave you?" Cindy asked.

"Six months ago."

"Oh." She had nothing else to say and so just sat quietly while he continued to cry.

The final bell rang, and she sagged in her chair. From the table next to her, Joseph gave her a little wave. They walked up together to the sign-in table and picked up the forms where they were supposed to put down who they were interested in.

"What if no one puts down my name?" Cindy whispered to Joseph.

"Unfortunately, you never know who puts down your name unless you put down theirs as well. Something tells me, though, that you don't want to put down every guy here."

"Heavens, no," she said.

"Yeah, same with the women."

"Are you putting any of them down?"

"A couple," he admitted, avoiding her eyes.

She took a deep breath and began writing on her form. B and C both had earned at least a chance. D seemed nice. R, the computer programmer, was the one who seemed the most interesting of the group. She hesitated for a moment and then blushed as she put down T, folding it quickly so that Joseph couldn't see that she'd put him down. After all, he was the nicest guy in the room, and Geanie's admonition that she should go out with him came to mind. *Wouldn't it be freaky if the newspaper caption turned out to be prophetic?*

They made it outside, and Joseph turned to look at her. "You want to get some coffee or some food? I don't really want to go home yet."

A wave of sympathy filled her. "I've been there. I would love to get something to eat. I was too nervous to eat earlier."

"Okay. Meet you at Outback Steakhouse?"

"All right."

Fifteen minutes later they gave the waitress their order and then settled back and began to dissect the evening.

"Did you see crying guy?" she asked.

Joseph winced. "He was hard to miss. I sat one table over from him the entire night. He cried most of the time. It was distracting, to say the least."

"I can imagine. So how did you come up with Animals to the Rescue?"

"Well, I've been a supporter of various charities around the country that have been taking dogs into hospitals, nursing homes, and retirement communities."

"I've heard of those," she said.

"They have had some phenomenal successes. One day last spring I was walking Clarice in the park, thinking about what else might be done with dogs in a therapeutic setting, when I saw this homeless man sitting on a bench. Some volunteers were giving out free sandwiches and passing out information about the homeless shelter. I watched this guy feed half his sandwich to the dog that was sitting with him. One bite for him, one bite for the dog. Well, I asked one of the volunteers about it, and she said that he had some severe mental problems and it used to be no one could get near him; he would just rant and scream and throw things. Then one day he showed up with the dog and asked for a sandwich. They said he'd been making marked improvement ever since."

"Amazing."

"That's what I thought. I talked to a few people around the country, and they all said that when a homeless person started caring for a dog, he took better care of the dog than himself. I theorized that it might be a way to reach out and start bringing these people back into society. Taking responsibility for something other than themselves has got to be a big step."

"Wow. This program could do so much good."

"Or fail miserably. There's obviously a lot of concern for the welfare of the animals and a lot of people who think I'm part of the problem instead of part of the solution."

"Yeah, but at least you're trying to do something to help. I mean, really help. Oftentimes all people need to change their lives is a reason."

"Give a man a fish . . ." He shrugged his shoulders. "Sorry, that was a rather long answer. I hope I didn't bore you."

"Not at all. I just kind of wish now that I had a dog."

"Feel the need to have a reason to change your life?" he asked with a sly smile.

"Something like that," she said with a laugh.

"Well, if you decide to take the plunge, I know a lot of great dogs that need a good home."

"I'll think about it."

Her phone rang, and she slid it out of her purse and looked at the caller ID. It was Mark. She frowned and flipped the phone open.

"Detective?"

"Listen, I need to know where your boyfriend is."

"Who are you talking about? I don't have a boyfriend."

"Joseph."

"Oh, um, just a second," she said, feeling herself flush. She held the phone out to Joseph. "For you."

Joseph listened for a moment, and then his face went completely white. "We're at Outback Steakhouse. Okay, we'll wait."

He hung up the phone and handed it back to Cindy. "What's going on?"

"There's been another murder."

Cindy sat up straight, and her heart pounded. "Did he say who?"

"No."

Deep, paralyzing fear reached inside her mind. Was it someone else connected to Joseph? It had to be if Mark was looking for him. Her mind swirled with possibilities, faces floating in her mind, people from the church, people from the event, Jeremiah.

Mark arrived within a few minutes and slid into the booth next to Cindy. His face was grim, and she gripped her soda hard, trying to read his expression.

"Is it bad?" she whispered.

"It's bad. You know that guy from the event last night, Randy Garcia?"

"The one I gave Duchess to?" Joseph asked.

"Yes. He was murdered."

Joseph began to shake uncontrollably. Cindy felt overwhelming relief that it wasn't Jeremiah or Geanie or someone else she knew. In her relief, though, one question came to her. "How is Duchess?"

Mark shook his head. "We don't know. When we got there, there was no sign of her. It's possible she was taken by the killer."

4

Jᴇʀᴇᴍɪᴀʜ ꜰɪxᴇᴅ ʜɪᴍꜱᴇʟꜰ ᴅɪɴɴᴇʀ ʙᴜᴛ ᴄᴏᴜʟᴅɴ'ᴛ ᴇᴀᴛ ᴍᴜᴄʜ ᴏꜰ ɪᴛ. Hɪꜱ ᴍɪɴᴅ kept drifting to the man in the park. Had he actually recognized him? What had happened to him? He looked like a homeless person, but Jeremiah had a hard time believing that was true.

The last time they had met had been five years earlier in Israel. Jeremiah remembered the details clearly. He could only imagine the other man did as well.

Could it actually be a coincidence, them being here in the same town? If it wasn't, then he would need to tread carefully. If it was, then what could Adonai possibly have in mind? He bowed his head and prayed, asking for strength and clarity as he figured out what it all meant.

The phone rang, interrupting his prayers. He answered it and heard his secretary, Marie, on the other end.

"Attendance was down today," Marie informed him.

"It looked a little thin," he said with a sigh. "But some people are probably getting out of town ahead of the Thanksgiving exodus." He smiled at his own joke.

"That better be what it is," she grumbled.

"Speaking of, aren't you leaving soon?" he asked.

"We're in the airport right now; we're taking the red-eye."

"Well, have fun visiting with your family."

"If I wanted fun, we'd be spending Thanksgiving at Disneyland or The Zone, not Jersey."

A thousand retorts filled his mind, about people who would give a lot to spend the holiday with family and that there were far worse places in the world than New Jersey. He bit his tongue, though. "At least have a safe trip."

"That would be remarkable. Two years ago everyone got food poisoning at Cousin Tina's house. It was miserable. You should have seen it."

"I'm kind of glad I didn't."

"You've got all the keys to the synagogue?" Marie asked.

"Yes."

"You remember where everything is?"

"I think so."

"If you get in trouble, you can call my cell phone."

"I'm sure it won't come to that."

"Just promise me."

"Okay, Marie, if I get in trouble, I'll call your cell phone."

"And you best be thinking about what we're going to do to make sure there are bigger crowds during Hanukkah. The numbers today don't bode well."

"Yes, Marie, I'll be thinking about it."

"Good. We can talk about it when I get back. Now, where are you going for Thanksgiving dinner?"

"I haven't decided yet," he said. The year before had been easy; he'd gone to her house.

"Do you want me to make a couple of calls?"

"No, I promise I'll figure it out myself. Be safe."

Jeremiah hung up the phone and realized he was more shaken than he had thought. He hadn't used *be safe* in lieu of *good-bye* in a long time.

⊙━╾┼╼━⊙

"I knew it!" Cindy burst out loud enough to startle herself as well as Mark and Joseph.

The second puppy had been taken. It had to be about the dogs.

"Do you know for certain that Duchess was stolen, that she didn't just run off?" Joseph asked.

Mark shrugged. "We don't know for sure, but a guy called the police station to complain about a dog barking like crazy in the alley next to his apartment. It took a while for an officer to go check it out. When he did, there was no dog, but there was a body. So, we're assuming the dog was still there right around the time Randy was killed. Now, she could have run off."

"She was stolen," Cindy insisted. She could feel it. Two men dead in twenty-four hours, both of them in possession of one of Joseph's puppies, couldn't be a coincidence. She tried to push from her mind the tears of joy on his face as Randy had accepted the dog the night before.

Joseph's cell phone rang and he answered it. A moment later he bolted up from the table, slamming into the waitress carrying a tray with their food. The plates crashed to the floor, showering Mark and Cindy with a spray of mashed potatoes and gravy.

"Look!" an excited patron shouted. "There's blooming onion all over the blooming floor!"

Mark lurched out of the booth, struggling to maintain his balance on the suddenly slippery floor. Joseph threw some bills down on the table and then took off for the door at a run. Mark ran after him, and Cindy scrambled to keep up, her stomach growling noisily as she saw what would have been a lovely dinner covering the floor.

When she made it out the door, Joseph was already in his car, pulling away. "What is it?" Mark yelled.

The window rolled down, and she heard Joseph shout back, "My alarm service. Someone broke into the house."

With an oath Mark lunged toward his car, and Cindy stood for a moment before running to hers. She yanked on her seat belt, started the car, threw it in reverse, and peeled out of the parking lot right behind Mark. That's when her mind stopped spinning long enough for her to wonder what in the world she was doing. *This is insanity. I'm not seriously speeding toward the scene of a crime! What am I doing?*

She could still feel the adrenaline rushing through her body, courtesy of Joseph's flight from the restaurant. *He hadn't wanted to go home. Maybe it's a good thing he didn't.* She remembered what it had been like when her home had been broken into—the fear, the violation—and she felt for Joseph. He shouldn't have to face that alone. She had had Jeremiah to lean on.

Jeremiah. Her hand moved to her cell phone, but then she hesitated. Aside from his being there the night before, this really didn't have anything to do with him. He would probably thank her to leave him out of it. Reluctantly, she let go of her phone and concentrated on following Mark to Joseph's house.

When they finally got there, she was relieved to discover that the police were already there ahead of them, apparently alerted by the alarm company. The front door was open wide, and lights blazed all over the mansion. Cindy followed Mark as he walked over to Joseph who was talking to a uniformed officer. She was stunned to discover that it was the guy from speed dating.

He looked equally surprised to see her but flashed a grin. "I just started work like half an hour ago," he informed her.

"Oh," she said, not sure what else to say.

The officer turned back to Joseph.

"What are you saying?" Joseph asked, looking bewildered.

"Whoever it was deactivated the alarm on their way in and then on their way out tried to reactivate it and failed to do so correctly. That's what alerted the security company."

"Are you saying someone has my access code and can come in whenever they like?"

"It looks that way. We're going to need a list of people who have that code."

"Nobody," Joseph said, pulling at his hair with his fists. "Just me. The only other person who had it was my personal assistant, Derek, and he was killed yesterday."

"Derek had the code?" Cindy and Mark asked in unison.

"Yes, of course."

"Is there anyone he would have given it to—a housekeeper, dog sitter, girlfriend, anyone?" Mark asked.

"No, absolutely not."

"You're sure about that?"

"Yes."

"Could it have been someone at the alarm company?" Cindy asked.

"No. I entered the code after installation. No one at the company knows the code."

"If someone from the company had used an override, it wouldn't look like this," the officer explained.

"Was anything taken, Vince?" Mark asked.

Vince—it was a good name for him, Cindy decided.

The officer shook his head. "We're still searching. Whoever this was probably knew exactly what they were after. Electronics, files in the office all seem to be undisturbed." Vince shifted his eyes to Joseph, "Sir, if you could help us check to see if any valuables like jewelry, cash, anything readily portable is missing, we can move this along."

"What about the puppies?" Cindy asked.

"Ma'am?"

"The puppies, are they safe?"

Vince shook his head. "We haven't seen any pets at all. Where would they be?"

Joseph pushed past him and sprinted into the house. Cindy and Mark followed as he passed the staircase and headed to the left. At the end of a hallway a door stood open, and they followed him inside.

The room was tiled. The left front corner of the room was covered with newspapers. In the back left corner there were food and water dishes. The right side of the room held a comfy-looking old couch, a couple of arm chairs, and almost a dozen different dog beds scattered around. In and on everything were a variety of dog toys. It was a dog's dream pad without the dogs.

"Where are the puppies?" Cindy asked again.

"Where is Clarice?" Joseph asked.

"It really was about the dogs," Mark muttered.

Vince joined them inside the room.

"Did you or anyone else open this door?" Joseph asked.

Vince shook his head. "I was the first one in the house, and I can tell you this door was open already."

"All right, let's spread out and search the grounds for any sign of those dogs," Mark said.

Mark and Vince left the room. Cindy watched Joseph. He stared vacantly at the sofa, and she wondered what it was he was seeing. She stepped forward and touched his arm. He jumped and turned to look at her.

"Is there anywhere Clarice would go if she was upset? Somewhere she would hide?" Cindy asked.

It was a long shot, but making off with a puppy was one thing, making off with a full-grown standard poodle was quite another.

He nodded and left the room, walking back toward the foyer. Outside she could hear men calling and whistling for dogs that weren't coming. She followed him upstairs and into what was probably his bedroom. Like the guest room, it was also large and elaborately decorated.

Joseph got down on the floor and peered underneath the giant four-poster bed. "Clarice?" he called.

He stood up, a look of desperation on his face. "This is where she hides when she's upset about something. She's not here. She's gone."

"If she ended up outside the house, where would she hide?" Cindy asked.

"There's an old work shed close to the tree line. She likes to crawl underneath it. I caught her hiding out there a couple of times when she was a puppy."

"Then let's go check it," Cindy said.

She had to keep Joseph thinking, moving, otherwise he was going to lose it. She recognized the look of despair on his face. She had seen that look in the mirror before and knew that she had to keep him busy for as long as she could.

They made it downstairs, where he grabbed a flashlight and a leash from the kitchen. Then they jogged across the lawn. After a minute they reached the shed, and Joseph flashed his light underneath.

"Clarice, are you there, girl? Come out. Here, Clarice."

Cindy held her breath. Several seconds passed, Joseph's shoulders began to droop, and then she heard a scratching sound coming from the dirt below the shed. A moment later Clarice emerged, limping. Her coat was matted and dirty, and when the flashlight hit her head Cindy gasped. The dog's muzzle and throat were covered in blood.

Joseph collapsed to his knees and wrapped his arms around Clarice. Cindy shouted, "Over here, we found the mother!"

As the officers descended, Clarice jerked and looked like she was trying to struggle out of Joseph's arms. He made soft noises to calm her.

"Any sign of the puppies?" Mark asked.

"No, but she's hurt," Cindy said, picking up the flashlight Joseph had dropped and playing it over the dog.

"I can't find any cuts on her face or neck," Joseph said. "Shine the light here."

Cindy obediently shined the light right at Clarice's muzzle. Joseph opened her mouth. Her tongue and teeth were also coated with blood. Joseph stared for what seemed an eternity. "I don't think there are any injuries inside her mouth either," he said at last.

"What does that mean?" Vince asked.

"It means that she bit the guy who stole her puppies," Mark said. "That's DNA evidence all over her." He turned to Vince, "Call in forensics." He turned his attention back to Joseph. "The dog is now evidence."

"Clarice isn't evidence. She's a dog, *my* dog," Joseph hissed at Mark.

"Be that as it may, she's also our first break in this case."

"Why don't we get her inside where the light is better?" Cindy suggested.

Joseph clipped the dog leash onto the poodle's collar, and she followed him back to the house.

They stopped inside the foyer. Cindy and Mark sat on the stairs while Joseph sat on the floor next to his dog and examined her carefully.

"So, if we are looking at a rival breeder," Mark asked, "why take the puppies when they could have taken Clarice? They'll have to wait to be able to breed the puppies."

"These puppies aren't just special because Clarice is their mother. Their father is an international champion. With him it's not about the money, although the stud fee is astronomical, but selectivity. His owner will only allow him to breed with females who are also champions. That makes these puppies especially unique."

"Aren't all of the dogs registered?" asked Cindy. "I mean, if they want them for their pedigrees, then it's kind of pointless to steal them, because they'll never be able to admit who the parents are without being discovered."

"The breeder could be looking for perfect show dogs. He can doctor their pedigrees and make some good money off winning shows. Once his dogs have a few wins, people will be lining up to pay stud fees, never dreaming the animals were stolen."

"Okay, so it's possible a rival breeder wanted the puppies badly enough to kill for them," Mark said. "But why just take the one yesterday? Why not take them all?"

"Maybe the killer thought he'd have plenty of time to grab the others and was only worried about the one he knew Joseph planned to give away," Cindy suggested.

"Ah, so when Joseph gave away a different puppy from the same litter, the killer had to get that one as well and then probably realized he couldn't waste any more time and take the chance of Joseph giving away or selling another puppy."

"It would make sense," Joseph said.

Vince arrived. Reluctantly, Joseph handed Vince Clarice's leash.

"We'll take really good care of her, have her checked out by a vet and everything. You'll have her back in a day or so," Vince promised.

Cindy stared at Clarice's collar as the dog reluctantly followed Vince out of the house. On Clarice the sparkly red collar seemed fitting; she was the queen of Joseph's household.

From everything Cindy had noticed, the dog was treated like a queen.

"What if there is a simpler answer to this riddle?" she asked as Vince led the dog out.

"How do you mean?" Mark asked.

"Joseph, those aren't by any chance *real* diamonds on Clarice's collar, are they?"

Joseph smiled. "Yes, they are. Why do you ask?"

"Because in my book that's a much more likely cause of murder than bloodlines," Mark said, coming fully alert. "Does anyone else know the stones are real?"

"Probably about a dozen people," Joseph guessed.

"What about the puppies?" Cindy asked.

"They all have collars that look like hers, but the stones are only crystal."

"What if the killer didn't know that? What if he thought the puppies were wearing diamond collars too?"

"That could lead to all sorts of unpleasantness," Mark said.

"But why not just grab the collars and leave the puppies?" Cindy asked.

"To divert suspicion, probably," Mark said.

"And why not take Clarice or her collar?" Cindy pressed.

"I'm guessing he tried and got mauled for his effort," Mark answered.

"That would certainly explain the blood," Joseph said with a sigh.

"So we're looking for someone who knew that one of the dog collars, at least, had diamonds," Cindy said.

"*I'm* looking for," Mark said, standing abruptly. "*You* need to go home."

<hr />

Mark headed outside for some fresh air. *Jewel thief?* It didn't make sense. Something about the whole thing felt wrong somehow.

"What is it?" Paul asked as he walked up to him.

"This whole thing stinks."

"Yeah, I have to agree with you there. So what do you think is really going on?"

"I don't know; I can't quite put my finger on it."

"Don't you mean your paw?" Paul joked.

Mark grimaced.

5

It was early Sunday morning when Mark showed up at the Humane Society. He recognized the woman working the desk from the charity event.

"Officer, is there something I can do for you?" she said, clearly puzzled at seeing him in T-shirt and jeans. He spent so much time in a suit that the casual clothes felt a bit odd to him too. But he had promised his wife she'd have the entire day, and he intended to keep that promise.

"I wanted to know if all of the dogs from the charity event were adopted."

"We brought seven of them back here, but six of them were adopted yesterday, I believe."

"The one that's left, is there any chance it's a beagle?" he asked, trying not to hope too much.

A grin spread across her face. "Every chance. Buster is still here and looking for a good home. Do you have any suggestions?"

He smiled. "Actually, I do."

"Why don't we go see him and make sure he's the one you're interested in?" she said, moving from behind the counter to lead him down a hallway.

He followed her and soon found himself in a room with large dog pens that each had small outdoor runs. There were a dozen dogs present, and in the last pen was Buster, the beagle he had been eyeing at the event.

He knelt down in front of the cage, and the dog threw himself against the bars, licking at Mark's hand.

"He's perfect," Mark said. "I'll take him."

"I'm so glad. He's a really great little dog. Beagles have a lot of energy, and the family that originally owned him just couldn't handle it."

"We shouldn't have any problem with that."

"All right, let's go fill out the paperwork."

Thirty minutes later Mark pulled up outside his house. Buster barked excitedly as Mark carried his crate up to the front door.

"You're going to blow the surprise," Mark said.

He walked into the house, put down the crate, and opened it. Buster bounded out with another joyous bark.

"Mark, is that you?" his wife, Traci, called from the back.

"Yes."

"Do you hear barking?" she asked.

"What?"

She appeared in the hallway, blonde hair up in a ponytail. "I said—" She stopped with a squeal as she saw Buster. She dropped to her knees and patted her legs. Buster went flying to her and began licking her face in a frenzy.

Mark followed and knelt down next to them in the hallway. "His name is Buster," he said, reaching out to scratch the dog's head.

"He's perfect," she said, tears gleaming in her blue eyes. "How did you know?"

Mark shrugged. "A lucky guess."

He thought of all the other tears of joy he had seen Friday night. Rich or poor, man or woman, all were moved by a bond with a furry creature who gave love unconditionally.

Cindy could hear her phone ringing as she tried to unlock her front door. She rushed inside and picked up the receiver just before the machine could.

"Hello?"

"Cindy Preston?"

"Yes," she said, tossing her purse and church bulletin on the counter.

"This is Jerry, the organizer of the speed dating event last night."

Was that really just last night? "Oh, yes?"

"We have your matches for you."

She sat down at the kitchen table, her heart actually pounding. "Okay."

"You had two matches."

Two was a lot better than zero.

"Do you have something to write with?"

"Yes," she said, reaching for pen and paper. "I'm ready."

"The first is Guy Randall, he's a computer programmer; you would know him as Gentleman R."

"Yes, he seemed quite nice."

Jerry gave her Guy's phone number, and she wrote it down.

"And the second. His name is Joseph Coulter. He was Gentleman T."

Cindy couldn't help the nervous laughter that bubbled to her lips.

Jerry gave her Joseph's phone number, and she wrote it down even though she already had it.

She sat for a moment, staring at the two names and phone numbers. She knew that Guy and Joseph would be getting her number.

Her phone rang and she jumped before she reached for it. "Hello?"

"Hi, Cindy? This is Guy Randall, from speed dating."

"The computer programmer, I remember," she said.

"And you're the church secretary."

"That's me. So what do we do now?"

"I think tradition dictates that we go out to dinner or something like that. However, I'm leaving in a couple of hours, and I'll be gone for the week, back next Sunday."

"Well, then I guess we'll have to wait until you get back," she said.

"Unless you feel like going to Aspen for the week."

"Oh, you're going to Aspen, to ski?"

"To visit family. Everyone takes turns hosting Thanksgiving, and this year it's Aspen."

"Oh, well, have a wonderful trip."

"I know you said you needed more excitement in your life too. My aunt has plenty of spare rooms in her house and she loves to entertain."

For one wild moment Cindy wondered what it would feel like to say yes, to just be spontaneous and go on the trip. *Kyle would go*, she thought.

"I'm sorry, Guy. I do need more excitement in my life, but I'm afraid that's just too much excitement."

"That's cool. If you change your mind, this is my cell number."

"Thanks."

"So would you be free a week from Friday?"

"I believe so."

"So dinner then?"

She took a deep breath. "Absolutely."

"Great, I'll give you a call next Sunday."

She hung up and discovered that her hands were shaking. "Lots of people go out on dates with people they barely know, you can do this," Cindy coached herself. She stared at Joseph's number and wondered how long until he called. She picked up the phone and dialed before she could change her mind.

"Hello?" He sounded tired. She didn't blame him.

"Hi, it's Cindy."

"I was just about to call you."

"Beat you to it."

"I'm sorry, I just couldn't cope with it this morning."

"Oh, I'm sorry, I just figured I'd get the call out of the way."

"I know. It's just with everything that has happened—"

"That's cool," she said, feeling slightly sick to her stomach. "We're friends."

"Yes, and I value your friendship more and more. Oh, call waiting. Can you hold on a second?"

"Sure."

Silence descended, and Cindy felt both relieved and embarrassed. She should never have put Joseph's name down. She didn't think of him in that way. It had just been so easy given that he was the nicest and least threatening guy in the room.

She heard a clicking sound and then Joseph's voice. "So something you want to tell me," he said, his voice amused.

"The speed dating people were on the other line, weren't they?" she said, feeling her cheeks burn.

"Yup. I was busy apologizing to you for missing church this morning, and you were . . . asking me out?"

"Getting the call over with is more like it," she retorted.

"It's been a terrible couple of days. There's nothing for me to do but wait. Do you want to go see a movie this afternoon?"

"Depends. Will it be a romantic comedy?"

"No, I swear."

"Cool."

"Meet you at Main Place in an hour?"

"Works for me."

She hung up and walked back toward her bedroom wondering whether this counted as a date.

When she arrived outside the theater and saw that he was casually attired in khaki Dockers and a black polo shirt, she was relieved that she had opted to go for the jeans and burgundy sweater instead of something dressier.

"Hey," he said, giving her a quick hug.

"How are you?" she asked.

He shrugged. They started walking toward the box office when he suddenly pointed toward a homeless woman, begging by the side of the theater.

"Look!" Joseph said.

"Who is she?" Cindy asked.

"That's one of the women I paired with a dog," Joseph said, heading in her direction.

"What are you going to do?" Cindy asked.

"I just want to ask her how it's going."

Cindy didn't want to, but she found herself walking next to Joseph as he approached the elderly woman. The dog was tiny and looked like some kind of Pomeranian mix with reddish fur.

"Could you spare a dollar for an old lady?" the woman asked as they approached, without looking up at them.

"That's a mighty fine-looking dog," Joseph said.

"Thank you!" the woman said, breaking into a smile. "This here is Ginger." She looked up and then scrambled to her feet when she realized who Joseph was. "And bless me, you're the man who made it possible for us to be together!"

"I only helped," Joseph said, accepting a hug from the old woman.

The woman turned to Cindy. "And you're the woman who's dating this sainted man. You keep a tight hold on him, missy."

"But—"

"Oh, you can't fool me. I seen you Friday, and your picture was in the newspaper. Ginger and I had a picture too," she said, proudly patting the little dog.

"What are you doing here?" Joseph asked.

"Ginger and I are just waiting for Sammy and his Buddy. We're all going to go for a walk in the park soon. They should be here anytime."

"Well, you kids have fun," Joseph said.

"You too," she said with a big wink.

Joseph took Cindy's elbow and steered her back toward the theater. "Well, there's one satisfied customer," he said.

"She certainly does seem crazy about Ginger," Cindy said.

True to his word, Joseph bought them both tickets to an action movie, not a romantic comedy. They grabbed some popcorn and sodas and sat down right as the previews began to play.

Previews were one of Cindy's favorite parts to the movies, but she found herself studying Joseph more than the screen. She couldn't believe how calm he looked, given everything that had happened. She wondered who the jewel thieves were and how they had come to target him and his dogs. Was it someone he knew or someone who had seen him at a dog show?

Somehow it was easier to conjure up images of an international jewel thief than it was some random criminal in Pine Springs. *Criminals*, she mentally corrected herself. Odds were good that there was more than one person in on it. *What if Derek was in on it, and that's why he's dead?* It was almost too clichéd to be true. Inside man tries to double-cross partners and gets killed for it. If that was the case, though, was it possible he had already stolen the real diamond-studded collar?

Did Joseph keep the real one locked up, or did Clarice wear it all the time? If so, was she wearing it the night before when the policeman took her in for examination? She froze at the thought. *Could someone be stealing the collar right now?* She chided herself for the errant thoughts. If the dog was wearing the real collar, who better to guard it and her than the police? Still, she would have to ask Joseph about it after the movie.

The film finally began, and thoughts of the murder and the diamond collar faded into the background as she became painfully aware that their action film had a strong romantic subplot. She slunk down in her seat, all too aware of the fact that she and Joseph were on a quasi-date. When things turned serious between the two onscreen characters, she could feel her cheeks burning, and she had an overwhelming urge to excuse herself to the bathroom and never come out.

Every time Joseph shifted in his seat, she jumped, worried that he would reach for her hand or put an arm around her. *Okay, this is so seventh grade.*

Joseph leaned close, and she tensed up. "Are you okay?" he whispered.

She nodded, and it seemed to satisfy him. As he straightened back up, she let out the breath she had been holding.

Okay, time to face the music. Tall, dark, rich, handsome, kind, funny, and absolutely no spark whatsoever. What's wrong with me? Maybe the perfect guy is Geanie's type but not mine. Okay, that's just stupid. Who isn't looking for the perfect guy?

She stole another glance at Joseph. Maybe he was a perfect guy, just not *her* perfect guy. The thought should have comforted her, but instead she just felt more uncomfortable and embarrassed. It was a complete mistake to put him down on the piece of paper at speed dating. It had been even more of a mistake to agree to go to the movies with him without specifying in what capacity they were going.

When the film ended, she leaped to her feet and headed for the doors instead of staying to see the credits as she normally would. Joseph caught up with her in the lobby.

"Hey, what's wrong?" he asked.

She looked up at him, not wanting to hurt him, but needing him to know what she was thinking.

He looked deep into her eyes and then smiled at her. "It's okay, you know."

"What is?"

"To just be friends."

"I'm sorry."

"Don't be. There's no spark for either of us, and that's okay. No reason to try and force it."

"You are a mind reader. And a good friend," she said, gripping his hand, and realizing how easy it was to do so now that there was no expectation behind it.

He laughed and swung her arm back and forth slightly as they walked outside.

She looked at him. "You are going to make some lucky woman very happy."

Suddenly, she heard a commotion and saw a flash go off. She turned and froze like a deer in the headlights when she saw reporters staring at them. A couple more flashes went off, and she instinctively pulled closer to Joseph until she remembered seeing the picture of them in the newspapers the morning before.

She dropped his hand and took a distancing step. "What's going on?" she asked.

"Whatever it is, it isn't good," Joseph muttered.

"Hey, that's him!" she heard one of the reporters shout.

Suddenly, they were at the center of a press of bodies, half of them with cameras or microphones.

"Joseph, care to explain how people keep ending up dead around you?"

"Is it just a coincidence that you're here today, or did the police call you?"

"First your assistant and now one of your charity cases. Are you cursed?"

Dead. Charity cases. The words echoed in Cindy's mind. She thought of the old woman they had talked with on their way into the theater. Had something happened to her?

Cindy turned her head, and through the crowd of reporters she saw a line of yellow police tape and some uniformed officers.

"No," she whispered, pushing her way forward. She had to know. The reporters pressed in harder against her, determined to get answers. She pushed back hard, and finally bodies began to give way. She broke free of the crowd and ran toward the barricade, where an officer grabbed her and stopped her from moving forward.

On the other side of the line, she saw the little dog, Ginger, pacing back and forth next to some huddled people. She felt her stomach lurch, and then her eyes fell on Ginger's owner. The old woman was alive and talking with Paul, the detective.

She felt someone brush up against her, and a moment later Joseph called out. Paul looked up and then waved them through. Cindy slipped under the tape and was grateful that the reporters could not follow.

"What happened?" she burst out.

"Bernadette here found a body," Paul said, scowling.

Cindy turned toward Bernadette. The old woman had clearly been crying. Her eyes were puffy and swollen. "Are you okay?"

Bernadette shook her head. "I knew something bad had happened to Sammy, I just knew it. I walked all around the theater looking for him and Buddy. I saw his hat first," she said, pointing.

Cindy turned to look, and by a row of bushes an old battered hat was lying on the ground, a handful of crinkled bills still inside it. An investigator stood over a dark shape in the bushes, which Cindy realized must be Sammy.

"He's dead?" she asked, even though she already knew the answer.

Bernadette nodded, and Joseph slipped an arm around her skinny shoulders. "I called 911 on my phone," Bernadette continued. "It's prepaid. Sammy gave it to me last year for emergencies. He always said to call 911 if I got in trouble or something bad happened. I never dreamed I'd be using it because something bad happened to him," she said, fresh tears streaking down her cheeks.

Cindy looked away as a lump formed in her throat. She knew what it was like to see the body of someone you cared about, to be shocked by sudden, tragic death. Her eyes roved the crime scene looking for another familiar figure but didn't find him.

Cindy turned to Paul. "Where's Mark?"

"He had more pressing concerns today," Paul said, grimacing.

She had no idea what could be more pressing, but she was sure she didn't want to know. Her eyes drifted back to the dark figure in the bushes and to the forsaken hat on the pavement.

"It can't have been a robbery. Otherwise they would have taken the money from the hat," Cindy said.

"Thanks, but I think we already came to that conclusion ourselves," Paul snapped.

"Are you okay?"

"No. Someone is dead. I'm never okay when faced with the destruction of human life. Also, unlike my partner, I don't have much tolerance for amateur detectives."

Cindy blinked at his brusque tone.

"I'm not an amateur detective. We talked to Bernadette before we went into the theater. I was afraid something had happened to her given what the reporters who mobbed us were saying."

Paul muttered something under his breath that sounded unflattering to the reporters.

Meanwhile Bernadette was still crying and talking. "And I called and called, but there was no sign of Buddy."

"His dog is missing?" Cindy asked sharply.

Bernadette nodded.

"Is it possible he ran away or Sammy left him someplace else?"

Bernadette shook her head and pointed toward the body.

Cindy looked and saw what she had missed earlier. There, in the pool of blood, were dog prints, much larger than any Ginger could have made. Whatever had happened to Buddy happened after Sammy was killed. "Another missing dog? And this one not one of Joseph's puppies?"

"Yeah, yet funny that the dog was still connected to him. It was one of the ones adopted Friday night."

And suddenly it struck her. "Joseph's a suspect, isn't he?"

"Lady, everyone's a suspect," Paul snapped. "Your boyfriend isn't anything special in that regard."

"He's not my boyfriend," Cindy protested, though it seemed such a foolish thing to quibble about as the coroner began to remove Sammy's body.

It made no sense. Buddy didn't have a diamond-studded collar or even a crystal one. This couldn't be the work of jewel thieves. Could it be completely unrelated? Somehow she didn't think so. The timing was just too weird. "Joseph, I wanted to ask you, do you know for sure that you still have Clarice's diamond collar?"

"What do you mean?"

"Are you sure that someone didn't steal it and leave a crystal one in its place?"

"I can find out as soon as I get her back. She's wearing the real one, or at least, she was."

"You know, even women know enough to leave the real jewels in the safe and wear the copies," Paul said.

Joseph shrugged, an embarrassed look on his face.

"Ms. Preston, you can go home. We're done with you for now," Paul said.

She opened her mouth to protest and then snapped it shut. She glanced uneasily over her shoulder at the mob of reporters. Paul followed her gaze. "I'll have someone escort you to your car."

"Thank you," she said.

A uniformed officer moved close and walked with her toward the parking lot. When they left the cordoned-off area, a couple of reporters rushed forward, but he shot them a look so full of menace that even Cindy wanted to run away from him.

"I'm glad you're on my side," she admitted as the reporters backed off.

"Just doing my job, ma'am," he said.

They made it to her car, and he stood guard as she put it in reverse and exited the parking space. As soon as she hit the boulevard, she relaxed slightly. She thought about the pictures that might show up in the paper, though, and realized she should make a couple of phone calls when she got home. The last thing she needed was another wake-up call from her mother.

6

As it turned out, she got an early-morning wake-up call anyway, but it was from Mark. She avoided asking him where he'd been the day before and agreed to meet with him and answer some more questions on her lunch break. After hanging up the phone, she dragged herself out of bed. Despite having played nearly two hours of solitaire trying to calm down, she hadn't fallen asleep until nearly four a.m., and then she had had nightmares about speed dating. Every time the bell rang, a different dog jumped up into the chair opposite her instead of a guy.

She checked her e-mail and saw the alert reminding her that she had signed up to go to a timeshare presentation that evening. She was sure she wasn't in the mood to go, no matter what prizes they tempted her with.

Nothing else caught her eye, so a couple of minutes later she climbed into the shower and promptly fell asleep sitting on the bench along the back while trying to shave her legs. She woke up when the hot water ran out. She considered walking to work, afraid that she'd fall asleep driving even though the church was only a couple of minutes away. Ultimately, she forced herself to run three times around the car, breathing in the cold air before getting behind the wheel.

She staggered into work a couple of minutes late, and Geanie looked up from her desk with a smirk. "Late night?"

"Don't ask," Cindy groaned as she sank into her chair. It was a Monday, and those never seemed to go well. She was sure there was some fresh disaster waiting in the pile of papers on her desk or in her e-mail, and she wished she could find a way to avoid it all and go back to bed.

"Oh, but inquiring minds want to know. Besides, it's more fun to hear about it from you than to read it in the paper."

Cindy groaned and slammed her head down onto her desk. She had managed not to think about the newspapers yet that morning. "What do they say?" she asked, without lifting her head.

"That a homeless man was murdered yesterday and that Joseph and his girlfriend, Cindy, were among the people questioned by police at the scene."

"Oh, no," she moaned. "Not good. No one will ever believe I'm not his girlfriend now."

"Aren't you?"

"No!"

"Didn't you go to the movies together yesterday?"

"Yes, but we realized we're nothing more than friends, and we're both happy that way."

"Oh. Really?"

"Yes, really," Cindy said, raising her head, wondering why Geanie was obsessing on that and not commenting that Cindy had managed to stumble into yet another crime scene. She cleared her throat. "So what fresh torture awaits us this morning?"

"Wildman is going a little crazy trying to nail down the last-minute details on the food drive."

"Of course he is."

71

Wildman was the nickname for the church's youth pastor, a great guy who had been accused more than once of being bipolar. Still, dealing with teenagers could make just about anyone that way, Cindy figured.

"So what exactly is the problem, and does it require us to do anything?"

"I don't know, and I don't know. Sorry, not very helpful."

Cindy sighed. "That's okay. Anything else I should know about?"

"Um. He also mentioned that deposit money is going to start coming in this week for the high school weekend camp in March."

"Oh, goody, deposit money. I think I'm sick."

"You're not sick."

"Well, I wish I was. Does homesick count?"

"Sorry, can't give it to you," Geanie said. "At least it's a short week thanks to Thanksgiving."

"Let us give thanks."

"Nice one."

Cindy turned on her computer and waited for it to boot up. Thanksgiving. Still no invitations, and she was beginning to wonder what she was going to do.

"Are you going to your folks' house for Thanksgiving?" Cindy asked.

Geanie shook her head. "They're celebrating their thirtieth wedding anniversary by taking a cruise. Looks like I'll be flying solo this year."

"Me too. Hey, I know, why don't you come over to my house, and we can do Thanksgiving together?"

"Seriously?"

Cindy knew it was probably the sleep deprivation talking, but it did seem like a good idea. "Yeah. I don't have anywhere to go this year, either. There's nothing to say we can't make Thanksgiving dinner ourselves."

"I don't know. You've never seen me in the kitchen."

"Okay, then I can make it. You can bring pie."

"Is it cool if it comes from a store?"

"Absolutely," Cindy said, turning to look as the office door opened and Joseph walked in. *Speak of the devil.*

"You're on," Geanie said.

"What's on?" Joseph asked.

"Thanksgiving at Cindy's," Geanie said.

"Really? What does a guy have to do to get an invite?"

"*You* don't have anywhere to go for Thanksgiving?" Cindy asked.

He shrugged. "I don't have any family, and I usually take the holiday to travel somewhere. The police want me sticking close by, though, in light of everything that's been happening."

"You're not a suspect?" Geanie asked, horrified.

"There are a lot of connections to me, and I guess they want to be able to get hold of me whenever they have a question."

Cindy wanted to know what they had asked Joseph after they had escorted her from the scene the night before. He looked almost as tired as she felt, but otherwise he seemed none the worse for wear. He turned to look at her and gave her a weary smile.

"We'd love to have you join our misfit Thanksgiving," Cindy said.

"But you have to bring sparkling cider," Geanie said.

"Easy enough. Will a case do?"

Cindy burst out laughing. "There's only going to be three of us."

"So far. These things have a way of spinning out of control," Joseph said, giving Geanie a wink.

"In that case, I'd better bring two pies," Geanie said, blushing.

"So what can we help you with today?" Cindy asked.

"I was driving by on my way to pick up Clarice, and I just wanted to make sure you were okay."

"I'm fine," she said. "You can pick her up?"

He frowned. "They called and said I could come get her. They got DNA samples off her. They think she was in a fight with another animal."

"It took long enough."

"Tell me about it."

"Let me know about the collar."

"You got it," he said. "Well, if everything is under control here, I'll be on my way."

"We're fine," Cindy assured him.

"See you Thursday," Geanie added.

Cindy watched the expression on Geanie's face as Geanie watched Joseph leave and suddenly knew why Geanie had questioned her so sharply about their relationship. "So, maybe *you* should date Joseph," she teased once the door had closed.

Geanie tossed her hair over her shoulder but refused to say a word.

Cindy briefly considered forcing Geanie to admit it, but her silence spoke volumes. Cindy stared at her contemplatively. Geanie was wild, unorthodox, and a bit of a free spirit. Cindy wondered how she would do paired up with the more practical, traditional Joseph.

Either it would be a match made in heaven or . . . someplace else, Cindy thought to herself.

She shrugged. It would be interesting to watch the two of them at the dinner. They were both great people, and if they could find happiness together, then she would be thrilled for them. *If they could be happy together, then maybe someday I'll find someone too.*

She thought of the computer programmer and their upcoming date. Then she instantly felt guilty about it as she thought of the dead men. That had always been her problem, though. When she was faced with death, she didn't know how to get on with life. She could feel a dark mood creeping over her, and she stood up abruptly, determined not to let it take root.

"Where are you going?"

"To find out what Wildman's problem is with the food drive."

"You're a braver soul than I."

Wanna bet?

She found the youth pastor in the teen room, scribbling furiously on the chalkboard. He didn't seem to hear her come in.

"Dave?"

He jumped, dropped the chalk, and spun to look at her, eyes bulging from his head.

She took a step backward. "Sorry to startle you."

He ran a hand through his hair. "Not your fault. I'm just concentrating too hard."

"The food drive?" she asked.

"Yeah," he said, retrieving the chalk.

"What seems to be the problem?"

"I'm trying to work out how I'm going to get enough teams to deliver all the food."

"Okay. Can you be a bit more specific?"

He waved at the board. "We've adopted ten families from the community and collected enough food to give them all really great Thanksgiving meals. We're scheduled to deliver all the boxes Wednesday afternoon, after the kids get out of school."

"All right, with you so far."

"We're only sending one team to each house and then all meeting afterward at the homeless shelter to donate some more food and to help with food preparation for the next day."

"Sounds like a great plan."

"It is. The problem is that only eight of the thirty-nine kids who have volunteered to deliver food have driver's licenses. I can take a group, but that still leaves us a driver and a car short."

"No other kids can do it?"

He shook his head. "A lot have extracurriculars at that time of day, or they're going out of town with their families, or don't have access to a car, or just really don't want to do it."

"How about one of the parents or one of the college kids who worked as camp counselors?"

"Believe me, I've tried everyone." He put down the chalk and turned to stare glumly at her. A second later a smile tugged at his lips.

"Dave, don't look at me like that."

"What, it would be work related."

"No."

"And you'd only have to leave work an hour early."

"No."

"And I'm sure I can get Geanie to cover for you."

"No."

"And you'd be doing me a huge favor."

"No!"

"And you could help a family that's not going to have a Thanksgiving without you."

She thought of Harry and Bernadette. They didn't even have families to share Thanksgiving with. She hung her head. "Okay. Just give me the route with the safest neighborhood and the smartest, quietest kids."

"Um, you realize that the smartest kids and the quietest kids aren't necessarily the same kids, right?"

"Whatever. I just don't want to be responsible for anyone who's going to do anything risky."

"Thank you, Cindy," he said, putting a hand on her shoulder.

"You're welcome."

And next time I'll make Geanie come find out what the problem is.

The morning flew by, and promptly at noon Mark walked through the door.

"There's my lunch date," Cindy said with grim humor. "I'm ready," she said, standing up.

"Great, let's go someplace we can talk. But I'm not going to the kindergarten room again."

She smiled. He was referencing an interview from months earlier. She could still picture him perched on one of the tiny plastic chairs.

"Okay, then, let's go to lunch. I'm starving."

A block away from the church was a stand that boasted enormous one-pound burritos. Mark seemed momentarily taken back by her choice but then ordered the beef burrito with extra sour cream. Cindy contented herself with chicken minus the peppers. The stand boasted a lot of outdoor seating, and they were able to find a table far enough away from the crowd that they had some privacy.

"Apparently I missed all the excitement yesterday," Mark began.

"I wish you hadn't. Your partner can be a jerk."

"Comes with the territory, I'm afraid. You know I can be a bit of a jerk."

"I hadn't noticed!"

"So humor me. Tell me what happened yesterday from your perspective."

Cindy took ten minutes to fill him in, trying to include every detail she could remember but only describing the things directly relating to Bernadette and Sammy.

"What were the two of you doing at the theater, anyway?"

"Seeing a movie."

"Obviously."

"We both needed some fun after everything that had happened, so it seemed like a good idea at the time."

"Was it a date?"

"No!"

He stared at her hard.

"Yes, I don't know. Sort of. But we're not dating. We're just friends. We worked that all out yesterday."

"Before or after you discovered someone had been killed?"

"Does it matter?"

"Humor me."

"Before."

"All right. What can you tell me about Joseph?"

"He's a good guy."

"You'll forgive me if I don't take your word on faith."

She bit her tongue. He was right. Her track record on knowing who was and wasn't a good guy wasn't exactly stellar. "He's been a member of First Shepherd since he was a kid. Parents died young—no other family in the area. He was raised wealthy, but he's still down-to-earth and humble. His dogs mean everything to him, particularly Clarice, and neither of us buys the fact that your lab guy says that she was in a fight with another animal and that's why she was all bloody Saturday night."

"I don't like that either," Mark said under his breath. He shook his head. "Not going to argue with the lab techs, though. What else?"

"He really does care about those less fortunate. He's been involved in half a dozen charities that I know of."

"Any financial difficulties, changes in mood or personality?"

"Nothing that I know of. But as far as personality, I probably wouldn't be the best judge. I've only been getting to know him more in the last couple of months."

"Since the Easter thing?"

She shrugged. "He's one of the few people I know who witnessed any part of that. We both needed to talk."

"I understand. Is there anything else you can think of?"

"I really don't know what else to tell you. I think it's ridiculous to view him as a suspect. He has no motive, and as I see it, he's been one of the victims in this whole mess."

"The only human victim who is alive," Mark pointed out.

"Let's hope he stays that way. If you ask me, you should have him, his house, and his dog under armed guard."

"What about the homeless who adopted dogs that day?"

"I—I don't know," she admitted.

"Let me know if you figure it out," he said.

They finished up their burritos, and Mark ran out of questions. They parted ways in the church parking lot, and Cindy walked back into the office.

The phones were ringing, and there were four parents trying to pay Geanie the deposits for the camp. Thoughts of her conversation with Mark evaporated as she threw herself back into work.

The next few hours flew by in a rush of noise and people and phones. At four-thirty things finally quieted down. She was able to get a few things done. It was almost five when her cell rang. Joseph.

"Hi. I just thought you'd like to hear the update."

"Yes, what did you find out?"

"Unfortunately, very little," he said, sounding discouraged. "My jeweler confirmed that Clarice is still wearing the original collar."

"The diamond one?"

"Yes, indeed."

"Okay, so if that's what the thieves were after, they didn't get it."

"Yeah, I guess. When I get home, it's going in the safe, just to make sure, and I'm putting a plain collar on her. If they come back looking for it, they'll at least leave her alone."

"Sounds like a smart idea. So what did the police say?"

"That's the really frustrating part. The lab guy said they couldn't get any clean DNA evidence."

"Are you kidding? There was all that blood. It wasn't hers. It couldn't have been—" Could it have belonged to one of the puppies? That much blood, though, would surely mean that the puppy would be dead.

"It wasn't human blood or dog blood. It was some other kind of animal. They're saying she must have tangled with something outside before we found her under the shed."

"I don't believe that."

"Neither do I, but what can you do? Blood doesn't lie."

"Are the two of you okay?"

"Yeah, but we're both anxious to get home."

"Okay, well, call me if anything else happens."

"I will," he promised. "I'll just be happy when the police straighten this out and the puppies are found safe and sound."

"Me too."

And in the silence between them, she knew they were both wondering if that would happen. The puppies might be dead. Even if they weren't, they might never be found. She wasn't sure she could live with not knowing, but she knew for certain that Joseph couldn't. "Take care, okay?"

"You too."

Cindy hung up. "That was Joseph. He got Clarice back," she told Geanie. She glanced at the clock. Three minutes until five. She scooped up the papers in front of her and piled them in her inbox to deal with in the morning.

"So what do you have planned for this evening?" Geanie asked as she shut down her computer.

Cindy yawned. "I signed up to go to a timeshare presentation."

"Ooh, one of those ones where they tempt you with prizes and trips?"

"Exactly. I think I'm going to bail."

"Why, you've got something else planned?"

"Sleeping."

"Sleep during the presentation. That's what my cousin did last year, and she won a trip to Hawaii."

"Hawaii is one of the prizes," Cindy admitted.

"See! You should go."

"You know, you're right. It's not like they're going to test me at the end of the spiel."

"Exactly. Ninety minutes of your time, and you'll at least get some kind of prize."

"You talked me into it," Cindy said, shutting down her computer. *Of course it has nothing to do with the fact that I can put off being alone with my thoughts about what's happened to those dogs.*

They walked out to the parking lot together. Once in her car Cindy turned toward downtown instead of home. Twenty minutes later she was walking out of a parking garage underneath the office building where the timeshare company had space.

On the sidewalk a puppy that was tied up to a bicycle rack jumped to his feet and barked joyously upon seeing her. It wasn't safe to pet strange dogs, but he was so cute she almost couldn't resist.

"Sorry, little fella," she said.

She took the elevator to the fifth floor. When she signed in at the front desk, she was directed to a large meeting room where a dozen other people already waited, clustered around a few tables. Cindy glanced around, trying to decide where to sit, when her eyes fell on a familiar figure.

"Harry?"

He looked up at her, and a smile lit up his face. "Hello. Here, have a seat at my table."

It couldn't do any harm to sit with him. Besides, he was the only one in the room who wasn't a complete stranger. She sat down and smiled. "I'm surprised to see you here," she said, trying to think of a polite way to question him. He wasn't someone who could rent his own apartment, let alone afford a timeshare.

"I love these things," Harry said. "Free food, free entertainment, and you always win something cool just for sitting here."

She smiled as she realized her motives were no less mercenary. "So what are you hoping to win?"

"I've got my eye on the portable television," Harry said.

"I'm hoping for the trip to Hawaii."

"I've been to Hawaii three times," he confessed.

"Wow. I've never been."

"It's nice. Lots of palm trees."

"I would imagine."

He fidgeted in his chair and kept glancing toward the door.

"Are you okay?"

"They made me leave Rascal outside. I don't like leaving him alone."

"The puppy tied up outside?"

"Yes."

"I'm sure he'll be fine."

He mumbled something under his breath. But then the speaker moved to the front of the room, the lights dimmed, and the slideshow began.

Cindy struggled to stay awake for the next ninety minutes, not because she wanted to hear what they were saying, but because she was afraid if she started to snore they would kick her out without giving her a chance to draw for a prize from the tantalizing decorated box up front. When the presentation was finally over, she was distraught to discover that she had to spend twenty minutes saying no to three different people who all tried to sell her a timeshare, failed, and sent her "up the sales chain" to the next person she had to say no to. By the end she was exhausted and pretty sure that whatever she won wasn't going to be worth the frustration.

Out of the corner of her eye, she watched Harry stroke his beard and nod his head a lot. Once she distinctly heard him say, "Very interesting, but if you don't mind I'll need to take the materials and think it over."

She was finally cleared to get her parting gift and leave, and she managed to drop her packet of information on an empty table as she approached the prize box.

"Feeling lucky?" the woman standing there asked.

"I hope so," Cindy muttered as she put her hand in and fished out a paper.

"Oh, congratulations, you won a portable television!" The woman reached under the table, pulled out a box, and handed it to Cindy.

It was heavier than it looked. Cindy grasped it awkwardly and made her way back downstairs and outside. There next to the door sat Harry's puppy.

"Hey, Rascal," she said, putting down the box and scratching him behind the ears. At least she knew now who he belonged to and that he'd had all his shots. "Glad to see no one's dognapped you." She wondered if it was a coincidence that the missing puppies were all purebreds from Joseph's prize dog, Clarice. Were they being stolen because they were valuable, or was there a rival breeder out there who would stop at nothing to get his hands on the bloodline? She shook her head. She liked dogs, but it was hard to imagine the enormous prices some people paid for them.

Besides, there was yet another missing dog, the one that had belonged to Sammy. Sure, he wasn't a puppy, but it couldn't be a coincidence. Maybe diamond collars and championship bloodlines were all red herrings. Maybe there was some other motivation for the killer, something else that linked all the dogs.

"He's sweet, isn't he?" Harry asked a minute later as he came out of the building.

"Very."

"You won the television?"

"Yeah. What did you get?"

"The Hawaii trip. I can't go, though. I wouldn't want to leave Rascal. Hey, you want to trade?"

"Are you sure, Harry?" she asked. "Yours is worth a lot more than mine."

"Not to me, it's not. It seems we just got each other's prizes by mistake," he said with a smile.

She found herself grinning back. "You've got a deal."

He handed her the voucher, and she slid the box toward him. "Will you be okay carrying this and walking the little guy?"

"Yup."

Cindy started for her car. "See you around, Harry. And thanks."

She was halfway to the car when she found herself turning around and walking back out of the parking garage. "Hey, Harry?"

"No tradebacks."

"No, nothing like that. I was just wondering. Do you have somewhere to go for Thanksgiving dinner?"

"Well, the shelter usually puts on a nice spread," he answered.

She bit her lip. The side of her that hated taking risks screamed at her to walk away, but watching Harry pet Rascal, she just couldn't. "Would you like to come to my house for dinner?"

"You mean it? Can Rascal come too?"

"Of course."

"Oh, yes! You hear that, boy? We've got someplace to be on Thursday."

She pulled a pen and a piece of paper out of her purse and wrote down her address before she could change her mind. "Do you know this street?" she asked as she handed it to him.

"Yes, ma'am."

"Okay. Dinner is at three."

"We'll be there."

"See you then!" She turned and headed back to her car, hoping she had done the right thing.

She couldn't help but think about what Joseph had said, and she realized it was true. These types of events certainly did have a way of spinning out of control.

7

Monday could have gone a lot better as far as Jeremiah was concerned. An endless stream of people had flowed in and out of the synagogue office all day. He didn't know how Marie juggled so many demands simultaneously. On top of that, every office machine in the place managed to break down.

At the end of the day, Robert's Paper had called to say that a shipment of paper ordered by Marie for the youth director had finally come in. At that point Jeremiah had a throbbing headache, a runny nose, and a suspicion that he might be sick. He opted to wait until the next day to pick up the order instead of trying to race there before the store closed.

When he finally dragged himself home, all he could manage was to heat up some chicken noodle soup before falling headfirst into bed.

⚓

After the timeshare presentation, Cindy felt too keyed up to go straight home. She stopped and grabbed a burger and shake at Bob's Giant Burgers and then decided to head to the grocery store to shop for Thanksgiving dinner.

Once she stepped foot inside, she instantly regretted it. More than a hundred shoppers prowled the aisles, ramming each other with carts, knocking over displays, and moaning loudly as they waited in seemingly endless lines at the checkout. She considered coming back later but realized that the closer to Thanksgiving, the worse it was going to get. She squared her shoulders, aimed her cart for the poultry section, and joined the fray.

What should have taken her fifteen minutes took three times as long, thanks to all the carts blocking the aisles. When she had finally filled her cart with everything she could think of, she headed to the front of the store.

She picked what appeared to be the shortest line, crossing her fingers that there wasn't a reason no one else wanted to be in it. Sure enough, she soon realized that the woman at the front of the line had a coupon for almost everything she had bought. Moments later Cindy saw the small sign next to the register that announced Cashier in Training and she slumped over her cart.

Finally the coupon queen had finished and moved on. The next two people made it through in what seemed a reasonable time. Finally the man in front of Cindy stepped up to the cashier. He then pulled out a plastic bag filled with change and began counting coins into neat little stacks.

The guy behind Cindy swore and demanded, "How come you didn't use the coin-counting machine?"

Cindy took in the man's ragged clothing and realized he had to be very poor. He looked vaguely familiar, and she wondered if he might even be homeless. She turned to the man behind her and said softly, "The coin-counting machine charges several cents per dollar. He might not be able to afford losing that money."

The man swore again, and Cindy turned away. Her eyes landed on the magazine rack, and her eyes widened in horror as she saw herself staring out from the cover of one of the tabloids.

It was a picture of her and Joseph holding hands outside the theater. The headline screamed *Spies Use Millionaire Couple's Dogs to Smuggle Information.*

"Oh, no," she whispered, as she snatched a paper from the stand. She flipped it open, trying to find the article.

Suddenly, the loudmouth behind her seemed to notice something other than the guy counting change.

"Hey, that's you! You're the chick dating that guy with the dogs who's killing homeless people!"

"What? No!" she gasped.

"Yeah, I seen you on the news!"

Other people turned to stare, including the man counting his coins. "You should be ashamed of yourself," he said.

And then pandemonium broke loose. People surrounded her, asking questions, shouting, pressing close. Someone shoved a pen into her hand and begged for an autograph. An old lady hit her with an umbrella.

Cindy backed up until she ran into the man in front of her, who pushed her into the arms of the man behind her.

Someone waved a fist in her face. She screamed. A manager appeared, pushing his way through the crowd and shouting for quiet. He reached Cindy, glanced from her to the tabloid cover still clutched in her hand, grabbed her elbow, and pushed her toward the exit. "You'd better leave. This crowd's not in a friendly mood."

She let him walk her outside. "My groceries," she protested.

"I'm sure you can get someone else to pick them up for you," he said, unable to hide the sarcasm in his voice.

"I'm not his girlfriend!" she snapped.

"Whatever. I don't really care. I just want order in my store."

Cindy pulled free of his grasp and then saw she still held the paper.

"Keep it," the manager said, backing away with his hands raised.

"But I didn't pay for it."

"Just take it and get out of here," he insisted.

A couple of people came out of the store looking their way, and Cindy decided it was a good suggestion. She turned and ran to her car. She peeled out of the parking lot and didn't look back.

⌇⟶⟶

It was still dark when Jeremiah got up. He felt much worse, and his body ached from head to toe. His stomach, which usually wasn't affected by anything, had gone into spasms, and he felt nauseous. He threw on sweats and grabbed his keys. It was time for a trip to the drugstore.

He walked outside, locked his front door, and then turned around. He froze. Something wasn't right. The hair on the back of his neck stood on end as he scanned the small yard slowly. Finally, he saw something out of place, a lump by the hedges close to the sidewalk.

He thought briefly about returning inside for a kitchen knife. Instead he crouched low and made his way toward the lump, eyes probing the darkness around him. Nothing moved in the inky blackness, and as his eyes adjusted, he realized that the lump was the body of a man.

He knew instinctively who it was before he saw the man's face. The homeless man from the park stared back at him with eyes that had seen their last. Jeremiah glanced around, but the German shepherd was nowhere to be seen.

The man had been shot in the left side of the stomach. It looked like he had done what he could to stop the bleeding, but with the location of the wound he would have only had about fifteen minutes before the toxins from the ruptured spleen and appendix killed him. He couldn't have traveled very far at any rate.

He knew where I lived. He was coming here. Jeremiah realized he should have been more careful at the park, followed the man, or at least made sure he hadn't been followed on his way home.

He only had about thirty minutes of darkness left; he would have to move fast. Jeremiah went back inside, yanked open a kitchen drawer, and pulled on a pair of disposable gloves and grabbed a penlight.

Back outside he knelt beside the body and committed it to memory, the way the limbs were angled, the drape of the material, everything, so that he could put it back the way he had found it.

He started with the obvious, pulling the contents out of front and back slacks pockets and the single shirt pocket. A piece of paper with the address of Pine Springs Veterinary Clinic scribbled on it, a fistful of dog treats, and a wallet came under his scrutiny. He shone the light through the piece of paper with the address of the veterinary clinic but couldn't detect anything else. *Was the dog there? Was he sick?* Jeremiah sniffed the dog bones, which appeared to be exactly what they seemed to be. He slid one back into the man's pocket, and then broke it open, careful to snap it off-center so it looked like an accident and not a deliberate break. Breaking it in the pocket ensured that crumbs were there, where they would be expected, and not on the lawn where they wouldn't be. Jeremiah shone his penlight into the pocket and examined the center of the broken bone, but it seemed ordinary.

Next he moved on to the wallet. There was a driver's license, expired by two years, bearing the name Peter Wallace. There was also a Pine Springs library card, the address of the local homeless shelter scribbled on a piece of paper, and a grocery store club card.

He put everything back and then checked for a locket, ring, or watch. The man didn't have any jewelry on him. He slid his hands along the clothes, squeezing, to see if anything was hidden in the linings. Finally he removed the shoes and examined them thoroughly. He even checked to see if the heels had false compartments. He couldn't help but smile to himself. *How very Maxwell Smart, but hey, it's a good hiding place for a reason.*

Satisfied at last that there was nothing on the body that could link the man to him, Jeremiah slipped the shoes back on and then took a couple of minutes to rearrange the body and the clothing until it was exactly as he remembered it.

He made it back inside just as the sky began to lighten. He coughed hard and his stomach twisted more. He had to get the flu medication soon.

He removed the gloves, returned the penlight to its location, and grabbed a pair of scissors. He walked into the bathroom and cut the gloves into tiny pieces into the toilet, flushing at intervals. Finally the gloves were gone.

He returned the scissors to the kitchen drawer, looked himself over, and took a deep breath. It was time to make a decision. Sooner or later neighbors would be leaving their houses and one of them was bound to spot the body and raise the alarm. As sick as he was, he could just go back to bed and wait for the police to come to him, where they would discover him bewildered and feverish.

He shook his head. That would only delay his trip to the drugstore. Better to take charge of the situation. He slipped his cell phone into his sweats' pocket, grabbed his keys, and headed out the door, exactly as he had earlier that morning.

He locked the door, turned, glanced toward the body, and yelled, "Hello?"

He walked slowly toward the body. "Excuse me, are you okay?"

He picked up his pace until he stood over the body. "Are you—"

The nausea he had been fighting for the last hour finally overcame him. He spun aside and fell to his knees, vomiting in the bushes.

When he was able to straighten up, he pulled out his cell phone and called Mark. The detective answered on the second ring.

"It's Jeremiah. I just found a body. Outside my house, 31 Oak Street."

"I'll be there in ten. Don't touch anything."

"Okay." Jeremiah stayed on his knees for a few more minutes before stumbling to the porch to sit down, shoving keys and cell phone into his pockets.

True to his word, the detective pulled up quickly, beating the squad cars by a good thirty seconds. He parked in the driveway, blocking in Jeremiah's car. Seconds later he crouched next to the body in nearly the identical posture that Jeremiah had taken.

Jeremiah watched as officers cordoned off his yard. *So much for keeping a low profile in the neighborhood.*

Finally Mark crossed the lawn to sit beside Jeremiah on the porch. "Heck of a lawn ornament you got for yourself. Did you know him?"

Jeremiah turned and looked the detective straight in the eyes and lied. "No. He does look a little like a guy I saw in the park Saturday playing with a German shepherd."

Mark sighed. "A dog? Are you sure?"

"I remember the dog, but I couldn't swear that this was the same man." Jeremiah said, keeping his voice even.

"There weren't any German shepherds at the charity event," Mark said.

Jeremiah shrugged. "I don't remember seeing any there. I don't know what to tell you."

"Any idea how he might have ended up in front of your house?"

"I wish I knew."

The detective looked at him shrewdly. "You seem to be pretty calm for a guy who just found a body in his yard."

Jeremiah shrugged. "Thanks to Cindy I had to get used to bodies popping up in strange places."

"Ain't that the truth."

"But it was a shock." He jerked his head toward the bushes. "I vomited."

The detective grunted. "Happens to the best of us."

Jeremiah noted the unconscious grouping of himself with the detective and his colleagues in the simple word *us*. He didn't like it, but he didn't draw attention to it.

"He was shot," Mark said.

Jeremiah frowned. "I didn't hear anything like a shot."

"There's some blood up the street. He was probably shot elsewhere and walked or dragged himself this far."

"Why didn't he just call for help or ring someone's doorbell?"

"We're checking to see if anyone else heard or saw anything. Maybe he tried but your neighbors didn't want to open the door in the middle of the night."

"To die for the want of a phone, that's tragic."

"He would have died anyway, where he was shot. Nothing anybody could have done for him."

"In a strange way that makes me feel better."

"Yeah, you're off the hook, Rabbi. Even if you had heard something, you couldn't have saved him."

Jeremiah took a deep breath. "What do you need from me?"

"The usual, unfortunately." Mark pulled a notepad out of his coat and poised a pen over it. "So when did you find him?"

"About three minutes before I called you. I threw up in between."

"Tell me what happened."

Jeremiah took a deep breath and told the revised version of the story. Mark didn't question any of it. He watched other officers examining the scene and the body as Jeremiah talked. The one named Paul pulled the piece of paper out of the shirt pocket with a pair of tweezers and brought it over to show Mark.

"Pine Springs Veterinary Clinic," Mark read.

"So this might have been the guy with the dog," Jeremiah said.

"I think we have to operate under that belief for now," Mark frowned. "This week it seems like everyone has a dog."

"More like everyone has lost a dog."

"True. You ever have a dog, Rabbi?"

"When I was young, my family had a mutt. Good dog."

"Yeah, I just got a dog for my wife yesterday. It was that beagle from Friday night that didn't get adopted."

"Must have been meant to be yours."

"I got to admit it kind of seems that way. I'll tell you, Rabbi, I'm not a big believer in destiny or divine plans or anything, but I really feel like that dog was waiting for me."

"Then that's what is important. Focus on that, and don't worry so much about whether or not it is true," Jeremiah advised.

"That what you do? Focus on your tradition, your rituals, and not worry so much about whether or not it's true?"

White hot anger poured through Jeremiah, and he nearly struck the detective. He stopped himself just in time with a jerk and squeezed his eyes shut as he tried to regain mastery over himself. Stress and illness, that's all it was. He couldn't let them get the better of him. He couldn't let them ruin everything he had worked so hard to build. The neat web of lies and half-truths so carefully constructed could still unravel in a heartbeat if he wasn't careful. Very quietly, struggling still to control the rage that burned within him, he answered, "No. I know that Adonai exists."

He opened his eyes and found Mark staring at him. "Are you okay?"

"It has not been a good morning," Jeremiah said. He let his breath out slowly, and when he looked Mark square in the eyes he had regained mastery of himself. "And, frankly, I'd rather go back to bed than face the rest of the day."

"I can respect that."

Mark's phone rang. The detective took one look at the caller display and groaned.

⁕

It was just after six-thirty in the morning when Cindy rolled her cart to the checkout stand. She wore a baseball cap pulled low over her eyes and intentionally avoided looking at the magazine rack that had caused such trouble the day before.

Fortunately, there were few shoppers that early, and the cashier stifled a yawn and looked bored as he scanned Cindy's items. With a sense of accomplishment, she paid and wheeled her cart outside. She breathed a sigh of relief as the cold morning air hit her. She had done it. She had successfully bought the things she needed for Thanksgiving and hadn't started a riot.

She turned her cart toward the parking lot and froze. The coin counter from the night before was taping up a sign on one of the light posts. It was none of her business, and she certainly didn't want him recognizing her. She tried to look away but couldn't. When he had finished and moved toward a different post, she read the word "Missing!" hand printed at the top of the paper.

She wheeled her cart over to read the rest. The man's dog was missing. A sick feeling twisted her stomach.

She didn't want to face him, but she had to know. "Excuse me, sir."

He turned. "Yeah?"

"When did your dog go missing?"

"Last night while I was here. I had him outside, and when I came out he was gone."

She didn't remember seeing any dogs outside the store when she went in or when she left. She licked her lips. "How long had you had him?"

"Since Friday."

Friday. She knew the man looked familiar. She was sure she had seen him at the charity event. "Have you called the police?"

"No. Do you think I should?"

"I do. In fact, I'll call for you," she said, grabbing her cell phone and calling Mark.

"Don't tell me you've found another body," the detective said without preamble.

"No, but there's another stolen dog. I'm with the owner right now outside of Ron's Grocery on Fifth."

"I'm a bit busy here, but I'll be there as soon as I can. Meantime I'll send someone over."

"Thanks." She turned back to the homeless man. "The police are on their way. They'll help you find your dog."

"You sure?" He looked uncomfortable.

"I'm positive," she assured him. "Let me put these things in my car, and then I'll wait with you."

By the time she had stashed her groceries and returned to the sidewalk in front of the store, a patrol car was pulling up. Vince and another guy got out. Vince saw her and smiled and headed her way.

She pointed toward the man with the missing dog, and the other officer immediately walked over to him. "Sir, your dog is missing?"

"That's right."

She slumped in relief. The police would help him, so she didn't have to. Now, too, if he recognized her, hopefully, he wouldn't make a scene.

"How are you?" Vince asked as he stopped in front of her.

"I've been better," she admitted. "How about you?"

He shrugged. "A little disappointed."

She raised an eyebrow.

"I was sorry when I realized you didn't want to go out with me," Vince explained.

"Excuse me?"

"The speed dating thing. I put you down but didn't get a match."

"Oh, sorry," she said, feeling herself turn red. "You seem like a great guy, it's just—" What could she say that wouldn't sound lame?

"Is it the uniform? Some women don't want to get involved with guys on the force because they're afraid something might happen to them on the job."

She nodded, relieved. "I'm really risk adverse, and you're right, dating a policeman is not without huge risks."

He shrugged. "That's cool. Good thing to know about your-self. Lots of people don't know how to play it safe, when to just stay home and do the smart thing. Nothing to be ashamed of. You won't get hurt that way."

Somehow she didn't like it when he said it like that. The vague, unsatisfied feeling that had been growing for a while twisted harder inside of her. Sure, playing it safe could keep her from getting hurt most of the time, but not all of the time. And maybe a little risk now and again was a good thing.

She bit her lip before she could say something rash. "I guess you're right," she said, forcing a smile.

She turned to look at the other two men, eager to change the subject. "I hope you can find his dog."

"Me too. I don't know what kind of world we're living in when people steal someone else's dog. I mean, I can't even imagine."

"I know. Who would do such a thing?"

"And why?" he asked, scratching his head. "It's beyond me."

"Well, hopefully, they'll catch whoever is behind all of this soon, before any more dogs go missing or anyone else gets killed."

"So you have any theories?" he asked, dropping his voice.

"No, why do you ask?"

He shrugged. "You're the one who thwarted the Passion Week killer. I figure your theories are worth listening to."

She shrugged. "I had a lot of help on that one."

"Yeah, I guess so. Okay, so did you see this guy's dog?"

"No," she admitted. "I was here last night, but I didn't see him. I don't know if that's because he wasn't here or I was just distracted. I didn't know the man had lost a dog until I saw him putting up the flyer this morning."

"So what can you tell me about last night?"

She crossed her arms, took a deep breath, and recounted the story.

Vince whistled at the end of it. "Brutal. You know, you ever have something like that happen again, you call the police."

"I will," she said.

"So you and Joseph?"

"Are just friends."

"Just asking," he said with a smile.

She glanced at her watch. "I have to get going or I'll be late for work."

"Okay, I think we've got it from here. If we have any questions, we'll call."

"Thanks. Do you need my number?"

"Yes."

He flashed her a toothy grin and a wink, and she blushed.

8

Cindy managed to drive home, put away her groceries, and just make it to work on time.

When she walked in, Geanie regarded her with surprise. "Two days in a row I beat you here. I think that's unprecedented."

Cindy was almost always the first one at work in the morning, sometimes beating the others by twenty minutes.

"I was grocery shopping for Thursday," she said, not wanting to explain further.

"Cool! I invited a friend who had nowhere to go either. I hope that's okay."

Cindy smiled. "Sure. Besides, I invited Harry, the homeless guy who occasionally falls asleep in the sanctuary."

"Wow, awesome. It should be a memorable Thanksgiving."

"Yeah, hopefully it's just not memorable for me setting the turkey on fire or anything like that."

"My dad did that once. It wasn't his fault, though. There was a stove malfunction," Geanie said. "It ended up being fine. We just ate around the seared parts. It gave the stuffing a funky smoky flavor, though."

"Eew."

"As long as the food Thursday is edible, you won't hear me complain."

A minute later Dave came into the office and made a bee-line for Cindy's desk. He handed her a piece of paper with a sheepish grin.

"What's this?"

"Address and directions for the house your team will be delivering food to tomorrow afternoon. I also put down the names of the kids who will be going in your car. I put the shyer kids in your car, so hopefully everything will go smoothly and quietly."

She wasn't sure if she should thank him or stick her tongue out at him. She was still unhappy about the way he had dragged her into driving for the event. She settled for a nod.

"We're all meeting up in the youth room tomorrow to do a quick rally and to grab the food before taking off. Extra boxes of food are going to be delivered to the homeless shelter after the event. If you could at least drop your kids off there, you don't have to stay. I can find them rides home at that point."

"No, that's okay," she said. The homeless shelter didn't bother her so much. Plus she still had some questions for Bernadette and hoped the woman would be there to answer them.

"Awesome! I'll see you then. Well, I'll probably see you before then. You know what I mean," the youth pastor finished in exasperation.

Cindy couldn't help but smile as he left the office. Whatever her problems were, at least she didn't have to deal with a hundred kids aggravating them each week.

It was almost ten in the morning before the detectives released Jeremiah and he made it to the drugstore. He stood for what felt like an hour staring at the rows of cold and flu medication and despite his best intentions, he just couldn't force his brain to compare them all and make a choice.

A clerk, seemingly sensing his uncertainty, finally approached. "Can I help you with something?"

Jeremiah gestured to the wall and slurred his dilemma. He hoped it was understandable to someone besides him. For a moment he wasn't even sure if he'd spoken in English.

The clerk cheerfully selected several different candy-colored packages and put them all in Jeremiah's basket. Jeremiah nodded gratefully, too out of it to even register what the man was saying about dosing. He added some water, microwaveable soup, saltine crackers, and 7-Up to his cart before heading for the register.

Once in his car he cracked open a bottle of water and sorted through his packages of pills until one that said "Cold" on it jumped out at him. He popped two tablets out of their sharp, plastic and metallic packaging and downed them, praying that they were fast acting. Then he headed to the synagogue, unsure of what was waiting for him there but convinced that somehow he would manage. He'd never hear the end of it from Marie otherwise.

There were twenty-three messages on the answering machine in the office by the time he got there, and half a dozen of them were from Marie checking to make sure that everything was all right and that he hadn't accidentally burned down the building or canceled Hanukkah services. From the sound of her voice and the increasing length of the messages, he couldn't help but wonder how much was actual concern and how much was her need to be away from her family for a couple of minutes and calling to check in at work was a good excuse for hiding out from them. Whatever the reason, it was strangely comforting to know that she cared so deeply about her job and about her synagogue.

After he had finished clearing out the answering machine, he turned his attention to his scribbled notes from the afternoon before. He had managed to forget about picking up the specialty paper. With a sigh he stared at the written address, which meant absolutely nothing to him. He tried calling the store to get a cross street, but the line was busy. He thought he vaguely remembered Marie saying something about the store being on the other side of the freeway. He locked the office and headed to the car, figuring he could continue trying to call as he drove. Hopefully they would pick up or he would stumble upon it before he had to cave and call Marie.

<hr />

It was half past eleven when Cindy grabbed her purse and hopped up from her chair.

"Where are you going?" Geanie asked.

"I'm heading to lunch a few minutes early."

"Cool. I'll take mine when you get back."

Cindy walked out to the parking lot. Staring at the list of kids and the address for the food delivery had been a good distraction, but her mind had quickly drifted back to the murders. She needed to clear her head, try and make sense of it all, and there was only one person she could think of who could help.

She saw Jeremiah walking toward his car and was glad that she had listened to the impulse to leave early, else she wouldn't have caught him. In the next breath, though, she felt a bit foolish. They hadn't talked but to exchange pleasantries for months before finding Derek's body.

She stared long and hard at Jeremiah. He looked haggard. His shoulders were hunched, and he didn't look well. He was scowling, which wasn't in keeping with how she normally pictured him.

Cindy stood on the other side of the hedge and marveled that a man she had felt so close to at Easter could be a stranger by Thanksgiving. He didn't look up and see her, just kept his head down as he pulled his keys out of his pocket. "Rabbi Silverman!" she called, feeling foolish.

He didn't move or turn, just unlocked his car and opened the door.

"Jeremiah?"

He spun around, dark circles under his eyes making them look sunken. His jaw was clenched, and his whole posture was tense. When he saw her, he relaxed slightly.

"Cindy, what's going on?"

"I was about to ask you that. Are you okay?"

"Actually, I'm sick."

"Oh, I'm sorry to hear that."

He shrugged. "Can I help you?"

She bit her lip. He really did look awful. She should just leave him alone. She shook her head.

He looked like he was just going to accept that and continue on his way. Something stopped him at the last minute, though, and he swept her with his piercing eyes.

"Cindy, is something wrong?" he asked finally, stepping closer.

She had the sudden, crazy urge to take a step back. It had to be because she didn't want to get whatever bug he had, she reasoned. There was something about him, though, in that moment, that reminded her of the night the serial killer held her hostage and Jeremiah killed him.

"Yes and no. I mean, I'm fine. I was just really hoping to talk some things over with you."

"As a rabbi?" he asked, lifting an eyebrow.

"No, as a friend. And, you know, someone I talk about crimes with," she added, forcing herself to smile. It sounded lame even to her ears, and she couldn't help but think of all the times she had made fun of mystery heroes who always managed to find trouble wherever they went. The truth was, she was frightened and frustrated. She had been able to put Easter behind her because she had managed to convince herself that it was all over, that it was in the past, and that life would return to normal and relative safety. Finding Derek the way she did had shattered those illusions, quite possibly for the rest of her life. She didn't want to be someone who jumped at shadows or expected tragedy around every corner. She'd had enough tragedy in her life to ever want to encounter any more ever again.

He nodded. "I understand. I'd be happy to talk with you. Unfortunately, now isn't exactly the best time."

"I understand. We can always talk later. Just be sure to drink plenty of hot liquids and go straight to bed."

"Excuse me?"

"For your flu. You're heading home, right?"

"I wish. I have to go buy some supplies for the week. Marie's on vacation, and unfortunately synagogue business won't wait for her return, no matter how much I wish it could."

"Anything I can help with?"

"Not unless you can tell me where on earth I can find Robert's Paper and Office Supply."

Cindy grinned. "I can help with that. Picking up specialty paper?" she guessed.

"How did you know?"

"I think every church in the area orders from them. I think they cornered the market early. In cleaning out old, old files, I found receipts from them dating back to the sixties."

"That is impressive. Since you know the store, would you be so kind as to give me directions?"

"How about I drive you? It will be easier that way. It will give us time to talk too."

"I don't want to infect you."

"I'm willing to risk it."

He looked like he wanted to argue with her, but he finally nodded, closed his door, and crossed over to her side of the parking lot. A minute later they were in her car and turning onto the street.

"You wanted to talk?"

"Yeah." She hesitated, not entirely sure where to start. "So Marie's out of town this week?"

"Visiting family."

"So where will you be having Thanksgiving?"

"I think the flu might be a blessing. It will save me from having to choose and risk angering the other eighty-seven families."

"Why don't you come over to my house? I'm having a couple of people over and attempting to cook Thanksgiving dinner. It's sort of a misfit holiday."

"Feeding the orphans, are you?" he asked with a weak smile.

"Something like that. I'd love it if you came."

"I wouldn't want to infect everyone."

"Nonsense. We can put you at the far end of the table. Besides, no one should be alone on Thanksgiving."

"Thanks. I'll think about it."

She could tell she wasn't going to get any firmer a commitment from him, so she moved on, taking a deep breath as she plunged into the topic that had been occupying most of her waking moments. "I've been thinking about all these killings lately."

"Yes, and . . . ?"

"It seems to me that the missing dogs are the common denominator. Sure, most of the victims have been homeless, but Derek wasn't. When thieves broke into Joseph's house, all they took were puppies."

"Derek was only holding onto one of the dogs. He didn't own the missing puppy. Maybe the true link is the charity event and not the dogs themselves."

"Yes, but then why steal the dogs?"

"Cause confusion, maybe?"

"If so, it's working," she admitted.

"What has Detective Mark said to you about all of this?"

She sighed. "As usual he thinks the whole thing is police business and that I shouldn't get myself involved."

"He has a point."

"I know he has a point, but how can I not get involved? These things didn't just happen—they weren't stories I heard from a second cousin's nephew's girlfriend's best friend's sister. These happened to me."

"I lost you at nephew," he admitted.

"Sorry. My point was that most people who think you shouldn't get involved are either professionals who don't want amateurs contaminating everything or people whose lives haven't been touched by deep, profound tragedy."

"You could be right."

<hr/>

They arrived at the store, and Jeremiah excused himself while he went inside to pick up the order. Cindy was nothing if not persistent, and he didn't think she would let go of the mystery anytime soon.

He didn't want to talk about the dead man on his lawn that morning. The less people knew about it, the better he'd feel. Sooner or later, though, it would come up, and she would find it suspicious that he hadn't told her. Then she might start digging in places best left untouched.

He would have to tread carefully, though. The flu was impairing his ability to think clearly, and one slipup could cost him the new life he had built for himself.

He walked back out and stowed the package in Cindy's trunk. Then he slid back into her passenger seat with a sigh.

"Everything okay?"

He closed his eyes. "Not really. I feel terrible and I had a really bad morning."

"What happened?"

"I found a body on my front lawn when I tried to leave the house this morning."

"What!" The shock in her voice was clear. He had waited too long to tell her. He opened his eyes. "I debated telling you about it because I didn't want to frighten you."

She set her jaw. "While I appreciate the thought, I'd rather know about danger when it's around."

"The police think he was homeless."

"One of the men from Friday?"

"No. It's possible that he had a dog, though."

"Then the link has to be the dogs. It can't just be about the charity."

Jeremiah wasn't convinced that the two killers were the same or connected by anything other than unfortunate similarities. Still, he wasn't about to admit that to anyone. "I'm sure the police will catch the killer soon enough," he said.

"I'm worried, though. I mean, these killings can't keep going on, and I know a couple of these homeless people. It scares me to think something might happen to them."

"That's understandable."

"It's just like Easter all over again."

"How do you mean?"

"The anxiety, the fear, the knowledge that death could strike wherever whenever. I can't take it." Her face was pale and her hands were shaking. For a moment he thought she might pass out, but she held on.

"You need to relax and learn to focus so these feelings don't overwhelm you," he said.

"That sounds lovely, but I have no idea how to do that," she said.

"I could show you a few breathing techniques you can use to calm yourself down quickly when you're stressed," he offered.

"I would really appreciate that."

"How do you relax now?"

"Well, I generally play solitaire or throw darts at a picture of my brother."

"Darts?" He had seen the dartboard when he had been in her house months before but feigned surprise for her benefit.

"Yeah. Don't tell my mom."

"About the solitaire?" he joked.

"Very funny."

"Okay, what else?"

"That's it."

"No wonder you have trouble relaxing. Both those activities are active instead of passive. They require you to do something instead of just be."

"I don't know how to just be," she said.

"It's a shame. You're missing out on a lot of peace, and your spiritual life isn't all that it could be."

"How do you mean?" she asked, clearly startled.

"'Be still and know that I am God.'"

"Psalm 46:10. That's my father's favorite verse."

Jeremiah smiled. "In our version it is the eleventh verse, not the tenth."

"That is so weird."

He shrugged. "It happens from time to time. The meaning is still the same regardless of whether you see it as verse ten or eleven."

"'Be still, and know that I am God: I will be exalted among the heathen, I will be exalted in the earth,'" she quoted.

"But more than that, I think Adonai desires to be exalted in your heart," Jeremiah said. "How can He be if you are not still and thinking on Him?"

She was quiet for a long time, and he finally looked over to see tears streaking down her cheeks.

"I did not intend to make you cry."

"And yet you did," she whispered. "You're right. I have no idea how to be still. I'm afraid to be."

"Then I shall teach you." They pulled into the church parking lot, and he saw Mark leaning against his car, which was parked on the other side of the hedge next to Jeremiah's car. "But not today," he added. "I think you're right about one thing, though."

"What's that?"

"I should have gone back to bed with a bowl of soup."

"Will you be okay?" Cindy asked as they got out of the car and Jeremiah retrieved the paper from the trunk.

"Fine. I'm sure you have things you need to get back to," Jeremiah said. The last thing he needed was a witness while he spoke to Mark. "Thank you for the ride."

"Something wrong with your car?" Mark asked pointedly as Jeremiah passed through the hedge.

"I didn't know where the paper store was, and Cindy offered to drive rather than try to give me directions," Jeremiah said, holding up his package.

He glanced back and saw that Cindy was halfway to the church office.

"That was nice of her," Mark said.

"Not entirely. She wanted to pick my brain about the murders," Jeremiah said, leading Mark toward the synagogue office.

"Did you tell her about the guy on your lawn?"

"Of course," Jeremiah said, grateful that he had. "I'm guessing you found something else out about him, which is why you're here?"

He unlocked the office and led the detective inside before again locking the door. Whatever happened next, he didn't want to be disturbed.

"We checked out his driver's license. It turns out that Peter Wallace wasn't his real name," Mark said.

Jeremiah could have told him that. "Really? What was his real name?"

"That we don't know yet."

"Then how do you know it isn't Peter Wallace?"

"Because the real Peter Wallace died of cancer three years ago in a hospital in Memphis. We were able to trace the alias back that far. Whoever he was, he knew people who knew a lot about how to steal an identity."

Among other things, Jeremiah thought.

"Rabbi, is there something you should be telling me?"

"Not that I'm aware of. Why don't you tell me why you're really here?"

"I checked with some of the people who spend a lot of time in the park. They remember him and a dog."

"I told you I thought there might have been a dog."

"Yeah, well, this dog doesn't fit our pattern. He wasn't adopted recently."

"I don't know what to tell you," Jeremiah said, struggling to keep his face, voice, and posture neutral.

"I can't shake the feeling that there's something I'm missing, that maybe that man was coming to see you about something."

"He could have been looking for a rabbi, I suppose," Jeremiah said, pretending to be deep in thought. "Of course it would be easier to find one here."

"Unless he wanted to talk to one in private."

"And why would he want to do that?"

"I don't know," Mark admitted.

"Now you've got me curious," Jeremiah said. "Maybe Cindy and I should put our heads together some more and see if we can come up with something."

"No, I'm sure it's nothing," Mark said hastily. "Last thing I need is her stumbling into harm's way again."

"But if the man was trying to see me—"

"No, he could have lasted a while with that injury. He might have been headed somewhere, but I doubt we'll ever know where since he didn't make it any farther than your lawn."

"Let me know if you do figure it out. It would make me feel better."

"You got it, Rabbi," Mark said, turning to leave.

"Thank you for your help," Jeremiah added for good measure.

Mark smiled. "That's what we're here for."

9

As Mark reached the parking lot, his cell phone rang. "Hello?"

"It's Paul. We've been called to investigate a possible homicide over on Shady Glen Drive."

Mark whistled low. Shady Glen Drive was in a private, gated community where the super wealthy lived. Sooner or later death claimed everyone, from those with no home to those with dozens of them. If this was a possible homicide, though, then death might have had help this time.

"It will take me a few minutes to get there."

"Sure, I'll be waiting."

When Mark arrived at Shady Glen Drive, it wasn't tough to figure out where to go. Half the street had been cordoned off, and his fellow officers were swarming like flies over every square inch of it.

At the epicenter of the activity he finally found Paul, sitting on the sidewalk next to a gray-haired man wearing an Armani suit and shoes that cost more than Mark made in a year. The man was visibly upset from the look of his puffy eyes and swollen red nose to the tear stains on his shirt.

Mark sat down on the sidewalk as well, quietly, waiting for Paul to clue him in to what had happened.

"His wife was hit by a car while she was out jogging," Paul finally said somberly.

"She went jogging every day," the man said. "About ten years now she's been jogging. We started doing it together after I had my heart attack. Six weeks into it I quit, but she kept going. She loved it. She said it was the only time she ever got to be by herself to think."

"Accident?" Mark asked Paul quietly.

"I don't think so," Paul said. "The car that hit her was a Mercedes, stolen from a couple up the block just moments before."

Mark raised an eyebrow. He couldn't even remember the last time a crime had been reported in the area. Politicians, entrepreneurs, even a few of Hollywood's A-list called the area home for just that reason.

"Did either of you have any enemies?" Paul asked. "Anyone who would want to do something like this?"

"Plenty. That's why we live here. We have a panic room in the house, bodyguards that live on property. She was right, you know; the only time she was ever truly alone was when she was jogging. Had I ever dreamed someone would do this, I never would have let—" He broke down sobbing.

Mark just sat quietly, head bowed like he had done with so many people before.

Husbands and wives, parents, children, friends, even unlucky strangers such as Cindy. He watched as they dealt with their pain and fear and struggled to put themselves together so that they could be helpful. *It sucks to be this guy, sitting here helpless after his wife has been the victim of a terrible crime. I am so glad I'm not this guy.* "Have we found the car?" he asked Paul.

Paul nodded. "A block outside the gate."

"So it definitely wasn't about taking the car."

"That's what I'm thinking."

The man started shaking. Mark stood up and signaled to one of the paramedics on scene. Mark and Paul moved away so they were out of earshot but could still observe the proceedings.

"He's in shock," Paul said.

"Yeah, hard to fake to that degree," Mark said.

"If he's faking, he should reconsider a career in theater."

"One of his neighbors could probably set him up."

"Yeah, really."

"So the usual, get a list of people who might have been capable of doing this?"

"Unless you've figured out a whole new way to do police work, then I guess so," Paul said, sarcasm edging his voice.

Mark scowled. It was going to take time away from their other investigation, and he didn't like it.

"Forensics find anything with the car?" he asked.

"Let's go find out," Paul suggested.

They opted to walk the three blocks instead of drive. Mark took in everything around him, wondering who might have seen something or how someone might have gained access without being caught or at least seen.

When they reached the car, they found the tech in charge and approached him. "Hey, Curtis, what do you have?" Mark asked, glancing inside the car while being careful not to touch it.

Curtis shook his head. "Wiped clean. Plus, the owners of this car kept it immaculate. The only thing I found here were a couple of tufts of dog hair in the backseat."

"Dog hair?" Paul asked.

Curtis nodded.

"Do the owners of the car have a dog?" Mark asked.

"I think we should find out," Paul said. He flipped open his phone and dialed. "Hi, yeah, it's Paul. Listen, are you still with the guy whose car was stolen? Yeah? Okay, ask him if they have any dogs or have transported any dogs in their car in the last six months."

Mark waited impatiently for the response to come back. After a moment Paul nodded and then continued speaking. "Thanks, no, that's it." He snapped his phone shut.

"No dogs, he's allergic."

Mark turned and began to run back toward the crime scene. Paul was right on his heels when he stopped in front of the husband, who seemed much calmer since the paramedic had begun checking him over. The man had a blanket wrapped around him, and Mark suspected he'd been given something to calm him down.

"Sir," Mark asked. "Did you and your wife have a dog?"

"Yes. Why do you ask?"

"Where's the dog now?" Paul asked.

The man looked confused. "I don't know. In the house maybe? Or I guess the backyard."

"Did she ever take him jogging?" Mark asked.

"I don't know. Maybe. I've been on a business trip, and I just got home last night. One of the security staff probably knows."

"Sir, when did you get the dog?" Mark asked, holding his breath as he waited for the reply.

"My wife got him while I was away. I think she said she got him Friday night."

Mark let out his breath and turned to look at Paul. A millionaire's wife, another millionaire's assistant, and two homeless men—it was improbable, but he could come to no other conclusion. "They're all connected."

◦━◆━◦

When Cindy got home, she had to fight the urge to call Jeremiah. She wanted to take him up on his offer to teach her some techniques to help her relax and focus. Still, if he had actually gone home to get some sleep, she would hate to wake him up.

She ate a quick dinner and then realized she had a lot to do to prepare to host Thanksgiving in two days. She began with the living room and started cleaning, trying to do a thorough job. Her mother would be so proud if she could see her.

As she worked, she couldn't keep her mind off the murders. They were a steady drum of worry in the back of her mind, even when she wasn't actively thinking about them.

When she finished in the living room, she cleaned the bathroom as well before calling it a night. After getting ready for bed, she hopped online and looked up the address that she would be driving the kids to the next day.

She knew the street, and she double-checked the cross streets for the exact address. Thinking about the event did little to calm her down, and she briefly considered playing a game of solitaire. Jeremiah was right, though; given that it was an active thing, it might not help her settle down to sleep.

She brought her iPod into the bedroom, found an hour-long track of the sound of ocean waves, and did her best to fall asleep.

❦

The next morning Cindy felt jittery. She wasn't sure if it was the unsolved murders, the food drive, or both that was bothering her. Again she thought about calling Jeremiah, and again she forced herself to take a deep breath and let him be. She would see him the next day, and maybe after dinner she could convince him to show her the breathing techniques he had mentioned.

She was the first one to work and took some small satisfaction in having the place to herself for fifteen minutes before the chaos of the day began. It turned out to be the only oasis of peace in a day otherwise dominated by people turning in camp money and ministry leaders scheduling holiday events.

When it was finally time to report to the youth room for duty, she was almost relieved. At least it would be a different kind of crazy than what she had been dealing with all day.

She walked into the room and thought that she was early but soon discovered that the few others present were the teen drivers. Dave was talking earnestly to all of them. He welcomed her into the group, and she also got the lecture on safety as well as another printout of the sheet he had given her the day before. The only difference was that he had added his cell phone number to the sheet this time.

"Okay, if you get in trouble, give me a call. If you get into real trouble, call 911. Got it?"

They all nodded as more teenagers arrived. Sitting on one of the couches and watching the proceedings, Cindy wondered if it was too late to back out of the whole driving thing. All around her were bright-eyed kids bursting with long-weekend excitement and pent-up energy. Dave wasn't helping. Standing at the front of the room, he led the group in a prayer for safety and thanksgiving. Then he proceeded to wind them up until they were all jumping up and down, screaming.

The air itself seemed to crackle with anticipation. She remembered what it was like to be part of just such a youth group. But it seemed so far away. It had been before her sister died. Afterward she couldn't stand to go. She told her parents it was because there were too many memories, too many people with pitying looks. The truth was that from their scavenger hunts to their sleepovers to their parties, youth groups participated in activities that she just found too dangerous. To make it worse, the people involved were almost completely unaware of the risks they took daily.

"Okay, so everyone's clear on what we're doing, where we're going, what this is all about?" Dave asked at last.

"Yes!" everyone around her shouted at once.

"I can't hear you!"

"Yes!"

"I don't know, maybe you guys really don't want to do this. I mean, I'm not feeling the energy here. Are you sure you're ready?"

When the group shouted "Yes!" for the third time, Cindy could swear her ears started to ring.

"Great. Now look up here on the board for your car assignment. Drivers, raise your hands and lead the way to your vehicles."

Cindy stood and raised her hand as instructed. She turned and headed for the parking lot, three teenage girls trailing after her.

Twin sisters Ai and Mai, exchange students from Japan, climbed into her backseat. The girls were seventeen and staying with one of the church's families for the year. Brenda, who was a couple of years younger, slid quietly into the passenger seat. Cindy glanced at her. She knew from Dave that Brenda was painfully shy and rarely talked. She also knew the girl never missed a Sunday or a youth group meeting. She always came alone by bus, and no one really knew anything about her parents.

"Everyone, put on your seatbelts," Cindy said, only to glance around and realize that everyone already had. She had been all prepared to give a speech about keeping the noise and the horseplay down but decided against it when she realized she'd be lucky if she could get her charges to speak if she wanted them to.

She waited a moment for all the cars with teenage drivers to exit the parking lot before she headed out to Canal Street to the Parker family. She had already mapped the way out in her head, but she also had directions in the glove compartment if she needed them. She knew Canal Street and had been relieved that it was where they were headed. It was a neighborhood where many families had fallen upon hard times, lives and houses in various states of disrepair, but in which drugs or gangs had not taken hold.

After ten minutes the unnatural silence finally got to her. "So how do you girls like America so far?" she addressed the twins, glancing at them in the rearview mirror.

They both nodded enthusiastically, smiles lighting up their faces, but they didn't say anything. Cindy glanced at Brenda. "You looking forward to Thanksgiving dinner?"

Brenda just shrugged and looked away.

Cindy returned her attention to the road. Dave had been true to his word, but she was surprised to discover that she was wishing she hadn't been so strict with her requirements. A little talking would have been preferable to the awkward silence that reigned in the car. The next fifteen minutes were some of the longest she could ever remember as they made their way through traffic that was already snarling up for the holiday weekend. She was grateful that once she got home she wouldn't have to be driving anywhere else until at least Friday.

At long last they turned onto Canal Street about a quarter of a mile from their destination. Next to her there was sudden movement as Brenda sat up straight and leaned forward, her hands on the dashboard, and her tiny face pinched with fear.

"Where are we going?" Brenda asked. "Which family?"

"The Parker family," Cindy said, startled.

Brenda shook her head fiercely. "I told Pastor Wyman I didn't want to come to this house."

"I'm sorry," Cindy said. "That's probably my fault. I asked for—never mind. We'll only be there a couple of minutes."

"Can I stay in the car?" Brenda asked.

Cindy didn't know how to respond to that, and for a moment she considered calling Dave's cell to ask him. *He put you in charge of these girls,* she reminded herself. *And this was strictly volunteer work for them. She doesn't have to be here, so it wouldn't hurt for her to not go inside, I guess.*

"Sure, you can stay in the car if you want to," she said.

"Thank you," Brenda said, sliding down in her seat until Cindy thought she was going to end up with her whole body in the foot well.

"Um . . ."

Then she spotted the address she was looking for, and she pulled over to the curb in front of a house where the weeds had long before supplanted the lawn. Two young boys played among the weeds with what looked like a ratty stuffed dog and a beat-up toy dump truck. A girl who looked about sixteen sat on the porch, smoking a cigarette openly.

"Stay here for a minute," she told the twins. Cindy got out of the car and walked up the path to the front porch. The boys jumped up and followed her, eyes wide.

"I'm from First Shepherd; I'm looking for the Parker residence," Cindy addressed the teenage girl.

"Mom! The chick's here with the turkey," the girl shouted.

Cindy took a step backward. A moment later a woman in her forties appeared in the front door. Her hair wasn't brushed, her cheeks were hollow, and she wiped her hands repeatedly, almost obsessively, on the yellowed apron she wore over her dress.

Hope has abandoned this family, Cindy thought.

"Hi, I'm here from First Shepherd."

"Please, come in."

"I just wanted to make sure I had the right house before we unpacked the car," Cindy explained.

"You do have the right house, and we are so grateful for it. I'm Mrs. Parker," the woman said.

"Okay, we'll be right in."

Cindy turned and hurried back to the car. She opened the back door. "Okay, girls, help me get the food out of the trunk."

Ai and Mai piled out, and between the three of them they managed to lift out the box and four bags of food that had been donated to give the family a real Thanksgiving dinner and a couple of other meals as well. Holding the box in one arm, Cindy managed to close the trunk without dumping the contents onto the ground. She thought she caught one of the girls grinning as the box wobbled.

As they walked back up to the house, Cindy glanced down at the dirty, broken toys and wished she had brought something the children could play with. She wondered if the church was going to do another charity drive for Christmas and whether or not this family would be included. She hoped so, because some new toys would certainly go a long way here. Mrs. Parker held open the screen door for them, and they trooped into the kitchen. They placed the box on the kitchen table and the bags on the counter.

Mrs. Parker started going through them gasping with excitement while her sons danced around the table asking over and over what was in the bags. The girl finally came in, and even though she acted uninterested Cindy could see that there was curiosity in her eyes as she, too, peered into the bags.

With the food delivered, Cindy had no idea what to do next. Were they supposed to stay for a few minutes, or would it be rude to drop the food and run? She glanced at the twins who watched the whole proceedings with fascinated expressions.

"Happy Thanksgiving," Cindy said.

"To you too," Mrs. Parker beamed. "The six of us will be eating fancy tomorrow."

"Six?"

"Yes, I'm sorry my husband and my other daughter couldn't be here to see this and thank you in person. He's working, and she's off somewhere, probably with her friends."

"Well, have a good day," Cindy said, putting a hand on each of the twins' shoulders and edging toward the door.

No one tried to stop them, and so they left the house and a moment later were climbing back in the car.

She heard running footsteps and turned to see the two boys chasing after them.

"Mom said to say thank you," the oldest one said as they screeched to a halt next to her car.

"Thank you," they chorused.

"You're welcome. And have a very happy Thanksgiving," Cindy said, wishing once more that she had something to give them.

They looked past her into the car, and their eyes widened.

"Brenda, what are you doing in there?" the youngest one asked.

Cindy turned and saw the girl sitting in her front seat, face buried in her hands.

And suddenly she realized why Brenda hadn't wanted to deliver food to the family. It was *her* family.

"Are you coming into the house now, Brenda?" the other brother asked, his voice a little sad.

Brenda shook her head almost imperceptibly, and Cindy bit her lip. She couldn't help but wonder if the girl's family knew she was going to church and youth group.

"She's got a couple of errands to run with us. She'll be home later," Cindy said at last when Brenda made no other move to answer her brother.

The boys nodded and then moved off as Cindy started the car and pulled away from the curb.

"Why didn't you say anything?"

"I didn't want anyone to know," Brenda said, her voice miserable. "It will ruin everything."

Cindy knew what it was like to have problems with her family. "No, it won't. Girls, it's our little secret that we saw Brenda's family today. Will you promise not to tell her secret?"

"We won't tell," Ai said.

"We understand," Mai echoed sweetly, putting a gentle hand on Brenda's shoulder.

"There, no one else has to know," Cindy said.

"Thank you," Brenda said, tears in her eyes.

"You're welcome," Cindy said, struggling not to let her own pain and sorrow show.

She drove toward the homeless shelter, and it occurred to her that there were so many with a home that were just as hungry as those with none. She thought of all the other kids who went to the church and their families. How many of them were suffering in silence, with none to know? It was a shame when there were many eager to help if only they knew of the need. She wondered what more she could do to help Brenda and her family without betraying the girl's trust.

They were within three blocks of the shelter when Mai suddenly bounced up and down in the backseat. "Doggie!" she shouted in Cindy's ear, pointing to the side of the road.

Cindy glanced over and saw a puppy covered with dirt and grime rooting in a garbage can that had been knocked over. Patches of the white, wavy fur showed through.

"We have to help him," Ai chimed in.

"We're not going to pull over—" Cindy started to say.

Brenda turned and looked at her, eyes full of pleading. She wondered how often the girl actually asked for anything from anybody. If it hadn't been for her, she would have been in someone else's car and delivering food to someone else's family. Cindy nodded slowly and signaled as she pulled over to the side of the road. "Everyone stay here; we don't know if he's violent or has rabies, or what," she said.

She got out of the car and wondered what was wrong with her. The dog probably had an owner. If he didn't, he probably wouldn't appreciate her interference in his dinner. She had had to get rabies shots once as a kid when a squirrel had bitten her on a family camping trip. She remembered the pain of the shots, and her stomach lurched.

God, please don't let the dog have rabies, she prayed as she walked toward him.

She saw a flash of red around the dog's neck. For a moment she panicked, thinking it was blood, until she realized it was a collar. She glanced around; there were no houses nearby. The puppy had an owner, then, but there was no one in sight, and given his filthy condition, it was likely he had run off. *If somebody owns him, he's probably had his rabies shots. Somebody is probably worried sick about him.*

She moved closer slowly and began making soft clucking sounds. When she was just a couple of feet away, the dog looked up at her and she jerked. It was a poodle. She could tell by the distinctive shape of his face.

"Here, boy," she said, holding out her hand.

The puppy sniffed at her and then bounced over to her and began licking her hand and whining. An ID tag dangled from a red collar studded with crystals, and with her other hand she twisted the tag around so she could see it. She gasped as she read the name out loud.

"Buff."

10

Cindy couldn't believe her eyes. The puppy was Buff, the one that Joseph had sent her to get when she had found Derek dead instead. He was alive, filthy, hungry, and far from home, but alive! She gazed at him in wonder for a moment, too astonished to do anything but pet him as he licked first her right hand then her left.

"How did you get here, Buff?" she asked him.

"Is he okay?" she heard Brenda call from the car.

Cindy half turned back. "Yeah. Can you bring me my purse?" Cindy called back.

A moment later all three girls were clustered around, cooing, and then they were on the ground petting Buff.

"I know this dog, or rather, his owner. We need some sort of leash so he can't get away from us if something spooks him," Cindy said, holding firmly to his collar. "Do you see anything we can use?"

"Here, how about this?" Ai asked, pulling the drawstring out of her hoodie and handing it to Cindy.

Cindy took the string, looped it through the metal circle on the collar, and tied it off. It was crude, but it would do for the moment until Mark or Joseph could arrive.

Holding the end of the string in her left hand, she dug her cell phone out of her purse with her right and called Mark and then Joseph. Both of them reacted with surprise and pledged to be there as soon as possible.

That done, she led Buff back toward the car and let the girls pet him while she turned off the engine.

"Whose dog is he?" Brenda asked.

"This is Buff. A member of the church owns him. His name is Joseph Coulter."

The twins startled giggling.

"What's so funny?" Cindy asked.

"Your boyfriend," Mai said.

"We saw your picture," Ai added.

"He's not my boyfriend," Cindy said, feeling herself turn bright red. "We're just friends."

They waited for a long time, and Cindy realized both of the men must have gotten caught in the holiday traffic. Finally Mark drove up, a siren flashing silently on top of his roof. She guessed traffic had to have been a nightmare for him to resort to using it.

He got out of the car and knelt down next to Buff. "So all this fuss started with you, huh, boy?"

The puppy licked his cheek, and a smile flitted across the detective's face. Cindy couldn't help but feel warmth at the sight.

Mark checked the puppy over and then finally looked at Cindy. "Where, exactly, did you find him?"

"The girls spotted him eating out of that trash can," Cindy said, pointing. "They begged me to pull over. I didn't realize it was him until I saw the ID tag on his collar."

Mark glanced around at the girls and then looked back at Cindy, eyebrows raised.

"I'm a driver for the youth group's food drive project. We're making our last stop at the homeless shelter. That's where we were headed when we stopped for him."

"Ah," he said, clearly uncomfortable with the girls being there.

"At least he doesn't seem hurt at all, just filthy," Cindy said. "That has to be a good thing, right? It bodes well for the other dogs—that they're okay and we might get them back safe and sound?"

"Maybe. In some ways it raises more questions than it provides answers. Doesn't it, boy?"

"Like what?"

"Well, for example, was he set loose or did he escape? If he was set loose, where and how far was it from where he was being held? For that matter, how long did they hold onto him before setting him loose? If he got away, how, where, when?"

"Oh," Cindy said, looking afresh at the puppy, who was happily licking Mark's fingers.

"Yeah. Either way is significant, but without knowing which it is, we're really operating in the dark here."

"If only Buff could speak and tell us what happened to him," Cindy said, giving the dog a quick scratch behind the ears.

"And humans haven't been wishing for that as long as they've had pets," Mark said with a small smile.

A car pulled over to the curb a few yards away, and Cindy recognized it as Joseph's. A moment later he was kneeling on the ground next to Buff. If she had thought the puppy was happy to see the rest of them, it was nothing compared to the way he greeted his master. Joyous licking and barking ensued, and the love was clear. Joseph responded in kind, picking him up and tickling his belly while praising him for being a good boy.

"Where have you been?" Joseph asked the puppy.

Buff barked in response.

Mark shrugged as he stood up. "On the other hand, maybe he can speak. The question is, can Joseph translate?"

"Not enough to tell you where he's been or who did this to him, I'm afraid," Joseph said. "Believe me, I wish I knew," he continued, his hands curling into fists and rage flashing in his eyes.

The relief Cindy had felt upon finding Buff faded slowly as she watched Joseph with him and remembered that all Buff's brothers and sisters were still missing, along with other dogs he wasn't related to in the least. Where were they? Would they escape or be released? She wrapped her arms around herself. And why were they taken in the first place? Mark was right about one thing. The reappearance of Buff didn't answer anything, but rather just made the whole picture fuzzier.

She glanced around and her eyes fell on the girls, and with a jolt she remembered her other responsibilities. They needed to get to the shelter and then back to the church before the twins' exchange family began to wonder what had happened to them or before Brenda missed her bus.

She cleared her throat. "Gentlemen, the ladies and I really do have to get going."

"Thank you, all of you," Joseph said, looking up earnestly at each girl in turn.

Ai and Brenda dropped their eyes, but Mai burst into excited laughter and clapped her hands together.

"That reminds me," Cindy said. "Joseph, would you care to explain to these young ladies that we are not dating, not now, not ever?"

"Why, whatever you do mean, darling?" Joseph teased, eyes all wide and innocent.

Cindy could have killed him. She glared until he smiled and shook his head. "Sorry, girls, I'm just teasing. Cindy and I are just really good friends, nothing more."

Both Ai and Mai sighed in disappointment while Brenda just continued to stare at the ground.

"Thank you," Cindy said. "Okay, everyone back in the car. We're going to be the last ones to the shelter at this rate."

They all turned obediently and got back in her car, strapping on seat belts before she could even open her own door.

⊙━◆━⊙

It was with a deep sense of relief that Jeremiah locked the office and headed out to the parking lot. Except for the services Saturday morning, he had nothing to do for four days but sleep and eat turkey. It seemed like an excellent plan to him. He was especially eager to get to the first stage of sleeping, even if it meant he wouldn't wake up until just before he had to go to Cindy's for Thanksgiving dinner.

That reminded him: he still needed to let her know he would actually be there. He still felt guilty going when he was sick, but she had been insistent. Thanksgiving, as an American holiday, was certainly something he wasn't used to celebrating, but he had found that the few he had partaken of since he had moved to the country had left a lasting impression and he didn't want to skip this one. Truly, turkey with stuffing and mashed potatoes was a wondrous thing not to be missed if one could help it. At the very thought his stomach rumbled and he began to salivate.

Not yet, he told himself as he climbed into his car. As he turned out of the parking lot, he found himself instantly enmeshed in a snarl of traffic. He sighed and leaned his head against the cool glass of his window. It felt good against his hot

130

forehead. Holidays had their downsides as well, and traffic was almost always one of them.

After a minute he turned on the radio, hoping to hear something about the traffic.

"And now, listeners, KPIN is pleased to bring you a very special song request that has just come in by e-mail. This one is for Jeremiah from an old colleague. The song is 'You Know My Name' by Chris Cornell. So, Jeremiah, this one is for you from H.S."

Jeremiah swore in Hebrew and nearly rear-ended the car in front of him.

As it turned out, Cindy and her group were the last ones in to the shelter. When they arrived, Dave was standing outside. He waved at them with a look of relief on his face. Cindy glanced at her watch and realized that they had spent nearly an hour with Buff.

He hurried over to her as the girls started unloading the rest of her trunk. "Is everything okay?"

She nodded. "Sorry, slight side trip, but we're all good. Food has been delivered to the family, and now food is being delivered here. All in all, the mission has been a success."

"I'm glad to hear it. I was about ready to call you. I was sure something had happened to you despite the fact that I gave you the best neighborhood and the most well-behaved kids."

"No, it was nothing to do with any of that. We found the dog that was stolen Friday at the charity event wandering the street. We stopped and called the police and Joseph."

Dave's eyes widened in real alarm. "You dragged the girls into the middle of a criminal investigation?"

"No, it wasn't anything like that. We saw the dog and he was dirty and they wanted me to stop, and ta-da, it turned out to be *the* dog. It was all really low-key with the detective and everything."

Dave still looked stricken after her explanation, and after a minute she decided not to try and explain any further. After all, if he was uncomfortable with what had happened, maybe it would get her out of future duty when they needed a driver for something else.

The girls had finished emptying her car. Cindy and Dave moved inside where shelter workers were unpacking the boxes and stacking them by the back door.

"Okay, so what can we help with?" Cindy asked.

"Nothing, it's all done. The shelter workers and volunteers can take it from here," Dave said.

"Oh, okay." Cindy turned and looked around, trying to find Bernadette. To her disappointment and concern, she didn't see any sign of the woman or her tiny canine companion. She turned back to Dave. "So what do we do now? Do we head back to the church?"

He nodded. "You're off the hook, though. It turns out Jeffrey has his mom's van, and he can take three more."

"Oh, then I guess I really am done," Cindy said.

"I wish I was," Dave said with a sigh as he glanced at his watch. "I've got to drop my kids back at the church and then pick up all these boxes and take them to recycling."

"I'll do it," Cindy said.

"Really?"

"Yeah, there's a recycling location just around the corner in the Plusmart parking lot. It'll take me five minutes to dump the stuff there."

"You're a lifesaver. What would I have done today without you?" Dave asked.

"Just remember that in a couple of weeks when you tell the review board I deserve a raise," she half-joked.

"Don't think I won't," he said earnestly. "If anyone goes above and beyond for First Shepherd, it's you."

Belatedly, Cindy realized that it would have been easier to volunteer to drive kids back to the church than to do the recycling. Fortunately, one of the workers helped her out by breaking down boxes and stacking them in her trunk and backseat as she carried them out to him. The last couple were really large when flattened out, and she was surprised he managed to make them fit in her already stuffed trunk.

"Thanks," she told him when the task was finally done.

"Glad to help. Happy Thanksgiving."

"Happy Thanksgiving," she replied, turning to look one last time for Bernadette.

"Who is it you keep expecting to see?" he asked.

"Is it that obvious?"

"Kind of, yeah."

"Sorry. I was hoping this one older woman was here. Her name's Bernadette, and she has a little dog."

"Ginger? Yeah, cute dog."

"So you know them?" Cindy asked.

"Yeah. Bernadette is a semi-regular, and now so is Ginger. Bernadette has introduced her to everyone here at least five times already. You know, I think the whole Animals to the Rescue thing is a great idea, especially for people like Bernadette who need someone to love. I think it will do a lot of good in the long run."

"I hope so. Could you give Bernadette a message from me when you see her?"

"Of course I can deliver it, but you might want to wait a couple of minutes and give it to her yourself. I think that's her coming down the street," he said, pointing.

Cindy turned to look and recognized first Ginger then Bernadette. She broke out in a smile. "Thank you, I think I will give her the message myself."

Cindy walked to meet the woman and dog. When she got close, she called out to them, and Bernadette's eyes lit up in recognition. "Cindy, what are you doing here, child?"

"I was hoping to get a chance to talk to you," Cindy confessed. "How have you been?"

"I've been better, but I've also been worse, so I guess that means middlin', as they say," Bernadette responded.

Cindy smiled. "What are you doing for Thanksgiving?"

"Ginger and I hadn't really thought a lot about it yet, but we'll probably spend it here with hot food and good company. That's what I've done the last two years, and it's pretty nice. Why do you ask?"

"I'm having a few friends over to my house for Thanksgiving dinner, and I was wondering if you and Ginger would like to come?"

"Will there be anyone I know there?"

"Um, well, Joseph will be there. And I don't know if you know Harry, but he's coming."

"Harry?" the old lady pursed her lips in thought. "Is that the Harry who volunteers here at the shelter?"

"I don't think so," Cindy said. "I think he's a regular here."

"Then it must not be the same Harry that we're thinking of. Joseph is coming, though, you said?"

"Yes, he is."

The old lady smiled. "Ginger and I would be honored to dine with you at your house. At what time will you expect us?"

"Two o'clock."

"Perfect."

Cindy was prepared, and she pulled a piece of paper out of her purse with her address and directions from the shelter to her house written on it. She winced at the scrawl. She had scribbled it down right before heading into the youth room that afternoon. It probably would have been much easier to read if she had typed it up and printed it out instead. "I hope you can read my writing, I wrote it in a hurry," she said apologetically.

Bernadette took it from her. "My dear, I was a teacher for thirty years, I assure you I can read anyone's handwriting."

A teacher? Cindy thought.

"What happened to you?" Cindy asked before she could stop herself. "No, don't answer, it's none of my business," she hastily added.

Bernadette patted her arm. "It's all right, dear. Five years ago I was living with my niece after my husband ran off to Argentina with his secretary and everything we had. My niece's husband was an abusive man, and I tried to take a stand, help her like I could never help myself. It backfired. She kicked me out of the house. I had nowhere to go, but I had a friend here who said I could come stay with her. Turned out she was nutty as a fruitcake, and they had to commit her to an institution. I had nothing—no family to go to, no job, and no place to stay. It wasn't long before I was on the streets. I made a few friends, like Sammy, who taught me the ropes, and made it all bearable. I just can't believe he's gone."

"I'm so sorry," Cindy said.

"Why? You didn't kick me out of your house. At least, not yet," Bernadette said, the hint of mischief sparkling in her eyes.

Cindy bit back a smile. "Well, seeing as you were a teacher, I'll expect nothing but impeccable manners from you."

"If you insist on being boring," Bernadette said. "I will be on my best behavior. However, I cannot make any promises for Ginger. She's her own lady in that regard."

Cindy spontaneously hugged Bernadette.

"What was that for?"

"Just because."

"That's a good enough reason for me." Bernadette glanced upward. "You better get home, it looks like rain."

"Okay. I'll see you tomorrow afternoon."

"Yes, you will. And thank you."

Ginger barked as though adding her own thank you, and Cindy grinned all the way back to her car.

A few minutes later she drove around to the side of the Plusmart and parked next to the recycling bin for cardboard, a large green container that looked like it should be used to ship cargo. Slits in it near the top ran the length of the container. Huge signs covered the outside of the container instructing recyclers to remove all staples, labels, and packing tape and to completely flatten boxes before dumping them inside.

As she stepped out of her car, the rain that had been threatening began to pour down.

"Give me a break!" she yelled to the sky as she scurried to open her trunk. She grabbed hold of the top box and yanked it as hard as she could. It half came out of her trunk before catching on the lip and starting to tear. She freed it and struggled to get it the rest of the way out.

The loose end came free and landed on the ground. She let go with her left hand, slammed the trunk, and then tried to grab halfway down it. She half-dragged, half-carried the box the five feet to the side of the dumpster. The slots for depositing the cardboard were horizontal and a foot from the top of the bin. She hoisted the cardboard up and angled the top into the opening of the dumpster. She then stooped, grabbed the bottom, and lifted, rain pelting her in the face, and started to slide it into the container. She gave it one hard shove, which should have finished the job, but it stuck halfway.

She grabbed the protruding edge and pushed hard. It didn't budge. The front end had dipped down and must have caught on some of the cardboard already stacked inside. She pushed upward, trying to lift the entire thing enough to unsnag it, and then pushed again. It wouldn't budge.

Rain began to pelt down harder, and she considered leaving it as it was. She let go and took a step backward, but the whole thing tilted and began to slide back her way. She caught it and craned her neck, trying to see what was blocking her way. It was too dark inside the container to see anything.

She got a better grip on the cardboard, lined it back up with the slot, and prepared to ram it in as hard and as fast as she could. She took a deep breath, tensed her muscles, pushed the cardboard forward, and a bloody hand reached out of the bin to block it.

11

CINDY SCREAMED, DROPPED THE CARDBOARD, AND RACED TO HER CAR. SHE locked the door and threw the car into reverse. Just as she was about to stomp the gas, a thought stopped her. Whoever was in that recycling bin was injured, and the odds were far better that it was someone who had been attacked than it was an attacker. Still, there was no way she was going to risk her life to go back and find out.

She turned and kept her eyes trained on the dumpster as she reached for her cell phone to call 911. As soon as she hung up, every fiber of her being urged her to drive as far away as she could as fast as she could. She hesitated, though, and waited, foot hovering between the brake and the gas pedal until she heard sirens.

She breathed deeply and put the car back into park. When the fire engine pulled up in the parking lot a few feet from her, she turned off her ignition and opened the door.

"Are you the one who called for help?" a man yelled to her.

She nodded and pointed toward the bin. "There's someone in there, and I think they're hurt."

As three firemen surrounded the dumpster, an ambulance and police arrived on the scene, as well. The rain was still coming down, but as she stood next to her car and watched the scene unfold, Cindy ceased to care.

One of them shone a flashlight into the darkness. "There's a man inside! Sir, are you okay, can you hear me?"

Cindy didn't know if he answered, but the fireman continued. "We'll have you out of there in a minute. Just hold on."

Cindy watched in fascinated horror as the firemen worked to open the bin. After a couple of minutes they were lifting a man out of it. They held him aloft for a moment before putting him down on a stretcher provided by the EMTs. Cindy stepped closer to see who it was that had been stuffed inside.

She gasped and then flipped her phone open and dialed Mark.

"What is it?" he asked.

"Firemen just pulled a man out of a cardboard recycling bin behind Plusmart grocery."

"I know, I've been following on the scanner. Somehow when I heard that a woman had called it in, I figured it had to be you. Glad to hear that it's ended okay. He probably has you to thank for that."

"I think you should get down here."

"Since he's alive, there's no need for homicide to get involved, so no need for me to come down."

"That's a mistake," she said.

"Why?" he asked sharply.

"Because I'm standing here looking at him. It's Harry, one of the homeless guys from the charity event. He's been beaten pretty badly, and I don't see his dog."

The paramedics moved the stretcher into the ambulance, and Cindy followed. "Can I see him for a minute?" she asked the paramedic who was hooking him up to a machine.

"Just a minute," he said.

Cindy hopped up in the ambulance and looked at Harry. The old man opened his eyes and saw her. The ghost of a smile flitted across his face. How could anyone have done this to him? He had never hurt a fly. She thought of how much he had loved his dog, and rage gripped her. The only hope she felt was in the fact that just a couple hours earlier Buff had been discovered alive. That meant there was a chance Harry's dog was alive and well somewhere and might find his way back.

"I know some people believe in reincarnation, but did they seriously have to try and recycle me?" Harry whispered.

She stared at him for a moment, wondering if she could possibly have heard him right. "Harry, was that a joke?"

"Sorry. Wasn't it funny? The people at the shelter keep telling me I've got to stop that."

"No, Harry, that's great. You keep it up," she said.

"I mean, I know what people think about me, but would another cardboard box really be an improvement?"

She was laughing while tears fell on her already wet cheeks.

Harry closed his eyes, and his face seemed to relax a bit. Panicked, she turned to look at the paramedic.

"The medication kicked in. He'll be out of it for a little while. I'll have to ask you to leave now. You can visit him at the hospital later if you want to."

"Okay, thank you," Cindy said, climbing down out of the ambulance reluctantly.

She stood and watched as another paramedic closed up the back of the ambulance before moving around to the front. A minute later the vehicle moved out of the parking lot. The siren and lights flicked on, and cars scattered on the street as the ambulance shot out into traffic.

Cindy started walking back toward her car but stopped as Mark drove up next to her. "Get in out of the rain so we can talk," he instructed, indicating his passenger seat with a jerk of his head.

"Tell me what happened," he said once she was inside.

She recounted the event; it took less than a minute to tell. When she was finished, he nodded.

"He'll probably be out for a couple of hours. We can question him later. Okay, thanks, you can go."

"What are you going to do?" Cindy asked.

"I'm meeting Paul at Joseph's house so we can ask him some more questions."

"I want to come."

"I didn't say we were going for dinner," Mark growled.

"I know, but I might be able to think of something else."

"Well, I can't stop you if you want to drive up there to visit him and it happens to coincide with our visit," he said in a tired voice.

"Thank you," she said, opening the door and dashing across the open ground to her car. She started the engine, cranked up the heater, and headed out of the parking lot.

Fortunately, Joseph's house wasn't that far away so it didn't take too long to get there. Both Mark and Paul had arrived before her. When she rang the doorbell, Joseph answered and escorted her into the living room, where the three of them were talking.

"So there goes the theory that this was somehow a robbery gone bad," Mark said. "The dogs provided by the shelter weren't wearing any kind of sparkles on their collars. Also, Buff was returned with his intact. If they took it thinking it was diamonds, I doubt they would have returned it to him when they discovered that it was only crystals."

"So what else could it be?" Joseph asked as he sat back down.

"Is there anyone who would want to sabotage this program or hurt you personally?" Paul asked.

"We've had a couple of angry letters from some of the animal rights' groups."

"Which ones? The ones legitimately trying to stamp out abuse or the radical ones that are against pet ownership entirely?"

"One from each, I believe. We sent the first one full details on our program, what veterinarians were participating, how we were planning on making sure the animals were fed, cared for, looked out for, and so on. We sent them details on the whole thing."

"The whole thing?" Mark asked. "That's an awful lot of detail. You didn't also happen to send them lists of the people involved, did you?"

"No, but they had a representative on hand that day just to observe the proceedings."

Mark and Paul exchanged a glance, and Cindy would have given a lot to know what it meant.

"What about the more radical group?" Mark asked. "How did you respond to them?"

Joseph shrugged. "Nothing, frankly. Until pet ownership is made illegal in this country, those people won't be happy with anything. And I wasn't about to give them information they could use against our participants."

"Any chance both letters actually came from the same group instead of two different ones?" Cindy asked.

Joseph shrugged. "I don't think so, but I really can't say for certain. I mean, if they were actually trying to hide their identity, I'm not sure we'd be able to tell if it was really one group instead of two."

"We're going to need to see all the correspondence you've had with both groups," Paul said.

"Of course," Joseph said, then hesitated. "It might take some time to find, though."

"And why is that?" Mark jumped in.

"Derek handled all those types of issues, and so far I haven't had a lot of success figuring out his filing system."

"I can help," Cindy heard herself volunteering.

Suddenly all eyes were on her. She shrugged. "I am a secretary, and I've worked with the major filing systems commonly used."

"You're drafted," Mark said. "I'll draw you up a list of everything I want found."

"What about the protestors who were present at the event?" Cindy asked, remembering the angry faces, the signs, and the guy who had jumped in front of her car.

"I think I have pictures of everyone who was there," Joseph said. "I can give you those if it would help," he said to Mark.

"They would. Maybe one of them has a history of radical protesting."

"You mean the kind of protesting that sinks boats and kills lumberjacks?" Cindy guessed.

"The very kind," Mark said grimly.

The police asked a few more questions and then left for the hospital, hoping that when Harry woke up he'd be able to tell them something about his assailant. Cindy fought the urge to go with them. There was a real chance Harry would be able to identify his attacker and the whole thing would be solved and the killer arrested. That would truly be something to be thankful about. In case Harry couldn't help them, though, they would still need the letters she had promised to help find.

She glanced at her watch. It was seven. Her stomach growled noisily just as Joseph returned from seeing the detectives out.

"I was going to make myself a sandwich, you want one?"

"Yes, please."

She followed him into the kitchen.

"It's getting late. You don't have to start on those files tonight," he said.

She shook her head. "I can't work on them tomorrow, and the sooner the police have them, the better. No, hopefully I can find what they need tonight."

"I certainly hope so, but I'm not holding my breath," Joseph admitted. "There's a lot of files."

She shrugged. "I'm sure it will be fine."

Joseph put together roast beef sandwiches and handed her one. Almost on cue Clarice trotted into the room with Buff at her heels. The two of them sat down, assuming the time-honored begging pose.

"I bet Clarice was happy to see you, little guy," Cindy said to Buff.

"Was she ever. She was much happier, though, once I gave him a bath. She didn't like whatever she smelled all over him."

"If he smelled anything like he looked, I can't blame her," Cindy said. "He was a mess."

They ate quickly, washing the sandwiches down with some milk. When they were finished, Cindy followed Joseph toward the stairs. "You know, I've never had a tour of your house. I've only seen just a couple of rooms."

"Remind me to give you the full tour later. I warn you, though, I'm not the best tour guide."

They reached the second floor landing and turned to the right. The doors along the hall were standing open. "My office you've seen," he said as they passed.

"How could I forget?"

"And the guest room the police used as a holding pen last week."

"Yup, won't be forgetting that one anytime soon," she confirmed.

"Here's another guest room."

She glanced in at the masculine room with lots of wood and deep red carpet and accents. It was a bit overpowering, and she wrinkled her nose as she backed out of it.

"It can be a bit much," Joseph said with the ghost of a smile. He paused outside the next door. "And this is the room where I keep all the things I don't know what else to do with."

She glanced in. The walls were decorated with plaques, display shelves held awards and what looked like at least two keys to cities, and on the floor there were a dozen signs and displays, including one full-size cardboard cutout of him.

"Wow, that's . . . weird."

"Tell me about it. The awards are great. Some of the displays are a little strange, but people give them to me and then I don't know what to do with them. It seems a little ungrateful to destroy them or toss them out, so I put them in here. I guess it's kind of a memento room."

"It's like a giant, three-dimensional scrapbook."

He tilted his head to the side. "You know, I think you just hit the nail on the head."

"You know, there are groups for this sort of thing," she joked. "If you need a support group, I'm sure I can find you a number."

"Careful, or I'll hire you to go through the tens of thousands of family photographs I've got stacked in closets around here."

Cindy groaned. "I think I'll pass."

"I can't say that I blame you. If I don't want to do it, why would anybody else?"

"If they really are family photos, you might consider contacting the historical society. After all, your family practically founded this town."

"You know, that's really not a bad idea. I'll definitely think about it. Okay, moving on," he said, ushering her to the next room. "Here's Derek's office."

They stepped into a large room lined with a couple dozen filing cabinets. A massive wooden desk dominated the center of the room.

"This was Derek's office?"

"Yup. Before him it was Tina's office. She was my last assistant. She was really good too. She got married to a guy on the East Coast and moved. This is where I keep all the files. My office is where I work but not where I store things. I find so many containers filled with paper to be a bit oppressive, certainly depressing."

"Given the sheer volume, I can see why," she said. She squared her shoulders and refused to despair over the task at hand. "Please tell me you have at least an idea of where I can start," she said. When she volunteered for the job, she never dreamed what an enormous task lay before her. It might take her through the long weekend to find what she was looking for unless she could figure out Derek's filing system.

"I wish I could," Joseph said grimly.

He walked over and indicated three filing cabinets standing side by side. "As you can see from the labels, these are supposed to be for charity work. That was how my last assistant set them up. However, I haven't been able to find a single thing in them about Friday's event or Animals to the Rescue."

He opened the top drawer of the desk and pulled out a set of keys. "These unlock the filing cabinets if you need them."

Cindy grabbed a scrunchie out of her purse and pulled her hair back into a ponytail. Her purse she stowed on the floor under the desk.

"Is there anything I can get you?" Joseph asked, his voice sheepish as he stared from her to the filing cabinets, where she would be looking for the proverbial needle in the haystack.

"Yeah. A Coke." She gazed around the room. "Better make that a twelve-pack. I have a feeling we're in for a long night."

A minute later when Joseph returned with the soda, she was bent over inside the first of the charity filing cabinets.

"Anything?" he asked, his voice hopeful.

She looked up at him. "Seriously, after less than a minute?"

"Sorry," he said, setting the drink down on the desk. He pointed to the phone. "If you dial 14, it will activate the intercom system and you can talk to me anywhere in the house."

"Cool feature."

"It's convenient."

"Okay, get out of here, I've got work to do. I'll call when I find anything or when I run out of soda." She was likely to be calling for soda long before she called to say she had found something.

Half an hour later she had skimmed through the three charity filing cabinets and concluded that Joseph was right. There was nothing in them relating to Animals to the Rescue. On a hunch she pulled out a file labeled YEARLY CHARITY RECEIPTS FOR TAXES. She had to give credit to Tina; she had set up a highly functional system.

Cindy flipped the folder open. The top paper was from March 24. She looked at the one behind it. March 21. She went slowly through the folder and found nothing later than March 24.

She put the file away and then moved to a different filing cabinet labeled BILLS. She slid the top drawer open and pulled out the file labeled CABLE. She opened it and found statements for cable television from January, February, and March. The first two each had a canceled check stapled to it for easy reference. The third one had PAID 3/15 stamped on it, but no check was attached.

She replaced the file, opened the third drawer, and pulled out the file labeled PHONE. It was the same with that file—nothing past March. She closed up that cabinet and then pulled files at random from two of the other filing cabinets. Nothing was filed past March.

She picked up the phone and dialed 14. "Hello?" she said after a second.

There was a click, and then Joseph asked, "Hi, you need more soda?"

"Not yet, but I have a question. When did Tina leave?"

"The end of March," he said. "Why?"

"I'll tell you when I finish figuring it out."

"Okay, do you need me to come in?"

"No, I'm good," she said. "Bye."

She hung up and, starting on the left-hand side, systematically opened every drawer, looking for files that didn't look like those put there by Tina. When she had finished, she turned toward the desk and began opening the drawers. She yanked the bottom one on the left-hand side open and saw a towering mound of loose paper in it.

She pulled it out and dumped it on the desk. She began to go through it piece by piece. Receipts, bank statements, bills, unopened junk mail, and an assortment of invitations were all piled in there haphazardly. The oldest item was two months old.

What kind of personal assistant doesn't file things? And what happened to all the papers from April through mid-September?

Still, there was nothing about Animals to the Rescue in the whole mess. She finished checking the drawers and then crossed to the closet. She opened the door and discovered office machines and supplies, some of the more common ones like staples and paper were in more disarray than the rolls of ten-key paper and felt-tip pens.

She closed the door and turned to survey the room. There was nowhere else that she could see that he would have been able to stash papers. She returned to the phone and dialed the intercom again.

"Yes?" Joseph asked.

"Can you come up?"

"Right there," he said.

A minute later he walked through the door with Clarice by his side, a hopeful look in his eyes. "Did you find them?"

"No, but I did find this," she said, waving her hand at the towering pile of paper.

"What is all that?"

"The filing for the last two months."

"I don't understand."

"I don't think I do, either, but Derek didn't file a single thing in these filing cabinets the entire time he worked for you as far as I can tell."

"What?" Joseph asked, turning pale.

"Yeah. I'm still trying to figure out what he did with most of them."

"Not good," Joseph muttered to himself.

"Did Derek actually live here, or did he have an apartment somewhere else?" she asked.

"He lived here. It's more convenient that way."

"Can you show me where?"

"Certainly."

Joseph led her to the third floor and down to the end of the hall. Clarice bounded past them to the closed door at the end and stood in front of the door, growling low in her throat and scratching at the door.

"Clarice, stop it."

Cindy saw several scratch marks on the door, more than could have been made in the last few seconds. Clarice clearly didn't like something about the door. "Does she always scratch at the door?" she asked.

"Not usually. It looks like she's had at this door, though." He grabbed the knob and twisted hard. Nothing happened, and a look of puzzlement came over him.

"What's wrong?"

"It's locked."

"Derek must have locked it the day of the event. He probably didn't want to risk anyone wandering into the house and going through his things."

"You don't understand. There's a lock on this door, yes, but the key has been lost since before I was a boy. The lock was disabled years ago so no one could accidentally lock themselves out."

Cindy felt her pulse quicken. "So Derek must have had the lock fixed without telling you."

Joseph nodded. "I don't like this. Why wouldn't he have told me? And when did he have it done?"

"I don't know, but you should call a locksmith right now."

Cindy wasn't sure what Joseph said when he called the locksmith, but the man was there in less than half an hour. She stood in the hallway with Joseph, waiting as the man worked. When the door finally swung open, she sucked in her breath, wondering what she would find.

A foul stench assaulted her nostrils, and all three of them took an involuntary step back. Cindy pulled her sleeve over her hand and then pressed it to her nose and mouth and forced herself to step into the room. As soon as she did, she regretted it and ran back into the hall, not stopping until she reached the stairs where she grabbed the banister for support.

"What is it, what's wrong?" Joseph asked as he and the locksmith caught up to her.

"Call the police. There's a body in there."

12

Why am I not even remotely surprised?" Mark asked when he had arrived on the scene.

Cindy shrugged but didn't have a witty comeback.

"Clearly I should stop investigating on my own and just follow you around instead."

She stared at him, still having nothing else to say.

"You realize the body count is really growing fast, right? It's starting to feel like Easter all over again."

"I don't think it's a serial killer. After all, a serial killer wouldn't have failed to kill Harry. I think it's all about the dogs. Like maybe one of them is special," she said.

"I get why champion purebreds would be special to someone, but what about the mutts?" Mark asked.

"I don't know," Cindy said. "Maybe one of them is stolen, or carrying something."

"Stolen from some drug lord or Mafioso maybe? Or carrying something? What, a microchip in their collar? Secret blueprints or maybe a treasure map leading to oil or to a buried Civil War payroll, tragically one from the South? Can we stop with the Scooby Doo plots?"

"Okay, and what do you have?" Cindy asked defensively.

"Apparently another body," Mark snapped. "So let's see it, so I can get on with my job."

Joseph, who had stood silent through the whole exchange, led the way to the stairs. As they climbed, Cindy turned to Mark. "Did Harry give you a description?" she asked hopefully.

"He's still out of it, probably won't be any help until morning. Man, this place needs an elevator."

She took a closer look at the detective and saw that he was exhausted. "Are you okay?" she asked.

"Fine," he grumbled. "Any luck finding those letters?"

"No. It turns out Derek hasn't filed anything in the six months he worked for Joseph. Some papers are just piled in his desk, but nothing we need. I can't even find the majority of the papers, which is why I asked Joseph to see Derek's room. I was hoping to find them in there."

"And instead you found another body. You have the darndest luck."

When they reached the third floor, Cindy lingered at the top of the landing as the two men walked toward the room.

Joseph handed Mark a CD. "I got those pictures of the protestors and everyone who was there Friday. I didn't see any homeless men amongst the protestors, though."

Mark tucked the CD into his jacket and then disappeared inside the room. Joseph stood just outside, looking slightly ill.

There was a pounding on the front door, and Cindy turned and headed back downstairs to open it. Paul and a forensics team stood there, and she let them in. Fortunately, Paul didn't say anything to her, as she was in no mood to bandy words with him as well.

She pointed them upstairs and then moved into the living room, where she sank onto one of the sofas. She was exhausted and desperately wanted to go home. She knew better, though. Before she would be free to leave, there would be yet another endless round of questions from the detectives. And there were still those missing letters.

Derek, what was your deal? If it had only been the pile of papers in the desk that were out of order, she would have put it down to being too busy with other events to do the maintenance work. To not file a single thing since taking the job, though? That made no sense. That was one of the first things every secretary or assistant learned to do and do well. You needed to be able to put your hands on whatever your boss needed without having to frantically search through piles and boxes to find it.

How had Derek managed to do his job without keeping the files in order? Joseph walked into the room and sank down in the chair opposite her with a sigh.

"Joseph, when you asked Derek for something, a bill, a receipt, or a piece of information, how long did it take him to get it to you?"

"Not very long. Usually only a couple of minutes," Joseph said.

How were you pulling that off, Derek? Did you have a photographic memory? Did you digitize everything and put it on your computer? She shook her head. He still would have needed hard copies of a lot of those things, and it didn't explain their absence. Even if he didn't want to file, he should have been storing the papers in boxes in his office.

She closed her eyes. *So how did you get Joseph what he needed? Did you make it up?* A shiver went up her spine. What if Derek wasn't a good guy? What if he wasn't an innocent victim?

"Joseph, how well did you know Derek?" Cindy asked.

He was so quiet that she opened her eyes to see if he was still awake. His eyes were wide open, and he was staring at the ceiling. "Not as well as I would have liked," he said after a minute. "Tina was great; she was fast, efficient, and we talked a lot about life, family, politics, religion, you name it. With Derek it was different. He wasn't very communicative unless it was about work, and he never spoke about himself. He was pleasant and courteous, but in reality I really didn't know that much about him."

"Did Tina interview candidates to replace her or did you?"

"A bit of both. I hadn't chosen someone by the time she left. That was a miserable two weeks."

"What about Derek?"

"It was funny. I met him at a dog show. He had impeccable references. He had been the personal assistant for Theodore, an older gentleman who bred collies, for six years. Theodore had just passed away, and Derek needed a new position and didn't have a problem relocating from the East Coast. It seemed like providence at the time."

It seemed awfully convenient to Cindy. Before she could ask him anything else, she heard steps on the stairs and twisted her head to see Mark coming toward them.

"Who was he?" Cindy asked, sitting up straighter as Mark walked into the room.

He gave her a weary sigh. "His name was Larry Van Horn. He was a tech at a veterinarian clinic downtown. He was reported missing this morning by a coworker when he didn't show up for work a third day in a row and they couldn't reach him."

"Which vet clinic? It wasn't Valley Animal Hospital, was it?" Joseph asked. "That's the one I use."

"No. It was AA Animal Clinic. They do a lot of work with the Humane Society."

"The Humane Society? Was it possible he was here on business Friday?" Cindy asked.

"I've got a call in to the clinic to see if he was scheduled to be here. Hopefully, we'll have something soon," Mark said. "It certainly looks like he's been dead a few days, so my bet is that he was here on Friday, whether he was supposed to be or not."

"Didn't officers search the whole house when they were investigating Derek's murder?" Cindy asked.

"They were supposed to," Mark growled. "Clearly someone made a mistake."

"I only keep the attic and the room with the safe locked during events," Joseph said. "An officer asked me to open them both, which I did, but no one ever mentioned that Derek's room was locked."

"Trust me, heads are going to roll over that one if we find out he's been in there since Friday," Mark said.

"Did you find any boxes in there?" Cindy asked.

Mark shook his head. "After what you said, I made sure and checked the closet and under the bed. No papers that I saw."

"What on earth did he do with them?"

"You got me."

Maybe he had digitized them and shredded the originals. It seemed absurd, but so did everything else she could think of. She didn't remember seeing a computer in his office, though.

"Joseph, did Derek have his own computer? I didn't see one in his office."

"Yeah, he used a laptop so that he could take it with him wherever he needed to. It wasn't in his office?"

"No. Did you see one in his room?" she asked Mark.

"No, but I'll take another look."

"Thanks. I'm getting a really bad feeling about Derek."

"What do you mean?" Mark asked.

"I don't think Derek was one of the victims. I think he was one of the villains."

Jeremiah wanted nothing more than to go to bed and sleep off the rest of the flu. After hearing the song dedication on the radio, though, he had known he would get no rest until he knew for sure that his old colleague was actually dead.

I saw him, I touched the body, inspected the wound. I don't know how he could have faked that, unless it wasn't really him.

There was only one way to find out. He stood and looked himself over in the mirror. He was dressed in all black from head to toe. There were no buttons, zippers, or any other identifying marks. The black was dull and flat, not even the shoes held any shine and neither did the gloves that he wore. He put on the cap and mask, which were made of the thin, black material used to hide a person's face in many of the Halloween costumes that were so popular. The effect was perfect. Even as he stared at himself in the mirror, he felt his eyes drifting slightly away from his own reflection. He could see just fine through the cloth, but no one could see him.

He gripped the edge of the sink as a wave of cold washed over him. The shape in the mirror was one he had not had reason to behold in a long time. What would Marie say if she could see her rabbi now?

He turned the television in his bedroom on low and piled pillows under his blankets that would pass a cursory inspection through the window. He had left the bottom quarter of the window uncovered by blinds. Finished, he moved to his office, and after a minute spent studying the world outside the window, he opened it and eased himself out and onto the ground below, feet touching down silently. He slid the window closed, leaving only a crack for him to be able to use his fingers to open it again.

He carried no wallet or keys. Strapped to his left leg was a small black knife, also dull black, and a tiny black tool set. He made his way to a street three over from his without being spotted and then from there walked to the local movie theater. It was only two miles, but they served to remind him of just how weak the flu had made him.

Once in the parking lot, he kept to the shadows, even though he could have walked freely and not been noticed by the moviegoers. With no bit of color or shine there was nothing for the human eye to track on. Even if someone did see him, they would never be able to tell someone even the most rudimentary information, such as his height or body shape.

He drifted close to a dark car as it parked. Three guys jumped out. "Hurry, dudes, the movie starts in like five minutes, and I don't want to miss the previews," the driver called as the three ran toward the theater. "It's gonna be awesome!"

Jeremiah waited three minutes to make sure none of them had left a wallet in the car and would come back for it. When they didn't return, he moved to the driver's side, pulled one of the lock-pick tools from the kit on his leg, and opened the door in seconds. He slid behind the wheel, reached under the steering column, and hotwired the car.

He wasn't proud of it, but he was at least pleased to see that none of his old skills had faded. A minute later he pulled out of the parking lot. He drove to the hospital, parked the car, and then proceeded to make his way down to the morgue.

He made short work of the lock, relocked the door once inside, and bypassed the light switch. He pulled a small penlight out of his pocket, the lens covered in cloth to diffuse the light. The room smelled of antiseptic, which could not cover the stench of death.

A minute later Jeremiah found the correct drawer and stared into a familiar face. The coroner had finished with the body, and it awaited transport. Jeremiah didn't care about the forensic work that had been done. He cared only about a positive identification.

The face was as he remembered it; a beard could not alter it enough to obscure it. But faces could be changed, and for all he knew the man might have had a brother. He should have checked while he was searching him, but he had believed him to be the man he thought him to be and had not questioned it until the radio dedication.

Jeremiah grabbed the right arm and shone the light on the skin just above the elbow. There, subtle enough that a plastic surgeon would not have bothered to duplicate it, was a one-inch scar, faded with age. It was a scar that Jeremiah had given him. He gently lowered the arm back down.

"Rest in peace, friend," he whispered.

He slid the drawer back in place. As he turned toward the door, he heard voices coming down the hallway outside the morgue, whisper-faint but drawing closer. He turned off the penlight, returned it to his pocket, and melted into the shadows.

A minute later the door opened, overhead lights flickered on, and two men entered with a body.

"Where was this one found?" the taller of the two men asked.

"Joseph Coulter's house, where the body was found on Friday."

"It looks like this guy's been dead a while too."

Jeremiah listened intently while pressed against a wall in the corner, not moving a muscle.

"Connected?"

"Dollars to donuts."

They placed the body on one of the examination tables and a minute later left.

Jeremiah glided over to the body, taking a moment to examine the face. He did not know the man, and he was quite sure he had not seen him before. He exited the room, locking the door behind him.

Within an hour he had returned the car to the parking lot and made it back home. He took a dose of flu medication and crawled into bed. A mystery still remained about the radio dedication, and it troubled him, but there was nothing he could do about it that night, and certainly nothing he could do about it while so sick. He had gotten lucky that he had managed to accomplish all he had. There was no way he was willing to risk more without pressing need.

⌐━━━⌐

"I've had it with this case," Paul said as they arrived back at the station.

"You and me both," Mark said with a sigh.

He pulled the CD out of his jacket and tossed it to one of the other officers. "I need to see if we can identify all the people in these pictures, particularly the protestors. And keep your eyes out for one of them who might be homeless as well."

"When do you need it?"

"First thing in the morning," Mark said with a sigh. "We need to question all of them as soon as possible."

The officer nodded and headed off with the disc.

"I don't like working Thanksgiving," Paul said.

"Who does? But criminals need catching, even if it is a holiday for the rest of the world."

"I should have listened to my mother and become a banker."

Mark snorted. "I have a hard time picturing that."

"Me too. That's why I became a cop. Catching killers instead of cashing checks."

"Well, I need to head home to Traci, or you'll be catching my killer."

"If Traci ever kills you, it will be justifiable homicide, of that I'm certain."

—✦—

"You really think Derek was involved in some sort of plot?" Joseph asked Cindy once the police had left.

"Did you ever check with that dog breeder's family to see if Derek actually worked for him?"

Joseph blinked several times. "I made a phone call, to a number he gave me. The man on the other end of the line verified it."

"But did you know who the man on the other end of the line was for sure?"

"No," Joseph admitted. "I'd only met the old man. I didn't know any of his family."

"I think Derek was involved in something. Why else would Larry, the vet tech, be dead in Derek's locked room? Why would Derek have had a new lock installed without informing you? I don't think he ever worked for that man on the East Coast. I think he sought you out on purpose."

"Why? What was his motive?"

"I don't know. Whatever it was, I bet Larry was his partner in some way."

"You think he double-crossed him?"

"Maybe."

Joseph shook his head. "I don't know if the thought that he was somehow part of a plot and that's what got him killed makes me feel any better about him being killed here in my house. I haven't slept well since all this started. My home has been broken into, and now I learn two people have been killed in it. How am I supposed to get any rest ever again? I've contacted a different security company to redo the entire system next week, but I'm not sure I'll feel better even after that happens."

"It will take time, but eventually it will get better," Cindy said, reaching out to grip his hand. "Believe me. Even though you're surrounded by death, even though your home has been broken into, you will get through this, and at some point you'll even be able to relax again, if you let yourself."

"I knew a lot of terrible things happened to you earlier this year. I don't think I ever really understood or appreciated what you went through until now. I'm so sorry. I should have been more sympathetic, tried to help out in some way."

"There was nothing you could have done," Cindy said. "And besides, we barely knew each other back then. Don't worry; I made it through. And because I do understand, I'll help you make it through this."

"Thank you. Again."

"No problem. If you could help me figure out what Derek might have been after, though, it will help us put this all behind us much faster."

"Well, we ruled out the diamond collar," he said ruefully.

"Yes. I would think if it was simple robbery, he would have been able to snatch whatever he was after months ago, without the help of accomplices."

"Tina always told me I was too trusting," Joseph said grimly. "Yes, it would have been easy for him to steal anything in this house at any time in the last several months."

"So let's rule out robbery."

"Okay, what does that leave us with?" he asked.

"I don't know," she said, racking her brain to think of something that Mark wouldn't call a Scooby Doo plot. "Blackmail?"

Joseph shrugged. "How, what? There's nothing in my life that I would pay to keep quiet."

"Good to know," she said with a wry smile. "Ransom?"

"No one demanded anything in return for the puppies. I would have gladly paid a ransom for their return."

"Revenge?"

"Again, for what? I have no enemies that I know of. Rivals, yes, enemies, no. And, even if I did, Derek had multiple opportunities to kill me, maim me, or harm me in any number of ways."

Cindy sat quietly. What else could there be? She had to be missing something. What other motive could drive a man to spend six months in the employ of someone, waiting and planning, and drive one or more people to kill? Why was Derek killed? Why was Larry killed?

"It's getting late," Joseph said softly. "And clearly you're not going to be able to find those letters. You should go home."

The letters. "If it was some activist that did this, why kill Derek and not you? Why allow the adoptions to happen at all?"

"Even if an activist did kill Derek or the vet tech, that doesn't explain what Derek was doing."

"Or where he put all your papers," Cindy said softly. "Are you sure he didn't have some other place, an apartment, a storage unit?"

"If he did, I don't know about it."

"I wish I knew what was on his laptop and where it is right now," she sighed.

"I wish I knew where six months of paperwork was. If I can't find it, then he's done more damage to me than stealing everything in this house."

13

CINDY WAS UP AT SIX A.M. ON THANKSGIVING MORNING STUFFING THE TURkey. When she finally slid it into the oven, she had a new found respect for her father, who had always been up before anyone else, prepping Thanksgiving dinner.

On a whim she called his cell phone as soon as she closed the oven door. "Hi, Dad," she said when he answered.

"Sweetheart, what are you doing up so early on Thanksgiving?"

"I just put the turkey in the oven."

"Ah. Me too. Bread's rising nicely."

She kicked herself. She had forgotten to prep the bread the night before. Oh, well, the sourdough loaf she had would have to do for sandwiches later. "I'm glad to hear it. I love your bread."

"You could come home and have some, you know. We'd love to have you for the holiday."

"Someday."

"Or maybe we could come sample your turkey, someday."

She smiled. "Happy Thanksgiving."

"Happy Thanksgiving."

She hung up with her father and headed off to the shower. Holidays at her home had always been somewhat strange, at least when she compared them to those of her friends. Half the time her dad was out of the country and missed the entire event. When he was home, her mother regaled him with tales of Kyle's adventures and praised him until Cindy felt like her presence was completely optional. She was still fairly certain that no one had even missed her the first holiday she hadn't gone.

Then again, her current holidays were starting to become even stranger than those of her childhood. It was destined to be one of the oddest, most memorable Thanksgivings in her history. She could feel it.

When she exited the shower, the phone was ringing and she hurried to answer it.

"Hello?"

"Hi, it's Geanie. Sorry to call so early, but you said you'd be up stuffing the turkey."

"What can I do for you?"

"Actually, it's more what I can do for you. I was wondering if you needed any help?"

"Actually, that would be fantastic."

"Cool. I'll be there in about half an hour."

"Works for me."

No sooner had she hung up than the phone rang again. She assumed it was Geanie and was surprised when she heard a male voice instead.

"It's Detective Paul," he said.

"Oh, hi. What can I do for you?" she asked.

"I need a better description of the homeless protestor who jumped in front of your car Friday night."

"I told you all I could remember," Cindy said. "He had dreadlocks. Haven't you found him yet?"

"No, we've circulated the description you gave us, but no one seems to know who he is. There must be something else, even if it's minor, that you overlooked."

"I just don't think so," Cindy said, her frustration mounting.

"Well, if you think of something, call Mark or me on our cells."

"I will," she promised.

Why can't they find him? Could he also be dead?

Geanie arrived a few minutes later with pies and enthusiasm and completely managed to distract Cindy from the grimmer questions of the week. She was in shorts and a tank top and had brought her dinner clothes with her. She dumped her stuff in Cindy's room and then returned to the kitchen.

"Okay, what can I do?"

Cindy nodded toward the refrigerator. "The list is up there of the dishes we're making, with approximate cook and prep times listed. Dinner is in six hours, so we need to plan accordingly. The turkey with the stuffing is already in the oven."

"Maybe we should set the table first, since a lot of this has to be done closer to eating."

"Good idea."

Together they moved Cindy's kitchen table into the living room.

"How many are we expecting?" Geanie asked.

"Seven, no, six," she corrected herself, remembering that Harry would still be in the hospital.

Geanie eyed the tiny table. "I'm not sure we're going to be able to fit six people around this table."

"I've got a card table in the office closet," Cindy said, moving to get it.

A minute later they had it set up next to the dining table. It turned out that Cindy's one and only tablecloth just fit over both of them. Together they set the table before returning to the kitchen.

"What's wrong?" Traci asked Mark.

He shrugged. They were watching the Thanksgiving Day parade on television while eating oatmeal. She was curled up on the couch, with Buster asleep on her legs.

"I wish I didn't have to work today," he admitted.

"Then don't."

"You know I can't do that. Another body turned up last night."

"This is getting as bad as that serial killer," she said.

"I know."

"I'm worried about you."

"I'm fine."

"No, I mean, I've just had an uneasy feeling all morning. Promise me you'll be safe."

"I promise," he said. He knew how hollow that promise could be. Cops were never safe, and she knew that as well as he did. He knew she lived in fear that one day he wouldn't come home, and that she'd answer the door and Paul or one of the other officers would tell her that he was dead. It was a terrible burden she carried being married to him, and he knew it.

"Dinner at my sister's house is at six, and I want to drive over together."

"I'll be home by five so I can clean up," he said.

She smiled at him, and it warmed his heart as it always did. "I love you," he said.

"Of course you do," she teased. "You'd be crazy not to."

He got up and kissed her.

"I love you too," she said.

Paul was at his desk when Mark got in. "Have you been here all night?"

"No."

"Liar."

"What gave me away? The bags under my eyes, or that I'm wearing the same suit?"

"Actually, it's the Styrofoam cups and dozens of packets of sugar in your trash can."

Paul shrugged. "Coffee is my friend."

"Okay, so what do you have? Other than a caffeine rush, I mean."

"We've managed to identify all the people in the photographs."

Mark blinked. "All of them?"

"All of them," Paul said emphatically. "The reporters, the volunteers, the donors, the recipients, the hired help all check out as people we interviewed after being called to the scene."

"Did you see any pictures of the homeless protestor Cindy said jumped in front of her car?"

"Not one."

"What about the other protestors? Did officers on the scene interview them as well?"

"None of them were present when we arrived; they had all left beforehand, and not by much either."

"Strange."

"That's not the half of it. All of them were petty criminals; that's how we identified them."

"They took off before the police could show. That doesn't sound like a coincidence to me. Did someone tip them off?"

"Possibly. It's also possible that they were only supposed to be there at a certain time, to cause confusion."

"But how would you organize this many?" Mark asked as Paul handed him a stack of mug shots.

"Simple. We've already run down half a dozen of them this morning, and their stories all match up."

"Yes?"

"They were paid to stage the protest."

"By whom?"

"You're going to hate this," Paul said.

"I bet I am."

"Joseph Coulter."

The doorbell rang, and Cindy went to answer it. Joseph stood there with a case of sparkling cider and Clarice and Buff. "I hope you don't mind; I brought Buff too. I didn't want to leave him alone."

"He's more than welcome," Cindy said, opening wide the door.

The dogs bounded inside and immediately made their way to her couch. She smiled at the sight. Joseph carried the sparkling cider into the kitchen, where Geanie squealed in delight. Cindy had her suspicions that the squeal was actually for Joseph and not the cider.

"We told you that was too much!" she heard Geanie giggle.

"And I told you these things have a way of spinning out of control," Joseph said.

As Cindy walked into the kitchen, she saw Geanie flicking Joseph with a dish towel. He grabbed another one and flicked her back until they were both laughing.

Cindy couldn't help but laugh as well at the two of them. The doorbell rang again, and she went to find Geanie's friend waiting there, a loaf of fresh-baked bread in her hands.

"How did you know we needed bread?" Cindy asked with a smile.

"I must be psychic," the woman said.

"More like psychotic," Geanie teased as she walked in and hugged her friend, then took the bread and ran back to the kitchen.

The oven timer went off, and Cindy hurried to the kitchen and removed the turkey from the oven. The aroma was overwhelming, and everyone around her made excited sounds. She put the turkey on the counter and loosely covered it with a clean dish towel. It had to cool a while before she could cut it.

She listened to the others chattering around her, and she realized that this was what Thanksgiving was all about. It was gathering together. Friends, family, strangers, all sharing the simple joys of talking and laughing and eating together.

She heard the front door open and turned. "Hello in the house?" a familiar voice called.

She went into the family room and was glad to see Jeremiah standing there. Next to him was Bernadette. Ginger jumped out of her arms and raced over to join the other dogs on the couch.

"Welcome, all," Cindy said.

"I brought flowers for the table," Bernadette said. "It isn't polite to show up empty-handed."

She handed Cindy a bunch of wildflowers that had been freshly picked. "Thank you," Cindy said, touched by the thoughtfulness.

"I guess that makes me the rude one," Jeremiah said sheepishly. "I didn't bring anything."

"Sure you did," Bernadette said. "You brought me!"

They both laughed at that while Cindy stared at them.

"He saw Ginger and me walking this way about two blocks back, and he gave us a ride," Bernadette said.

"Well, I'm certainly glad he did. Now we're all here," Cindy said.

She took the flowers and found her only vase under the sink. Soon the flowers graced the table, and to her they were more beautiful than all the expensive decorations her mom always had.

Together she and Geanie shooed everyone else out of the kitchen. The others went into the living room and played with the dogs. Cindy had Jeremiah lie down on the couch previously vacated by the dogs.

"How are you feeling?"

"I've been a lot better," he admitted. "I shouldn't be here."

"Nonsense. No one should be alone on Thanksgiving. We've got about half an hour until dinner; rest until then and rest afterward."

Cindy returned to the kitchen and found Geanie making gravy.

"I thought you couldn't cook?"

"It's the one and only thing I can do. I watched my grandmother do this for years."

"Frankly, I'm relieved. I was not looking forward to tackling that."

"I'd far rather try this than carve the turkey."

"Yeah, this should be interesting," Cindy said as she uncovered the bird.

Geanie walked out into the living room. "Anyone here know how to carve a turkey?"

"I do," Bernadette said.

"You're drafted."

Bernadette came into the kitchen, washed her hands thoroughly, and then took the carving knife from Cindy reverently. "It's been a long time since I was asked to carve a bird."

"We're grateful to you for doing it," Cindy said.

"Here, let me show you how," Bernadette said.

Cindy watched, fascinated, as Bernadette carved the bird, and by the end she wasn't entirely convinced that she could replicate the method, but she thought she might be willing to try.

As Cindy carried the platter of meat to the table, she called everyone to sit down.

"Jeremiah, would you offer up a prayer for us?" she asked once they were all seated.

He looked at her, startled. "Me?"

"Unless there's another rabbi in the room," she said.

"Adonai, we ask your blessing upon us this day and this meal we share. May it honor you."

"Amen," the others chorused.

Jeremiah picked up a glass of sparkling cider. "*L'chaim.*"

"To life!" everyone else roared in unison.

They all drank, and as Jeremiah set down his glass, he remarked, "Everyone here has seen *Fiddler on the Roof*, I take it?"

Cindy nearly spewed her cider. She managed to swallow it and laughed along with everyone else.

Silence descended as they all began to eat.

⟡━✦━⟡

When they were finished eating, Joseph began clearing the table. Geanie stood up and grabbed Cindy's hand, dragging her toward the back of the house.

She pulled her into the bathroom and closed the door behind them.

"Geanie, what's up?" Cindy demanded.

"I needed to talk to you in private."

"And we couldn't have talked in the bedroom or the office?" Cindy asked, incredulous.

"I have a problem. I think Joseph likes me."

Cindy smirked. "Yes, because tall, dark, and rich is sooo unattractive."

"I'm serious! I don't date people from work."

"Joseph doesn't work at the church."

"I know, but he's a member, so it's kind of like dating a coworker."

Cindy looked her in the eyes. "Geanie, sometimes you just have to take a chance."

Geanie took a deep breath. "You're right. Some things are worth the risk."

"That's right, now go get him."

They exited the bathroom and walked back into the living room. Geanie approached Joseph, who was just putting the pies down on the table. When his hands were free, he turned to her. Geanie put her hands on his shoulders, stood on tiptoe, and kissed him.

Cindy blinked in surprise.

Geanie stepped away, and Joseph stared at her for a moment before putting a hand behind her head and pulling her back.

"What on earth did you say to her?" Jeremiah asked Cindy as Joseph and Geanie kissed.

"Go get him. I thought maybe she'd flirt, or ask him out to coffee or something."

"Well, that's definitely something," he said, laughing and coughing all at once.

"Yeah, it sure is. Can I get you apple or pumpkin?"

"Pumpkin, please."

Cindy walked over to the table, cut a slice of the pumpkin pie, and put it on a plate. She carried it back to Jeremiah, along with a clean fork.

"Thanks," he said.

"You're welcome."

She returned to the table and took her seat. Geanie and Joseph both took theirs as well, and Geanie set about serving the pie. A minute later Cindy was biting into apple pie that was surprisingly good.

"Wow, Geanie, you'd never know this wasn't homemade," Cindy said.

"Thanks."

There was a loud knock on the door. Cindy jumped up to get it. When she opened the door, she was stunned to see Mark and Paul standing there, a couple of uniformed officers behind them.

"What's happened?" she asked, fear flooding through her. "Has someone else been killed?"

"We need to come in," Mark said, not looking her in the eyes.

She stepped back and opened the door wide. The policemen rushed inside, and the uniformed officers pulled Joseph up from his seat at the table. Out of the corner of her eye she saw Jeremiah sit up with a start.

"Joseph Coulter, you're under arrest for the murder of Derek, Larry, and several others," Mark began.

"What?" Cindy gasped. Joseph turned to look at her, shock and fear mingling together on his face.

"This is preposterous," Geanie flared, standing up.

"Everyone settle down!" Paul said, his deep voice booming and freezing everyone in place.

"You have to be kidding, you know he couldn't have done this," Cindy pleaded, staring at Mark.

"You have the right to remain silent," Mark continued as Joseph was handcuffed. "Anything you say can and will be used against you in a court of law."

Cindy turned to look at Jeremiah. His eyes were cold, hard, and when he caught her gaze he shook his head, almost imperceptibly.

"You have the right to an attorney. If you cannot afford an attorney, one will be appointed to you by the court," Mark kept going.

The officers were at the door, hauling Joseph outside. Cindy turned and looked, and realized that the squad car was parked on her lawn. Clarice appeared next to her, and a low, rumbling growl came from the dog.

"Cindy! Take care of Clarice," Joseph begged.

Cindy laid her hand on the dog's head, and then slipped her fingers around the plain red collar she now wore. She could feel the tension running through the dog. If she attacked the police, though, it would just make the whole situation worse for everyone involved.

"Ssh," she soothed.

She watched, helpless, as they pushed Joseph into the back of the squad car. With a sob Geanie finally moved, racing over next to Cindy. Together they stood and watched as the car left, Joseph slumped in the back of it.

Cindy turned to Mark. "How could you?" she demanded.

"It's nothing personal," he said. "We have evidence that he did it, and we had to move before anyone else got hurt."

"You could have warned me, called, something."

"That's not how we do things," Paul said. "Come on, Mark, they'll need us at the station."

As the detectives drove away, Geanie began to sob uncontrollably. Cindy felt a hand descend on her shoulder and twisted around to see Jeremiah staring intently at her.

"If he's guilty, this is for the best. If he's innocent, we'll make sure he's cleared," he promised.

"Thank you," she whispered.

She closed the door and let go of Clarice, who whined and scratched at it. Geanie staggered over to the table and collapsed back into her chair. Everyone pushed their half-eaten pie away from them. It was a shame, Cindy thought, it had been really good pie. Joseph had been right. Thanksgiving had spun completely and utterly out of control.

14

After everyone had finished picking at their desserts and the food had all been put away and the dishes washed, the party broke up.

Geanie's friend left, offering to drive Bernadette and Ginger to the shelter, and they went with her. For a minute Geanie, Jeremiah, and Cindy just stared at each other. Clarice finally stopped whining and settled down with a look of misery on her face.

Cindy looked at her and felt bad for the dog. She glanced around the room. "Where's Buff?" she asked, suddenly realizing that she hadn't seen the puppy since the police arrived.

The other two looked around as well and then shook their heads. Cindy lurched to her feet. "Buff?"

Oh, please, not again. "Buff!"

Clarice jumped to her feet and whined.

"Did he run outside when the door was open?" Geanie asked. "We might not have seen him in the confusion."

"I don't know," Cindy said, looking under the table and then checking behind the sofa.

"I'll check outside," Geanie said, exiting the front door.

Jeremiah stood up from the couch. "Let's check the back, start closing off rooms as we clear them."

She nodded, and together they moved down the hall. A quick look in the bathroom and they were able to close the door. Next they searched her bedroom, checking under the bed and behind the furniture. Finally they closed the door and moved on to her office.

Fear was mounting in Cindy. They were running out of places to look. What if he had gotten outside and was lost again? It had been such a triumph to find him, and it would be devastating to lose him again, especially given what had just happened to his owner.

Cindy checked behind the filing cabinet while Jeremiah crawled under her desk.

"Found him," Jeremiah said at last. "He's wedged between the computer and the wall."

Relief flooded through her, and she crossed to him. Jeremiah pulled the puppy out and then handed him up to her. She took Buff from him, and then Jeremiah stood up.

"I'll tell Geanie we found him," he said.

Cindy followed him into the living room and then sat on a chair, still holding the puppy. He was shaking and whimpering deep in his throat. Every time she petted him, he jerked.

"What's wrong?" she asked him.

Jeremiah returned with Geanie.

"Something really terrified him," Cindy said.

"Well, it could be because he just saw his owner arrested," Geanie said, voice cracking.

Cindy glanced up at Geanie and realized that the other woman had been crying.

"He saw him leave, gut I doubt he would have understood the context," Jeremiah said.

"And he wasn't shaking like this when we found him wandering the streets, lost and hungry," Cindy said. "No, I think it's something else. I just don't know what it could be."

"If only he could tell us," Jeremiah said.

"I think I need to go home," Geanie said.

"Are you going to be okay?" Cindy asked.

Geanie nodded.

"Will you be okay with the dogs?"

Cindy looked at Buff and Clarice and realized that even if she had a way to get them into Joseph's home, there was no one to look after them. "I guess I'm going to have to be," she said.

"Do you need me to drive you?" Jeremiah asked.

"No, I've got it. Thanks," Geanie said. "It was a great dinner," she said, looking at Cindy.

Cindy nodded.

Geanie left a moment later, and Cindy and Jeremiah were alone with the dogs. Cindy petted Buff, stroking his head and then his back. There was a rough spot on the back of his neck and she glanced down at it. The fur had been shaved in one small spot.

"What is it?" Jeremiah asked.

"There's a small shaved spot here," she said, pointing.

"I noticed that Ginger had one as well. Bernadette told me the people she adopted him from said that was where they inserted the needle when they chipped her. They said the fur would grow back in a week or two."

"That's right. Joseph said all the dogs that were going to be adopted were chipped."

"Mystery solved," he said and then began to cough.

"You don't look so good."

"I'm feeling worse."

"I'm sorry, you probably should have stayed in bed all day. I shouldn't have forced you to come."

"No, I was glad to be here. And trust me, you didn't force me to do anything."

"Do you need me to drive you home?"

"I can manage."

"If you want to crash on the couch, you're welcome to," she said. "I've got flu medication and plenty of food."

He smiled. "Is this the same woman who was worried that it would create a scandal if she had pizza at my house?"

Cindy shrugged. "I doubt there's much else we could do today to cause more scandal here than has already happened."

"You might be right. Just the same, I think I just want to go home and fall asleep in my own bed."

"Fair enough. Can I send some leftovers home with you? I forgot to ask anyone else."

"Sure."

Cindy got up and prepared him a couple of plates of food, which he accepted with a smile before heading on his way.

With the house quiet, Cindy found herself at a complete loss. She fed and walked Clarice and Buff, but Clarice's anxiety over the absence of her master communicated itself to Cindy until she found herself pacing her apartment alongside the dog.

Joseph couldn't possibly be involved in whatever had been happening. There was just no way he was a killer. Or was he? Was it actually possible that every guy she'd had dinner with in the past year, possibly in her entire life, was a killer and she just couldn't see it? After all, she had gone to dinner with a killer over Easter.

She shook her head emphatically. Not every guy. She had shared pizza with Jeremiah and he was certainly no––

She stopped pacing and sunk down onto the couch. Jeremiah *was* a killer. He had shot and killed the serial killer at Easter when the man had been holding her captive with a knife at her throat. That was different, though, he had acted because he had to. There was nothing cold-blooded, illegal, or immoral about his actions.

She closed her eyes and relived that moment. Jeremiah had moved incredibly fast. She hadn't even had time to see the gun, but she had heard the crash and felt the impact on the body of the man who held her captive. She would always remember the look in his eyes, though, so cold and hard. Nor would she forget the confusion afterward about who had actually fired and hit the killer.

She shuddered and felt as though she was going to be sick. She had fought so hard for so many years to be safe, to stay away from death and danger, and yet she found herself completely immersed in both. She stood up. She had to do something before she went crazy.

With an apology to Clarice and Buff, she closed off her bedroom, bathroom, and office and left the dogs free to roam the rest of the house. She piled a plate with leftover food, grabbed a napkin and some plastic utensils, and then headed out the door.

She had too many questions that needed answers. Who was behind the murders and why? What, if anything, was Joseph's involvement? Why had the police not been able to find the homeless man who had jumped in front of her car in protest?

There was one question, though, that she hoped she could get an answer to. What had Harry witnessed when he was attacked?

When she arrived at the hospital, she discovered a policeman standing guard outside Harry's door. She recognized him as one of the officers who had been there when Harry was removed from the recycling bin. He recognized her as well and gave her a friendly smile.

"That smells like turkey," the policeman said, waving to her plate.

"It is."

"Any chance you brought enough for two?"

"I'm sorry," she said, feeling guilty.

"That's okay. I'm being relieved in twenty minutes, and my family is waiting dinner for me."

"That's nice of them."

He shrugged. "What can I say? I've got a great family."

"You're very lucky."

"I know. So is Harry if that's for him."

"It is." She hesitated. "Is it okay?"

"Yeah, you're on the approved visitor list."

"Really?" she asked, startled.

"Yeah, the detective said he figured you'd be along soon enough to check on Harry and ask him questions."

"I guess the detective knows me better than I know myself."

"Seems as though. Go right in."

He opened the door for her, and Cindy walked inside. Harry lay still, eyes closed in a badly swollen face.

She gently put the food down on the tray beside the bed and then took a seat on one of the hard, plastic chairs in the room.

"I smell turkey," Harry said, making her jump slightly.

"Not just turkey, but stuffing, mashed potatoes, and gravy too."

"Now, that's worth waking up for," he said, slowly opening his eyes and blinking in the brightness.

He turned his head slightly so he could look at her. "I guess I missed Thanksgiving dinner?"

"Not really. The dinner didn't go very well. But you get the food, which was the best part."

"Then I'm a lucky man."

Looking at him lying there so helpless, she couldn't agree with him. He had to be one of the most unlucky men she knew. She bit her lip and didn't know how to respond.

The door opened, and a male nurse walked in briskly, saving Cindy from having to say anything. He quickly checked Harry's vitals.

"Looks like Thanksgiving dinner came to you," the man said.

"Yup," Harry agreed.

The nurse helped Harry work the remote control for the bed and then maneuvered the pillows and pulled the tray in front of him so he could eat. "I'll be back in a while to check on you," the nurse said before exiting.

Harry began to eat, and Cindy contented herself with sitting quietly as he took his first few bites. "You're a good cook," he said at last.

"Thank you. I got lucky."

He smiled. "It doesn't pay to be too modest."

"A lot of people would disagree with you on that."

He laughed, a sharp, biting sound. "A lot of them haven't suffered because of it. You know what my favorite Bible verse is?"

"No."

"First Hesitations 1:3. He who does not toot his own horn, whereby shall it be tooted?"

"That's not a real verse!" she burst out. "That's not even a real book in the Bible!"

"I heard it once in youth group years ago, and it always stuck with me. You'd be surprised how many people go scurrying for their Bible trying to look it up when I tell them."

"You're kidding."

"Wish I was. You know my IQ is 170?"

She blinked at him. "Seriously?"

"Yeah. When I was young, I was modest to a fault. You know what happened?"

"No."

"I lost my job to a guy who took credit for my work, lost my wife to a man who boasted about being in Mensa because she didn't think I was very smart, and couldn't get a new job because I was always quick to point out my shortcomings and slow to point out my strengths in job interviews."

"That's awful!"

"Yup. But you know what?"

She shook her head.

"I'm better at being homeless than anyone else I know."

"That seems like the last thing you'd want to be proud of," she said before she could stop herself.

"I consider it good training. Ask me what else I'm good at."

"What else are you good at?"

"Taking advantage of every system I can get my hands on, as well as physics, math, and reading people. And I can tell you didn't just come down here to bring me Thanksgiving dinner."

She flushed with guilt. "You're right," she admitted.

"Of course I am. Excuse me, but I have a killer headache that doesn't lend itself too well to civilities and formalities. So what is it that you want to ask me?"

"Did you see the person who attacked you?"

"No. Wish I had. I got a good whiff of him, though. He was wearing Old Spice. I can also tell you he was devilish strong."

"How do you know?"

"He had to be to get me in that dumpster."

"It was a recycling bin," she corrected.

"You think that makes it any better?" he asked incredulously.

"No."

"So I smelled him but didn't see or hear him."

"Well, that's at least something."

"Yeah. What else you got on your mind?" he asked, taking a bite of potatoes and gravy.

"There was a homeless guy, a protestor, at the charity event Friday night. The police can't find him, and they need to ask him some questions."

"And you assumed since I'm also homeless I would know him?"

"I was hoping you'd seen him before, at a shelter, the park, somewhere," she admitted.

"What does he look like?"

"He's got dreadlocks."

"Okay, what else?"

Cindy shrugged. "I really don't know. He was right in front of me, and yet for some reason that's all I remember."

"It's because you didn't really look at him."

"I couldn't help but look at him; he jumped out right in front of me."

"You saw him, but you didn't look at him."

"I don't understand," Cindy said.

"The more uncomfortable a homeless person makes someone, the less they look at him," Harry said.

Cindy shook her head. "I still don't understand."

"Close your eyes."

She hesitated, but then did as he said.

"Now, tell me what I look like."

"Ummm . . . you have long, no, medium, dark-blonde hair . . . it's kinda wavy, I think. Your eyes are brown," she said, straining to remember.

"Okay, open your eyes and look at me."

"I got your eye color wrong," she realized. His eyes were a pale green and not the brown she had envisioned.

He nodded. "And you know me. On a scale of 1 to 10, 10 being very, how much do I freak you out?"

"One."

"Tell the truth."

"Four," she said, flushing.

"Uh-huh. Now you know that nurse who was in here?"

"Yeah."

"Describe him."

She found it easier to do so.

Harry nodded. "You got him right, and you've only seen him once. Difference is, you looked at him—really looked at him. People don't want to look at what makes them uncomfortable. How much did he freak you out?"

"One," she admitted.

"Even though you don't know him. He could be a crazy killer guy for all you know."

"You're right," she said, thinking about her own experiences with killers she had never suspected until too late.

"The harder someone begs off of you, the less you're likely to look at them because they make you uncomfortable. It's easier to not deal with them as a human being because then you'd have to do something about it."

"Do something, like what?" she asked, startled at the thought.

"It depends. You might have to realize that he's a human and hurting and you might have to open your wallet or your home or involve yourself in charity work. Or you might also realize that he's human but that he's crossed a line and is being an ass and you might have to push back, tell him to back off, yell, put him in his place. Most folks don't want to do that with homeless people because it would make them feel too guilty."

"What's the solution?"

"To homelessness? Hell if I know. To the personal problem? See them as people, give them a buck if you feel like it, or call the cops if they're whack jobs who are threatening and harassing you. We homeless get used to being dehumanized. People throw money at us or run from us, but they don't treat us like humans. They don't expect us to behave like citizens. They treat us and expect us to be no better than dogs, loud, aggressive, mean dogs oftentimes, but dogs nonetheless. You want to give the homeless man some dignity and self-worth? Look him in the eye and talk to him like you would any other human being in that situation."

What he said shook Cindy to her core. It also had her thinking, though, about more than just Harry, about more than the homeless, but specifically about that idea of making people uncomfortable and becoming almost invisible.

Like the homeless protestor who had jumped out in front of her car. All she had really seen of him was his dreadlocks. She hadn't wanted to look at him. She bet nobody else had wanted to, either. Maybe the reason Mark couldn't find him was because he knew how to disappear. Maybe he wasn't even really homeless, but someone who understood them, and how others related to them, really well.

Maybe it was a shelter worker.

Or a cop, the thought came to her.

"Thank you, Harry," she said, as she jumped to her feet.

"Where are you going?" he asked.

"To the store. I need to sniff some Old Spice."

"You think you know who attacked me?" Harry asked.

She tapped her nose. "I'll know soon enough."

⌖

Mark glanced at his watch. He had under half an hour before he had promised Traci he would be home. He hoped Joseph would just confess and make everything easier on all of them, but he couldn't count on that happening. Something seemed off about the whole thing, anyway.

He steeled himself to head into the interrogation room and began walking in that direction.

"Mark!"

He swiveled, something cold and hard stealing over him. There was a quality in the tone of Paul's voice that he had never heard before. It sounded like panic.

"What?"

Paul stopped before him, a stricken look on his face. "911 just received a call from a woman saying that someone kidnapped her neighbor a minute ago. Squad cars are on the way."

"Who?"

"The woman, she was your neighbor. Mark, someone's kidnapped your wife."

15

MARK STOOD IN HIS OWN LIVING ROOM AND FELT LIKE HE WAS LIVING A dream. Everything around him was his, but none of it looked familiar. The dining room table had papers scattered on top of and around it. He picked one of them up. Traci had been working on the bills. Her checkbook lay open on the table, her signature half signed on the cable bill. A drop of blood obscured the date.

Three of the chairs had been knocked over in the struggle; the legs on one of them had been smashed. One of the doors on the china hutch had been pulled off its hinges and lay across the room as though flung there.

Deep marks in the carpet looked as though someone had been clawing at it, trying to grab hold of something as they were dragged across the floor. More drops of blood were splattered along the path.

A wall close to the front door had been bashed in about a foot above the ground, cracks radiating out from around the impression. He crouched down to better study it. What had hit the wall with such force? There were no objects lying anywhere near. Was it a fist, a foot, a head?

He shuddered and rose to his feet. He couldn't think of it as Traci—couldn't think of this as having happened in his home to his wife.

"What does the neighbor woman have to say?"

"Her name is Alice," Paul said softly.

Mark knew her name. He had more than once helped her clean her gutters in anticipation of winter or helped carry packages that were too heavy for her stooped frame. But if he thought of her as Alice, then he would know that the woman who had been taken was Traci. And he couldn't know that, not if he was going to find her.

"What did she say?"

Paul took a step back, cleared his throat, and pulled out his notepad. "She heard a dog barking. She had fallen asleep watching television when she was awakened by the sound of a dog barking. At first she thought it was the television, but the barking continued when she turned it off. She says she knows the difference between the sound of a dog barking over a cat and a dog barking over danger, and she knew there was trouble. Next, she heard a scream. She went to her window and saw a man, tall, over six feet, with short dark hair, drag Tra— the woman who lives here out of the house and toss her into the trunk of his car. He drove off while she was trying to dial 911. She never saw his face but maintains that she could recognize him by a scar on the back of his neck, just below his hairline. He was dressed all in black."

Paul turned the notepad toward him where there was a rough sketch of a gently waving line with a sharp downward turn at the end—the scar. Something about it seemed familiar, like he had seen it somewhere before. He racked his brain wishing he could remember where he had seen it. Had it been on one of the people he had interviewed in the last few days? A criminal he had captured in the past?

Think!

He heard someone shout something, and he saw Paul turn and walk quickly outside. They might have found something; he needed to follow him. Before Mark could move, Paul returned, his face ashen.

Please, let them not have found a body. In that moment Mark wished he and God were on speaking terms, that he might pray and He would answer.

And then someone else walked into the room, a tall African American man with a cool demeanor and an expensive suit, and an icy hand wrapped itself around Mark's heart. He couldn't deal with what had happened in this room, but he knew the man talking with Paul would make him.

"Mr. Walters?"

"Detective," he corrected.

"*Mr.* Walters, I am Percy Grayhorn. I am the one they call in when there's been a kidnapping. I'm in charge of this investigation, and I need to speak with you for a few minutes."

"No, I'm in charge of this investigation," Mark corrected. "I believe it is tied to an ongoing murder investigation."

"That will be for my team to decide," Percy said in a tone that broached no argument.

He grabbed Mark by the elbow and moved him toward the kitchen, which seemed to have been untouched. He pulled out stools for both of them, and Mark sat after a moment.

Percy folded his hands on the counter and looked him in the eyes. "Now, generally, in a kidnapping situation, we can expect a ransom call fairly quickly. Do you or your wife, Traci, have any substantial assets or means of getting them?"

"No," Mark whispered, shaking his head.

Why does he say her name like that? He has no right to say her name, none at all. He has no right to be here. Mark squeezed his eyes shut. They had nothing, there would be no ransom call, he was sure of it. What would someone have to gain?

"I understand that Traci was kidnapped less than an hour ago."

Traci. Traci was kidnapped. His Traci. Mark dropped his head into his hands. *I'm not this man, I'm not the hapless husband, the victim waiting, I'm not, I'm not, I'm not. I'm the one in charge. I'm the one who gives bad news, not the one who gets it. I'm not the one whose wife, whose Traci, has been kidnapped.*

"I'm not this man," he groaned.

"Well, Mr. Walters, today you are."

"Excuse me," Paul interrupted, and Mark was grateful for his partner's presence. It would be all right, not because of well-dressed Percy and his team, but because of *his* team, the homicide team.

"I just need to ask Mark a quick question."

Please, ask me a million, just get me away from this guy, Mark wanted to beg.

Percy nodded, and Paul put a hand on Mark's shoulder, shaking him slightly as though to wake him up, or remind him of who he was.

"Is there anything missing?" Paul asked.

Missing? Mark glanced around and then back at Paul. Paul already knew the answer; he just needed Mark to confirm it. He tried to read his partner's eyes. What was missing? He thought of Alice's description of what she had seen and then it struck him. Mark cleared his throat. "Yes. Buster is missing."

"What?"

"Our dog, Buster."

And from somewhere inside him he found a calm he didn't know he had. He stood to his feet. "I am not this man," he said, slowly and emphatically to Percy. "Not today, not ever. I am Detective Mark Walters and this is another crime scene related to my ongoing investigation. You do whatever you have to do, but I'll thank you to stay out of my team's way."

"I'm afraid I can't do that. You're too close."

"You're absolutely right I'm too close. I'm too close to catching this killer, and I'm not going to let this stop me. I catch the killer; I find my wife. Now, you can either be part of the solution or part of the problem. There's a lot we could do working together. But if you want to report me, feel free to do so. Meanwhile I'm going to do my job."

He turned on his heel. Forensics had moved in and was sweeping the place. They wouldn't find much, if the other crime scenes were any indicators. Then again, the guy had had to hurry with this one, so there was always a chance. Best to get out of their way and let them do what they did best while he did what he did best.

"Come on, Paul, I have a hunch," Mark said, heading for the front door. He had Buster to thank for that.

⌁

After Jeremiah got home, he fell asleep in front of the television, something he almost never did. When he awoke, night had fallen. He turned off the television and stood up, ready to head off to bed. He coughed hard enough that he nearly fell over.

He finally stopped and in the silence that ensued he heard something, a high-pitched whining sound. It took him a moment to realize it was coming from outside. He pulled back the curtains on the front window just an inch so he could see outside.

Across the lawn, in the same spot that he had found the body, was another dark lump. This one moved slightly, and he realized whatever it was, it was very much alive.

He grabbed the butcher knife from the kitchen, secured it in the back of his waistband, and walked onto the porch. He walked quietly across the lawn, straining to see what it was that was moving in the corner. When he had closed the distance by half, he finally recognized it as a dog.

He held out his hand and whistled low, wondering if the animal was hurt and knowing better than to approach too close if he was.

The animal whined again and then stood up slowly and took a step toward him, then stopped.

It was the German shepherd he had seen in the park. Somehow the dog had managed to follow the trail left by its dead master and was lying in the spot where the man had died.

Jeremiah squatted down and said softly, "He's not there anymore, boy. I'm sorry. Come here, though, and I can get you some food and we can figure out what to do together."

Slowly, one step at a time, the dog came to him. Jeremiah scratched behind his ears before carefully standing up and taking a step toward the house, patting his leg so the dog would follow him. The dog began to move, flinching occasionally, and Jeremiah could tell he was in pain. He wondered what the extent of his injuries were.

They made it on to the porch, and Jeremiah opened the door into the house. The dog whimpered and then turned to look over his shoulder, clearly trying to decide what to do.

Jeremiah stood for a moment before walking inside. "Come on in, boy. I have turkey."

The dog turned back and walked inside. Jeremiah closed the door behind him and moved toward the kitchen. The dog didn't follow but instead stood rigid by the door. He began to scratch at it.

Jeremiah pulled one of the plates of leftovers out of the refrigerator and put some of the turkey meat on a smaller plate. He set it on the floor in full view of the dog.

The dog's nose twitched once, twice, and then he limped over to the plate and began to wolf down the turkey.

In the light of the kitchen Jeremiah was able to look him over. The dog was filthy, and dried blood covered both front feet, as if he had torn them up scratching his way through something.

Jeremiah got a bowl of water and set it down on the floor, as well. The dog turned, saw it, and then drank half the bowl before returning to his food.

"Just as thirsty as you are hungry, huh, boy? So what exactly happened to you out there? Your master, was he killed because of something he was involved in or because someone wanted to get to you?"

When the dog had finished the turkey, he turned again to the water, draining the bowl. Jeremiah refilled it, and the dog had one more quick drink before lying down on the kitchen floor with a weary groan.

Jeremiah took silent stock of the dog as he tried to decide what to do. A hacking cough racked his body, a painful reminder that he had been on his way to bed before discovering the animal.

He should call the police, feign ignorance again, and let them figure out where the dog had been and why he had tracked down his former owner a couple days later. They'd be able to get the dog the medical attention he needed and check him thoroughly for any evidence.

That was what worried him. If the murder wasn't connected, then the last thing Jeremiah wanted was the police figuring that out and asking a bunch of questions he wasn't prepared to answer.

No, he had to examine the dog himself first. He coughed again, so hard he had to lean against the counter for support. He was clearly in no shape to do it at the moment, though.

He didn't want to go to bed, though, until he had at least figured out if the dog was injured and needed his paws bandaged.

He filled a large pan with lukewarm water, grabbed a couple of dish towels, and sat down gingerly on the floor next to the dog.

He looked the dog in the eyes. "I'm not trying to hurt you; I only want to help. I realize that I don't know you and you don't know me, but you need to trust me."

He picked up the dog's left front paw. The dog winced but didn't growl. Carefully, Jeremiah lowered it into the bowl of water and held it there, letting the water loosen the dirt and blood that were matted onto it.

After a minute the dog relaxed slightly and then sneezed on him.

"Well, aren't we a pair? It looks like we're both sick as dogs," Jeremiah said with a smile.

He forced himself to be calm while he worked, to not feel fear or anger or any of the other negative emotions that had been plaguing him. Animals could sense emotions and would respond accordingly. So he worked hard to transmit a feeling of peace to the dog next to him. After a minute the dog began to close his eyes, and his head dropped to the floor.

"It's okay," Jeremiah soothed. "I think you need the sleep even more than I do."

After about ten minutes he was able to remove most of the dirt and blood from the paw. He took it out of the water and looked closely. There were scabs on the pads of his foot that seemed to be healing over.

After getting fresh water in the pan, Jeremiah repeated the process with the other front foot. When he finally examined that one, he discovered a bit of glass wedged in between two of the dog's toes. He got some tweezers and peroxide and carefully removed and sterilized the injured area.

The dog yelped once and started to lurch to his feet, but Jeremiah was ready for the movement and pressed him steadily back to the floor. Once the glass had been removed, the dog relaxed again.

Satisfied that he had done what he could for him until morning, Jeremiah turned out the lights and headed for bed.

He had been lying down for five minutes when he heard the dog walk into his room whimpering.

"What is it?" Jeremiah asked groggily.

The dog jumped up onto the bed and lay down next to Jeremiah's feet and within a minute was snoring softly.

❦

With a frustrated sigh Cindy finally had to admit that "soon enough" was shaping up to be "tomorrow." Every store she drove by seemed to have closed early for the holiday. The one drugstore that was open didn't carry any Old Spice products at all.

So much for avoiding the stores on Black Friday, she thought grimly as she pulled up outside her house.

Clarice and Buff were thrilled to see her, and she took them both for a quick walk in the front yard. Once back inside, she had no sooner unclipped the leashes than the phone rang.

"Hello?" she asked as she picked up her cordless.

"Hi Cindy, it's Guy."

"What guy?"

"Uh, Guy Randall from speed dating?"

"Oh, I am so sorry!"

"Did I catch you at a bad time?"

"A little bit, sorry."

"I can call back."

"No, now is fine," Cindy said, forcing herself to take a deep breath and sit down on the couch. Clarice jumped up beside her, and she petted the dog absentmindedly.

"I know I wasn't supposed to call until Sunday, but I just wanted to wish you Happy Thanksgiving."

"Happy Thanksgiving," she replied automatically. "How's your family?"

"Well, thank you. How is yours?"

"Okay, I guess."

"Good." He paused and then continued, "Is there anything wrong?"

"One of my friends just got arrested for murder. I'm sure he's innocent, but the police came to arrest him at my house during dinner."

"Ouch! I'm sorry."

"Me too."

"Is there anything I can do?"

"Are you serious?" she burst out.

"Yes, why?"

"Well, for one, you're out of state, and for another, you don't even know me."

"But I want to."

She blushed. "That's sweet."

"I'll take sweet. At least you didn't call me nice."

"Why?"

"That's the kiss of death from a girl. Whenever a girl tells a guy he's nice, that means she won't go out with him."

"I don't believe that for a second."

"Really? Can you think of the last guy you called nice?"

Joseph. "Uh-huh."

"Did you want to go out with him?"

"No."

"There you are."

Clarice shifted slightly, and Cindy's fingers ran over the back of her neck. Amidst the soft fur there was the sensation of smoothness, and Cindy stopped and looked down, parting the dog's thick fur with her fingers.

There on the back of Clarice's neck was a tiny shaved spot.

"Oh, my gosh," Cindy breathed as she stared at the shaved spot on the back of Clarice's neck. "Guy, I've got to go. Can I call you back?"

"Sure."

She examined the dog more carefully. Clarice had the same sort of shaved spot that the other dogs did. It made no sense, though. Joseph would have had Clarice chipped when she was younger. There was no reason she should have a shaved mark too.

"What happened to you?" she asked.

The dog just looked at her with dark, mournful eyes. Buff had discovered a catalog and was happily shredding it in a corner, not at all the frightened puppy of a couple hours earlier.

"What scared you, Buff?"

He glanced up briefly then went back to shredding the glossy pages. She knew she should stop him, but she couldn't bring herself to do it.

Why would someone be sticking a needle in Clarice? And who could have done it? It was possible that the person who had broken into Joseph's house whom she had bitten could have done it. The only other time the dog had really been vulnerable that she could think of was when the police had taken her into custody to check the DNA evidence from the blood on her.

And what about Buff? Who or what had scared him so badly when the police came to arrest Joseph? He had already met Mark the day she found him. She couldn't see where Paul would have been any more threatening.

It was the uniforms, she realized. Buff had been terrified of one or all of the uniformed officers. Had he seen or smelled one of them before? Or had he a reason to be afraid of the uniform?

She began to shake as the truth dawned on her. A policeman was involved.

16

MARK CALLED IN AND ASKED FOR THE HOME ADDRESS OF JUNE, THE DIREC-
tor of the animal shelter.

"They'll have it for us in five minutes," he said as he hung
up.

He considered hurling his phone out the window or smashing it against the dashboard, but stopped himself since he
needed it to receive the call back. Plus, Traci had the number.
She might manage to get free just for a second or two and
call.

Mark flipped the phone open and checked the battery. He
had full bars still.

Paul swerved the car into a parking spot in front of a 7-11.
"I need coffee and something to eat. So do you."

"I'm not hungry."

Another officer Lou, who had been at the scene, pulled up.
He glanced at Paul and Mark with an apologetic grimace. Paul
and he walked inside together, and Mark tried not to scream at
the delay. He sat, staring at his cell, willing it to ring.

Finally Paul and Lou exited, and Mark could hear the tail
end of their conversation.

"If it was about the dog, why didn't they kill Traci like everyone else?" he heard Lou ask.

"Could it be the guy doesn't want to cross the line by killing a cop's wife?" Paul asked.

"Why not just knock her out if he didn't want to kill her?" Lou countered. "Why kidnap her?"

"Maybe because she could identify him?" Paul said as he opened his car door.

"It was a cop," Mark said.

"What?" Paul and Lou asked in unison.

"A cop is behind all of this," Mark repeated, turning to look at his partner, who looked as stricken as he felt.

"How can you be sure?"

"This guy has killed too many people, both homeless and not. The only way he cares about kidnapping her instead of killing her is if he needs a hostage or he feels too guilty to kill her."

"Just because she's a cop's wife?"

"No," Mark said, as the full horror of it dawned on him. "No, because she's a cop's wife and because he knows her."

His cell rang, making him jump. He flipped it open as he reached for his pen. He jotted down the address the woman on the other end gave him and then hung up. "Let's go, I've got the address."

Paul slid into the driver's seat, carefully stowing the coffees in his hands in the twin cup holders. He stuffed a couple of high protein energy bars and a bag of gummi bears into the glove compartment and then tossed a hot dog at Mark as he put the car in reverse.

Even though the thought of food was making him a bit sick, Mark forced himself to down the hot dog. He would need to keep up his energy until this was over.

It only took them a few minutes to find the address they were looking for. As it turned out, Mark and Paul interrupted the director of the animal shelter during her holiday festivities. She came out on the porch, closing the door behind her as the evening seemed to still be in full swing. Through an open window somewhere Mark could hear the sounds of a game being played.

He winced, realizing he hadn't called his sister-in-law and that she would be wondering where they were. He almost didn't want to call her with the news that he had, but he knew he had to.

"What is it?" she asked, wrapping her arms around herself, and staring intently into their faces.

"We need to ask you a few more questions," Paul said.

"Now?" she blinked in surprise.

"Crime never sleeps and neither do we," Paul said grimly.

"Okay. Are these questions about the murder or about the break-in?" she asked.

Paul and Mark exchanged a surprised glance. "What break-in?" Mark asked quietly.

She looked surprised. "The one Sunday night. When I showed up for work Monday morning, the place had been broken into. The cat rooms had been opened and a couple of the dog pens too. It was a mess; fur and feces everywhere. The dogs were chasing the cats, and the cats were hiding everywhere they could. It took us hours to round everyone up and get them back where they belonged. Thank goodness there were only minor injuries. We called the police right away and filled out a whole report."

Mark felt a chill and couldn't help but wonder if he hadn't heard about it because the officers working that unit hadn't thought or realized they needed to alert homicide of a possible connection or if the officers who had taken her statement had conveniently lost the report.

"Did you get the names of the officers who responded to the call?" Paul asked.

She shook her head. "I was too upset to pay attention."

"Can you describe them for us?" Mark asked.

"One was tall, good-looking, wore a hat pulled down over his eyes, and the other was shorter and kind of fidgety."

As Paul scribbled down the descriptions on his notepad, Mark fought to control his temper.

"Anything more than that? Hair color, eye color? Light skin, dark skin? Could you sketch them?"

She shook her head. "I'm terribly sorry, no. I can remember every dog that's come through our shelter, but I have a terrible memory for people's faces. But why would that be important? It can't be that difficult to figure out who came out that morning."

It could be if they were trying to hide their tracks, Mark thought. Still, there was a chance someone at dispatch would know who it was who had taken the call.

"Was there anything taken?" Paul asked.

"Nothing physical, but I'm fairly certain information was stolen. The main computer was on and it had been hacked into. Not that that's too hard to do, though. We are pretty sloppy about passwords and the like. I've since implemented new safety precautions."

"What information?" Mark asked.

"Names and addresses of everyone that adopted a dog involved with the Animals to the Rescue program."

Mark felt the world tilt sideways. "Including the non-homeless who ended up adopting one of the extra dogs, like me?"

"Yes, Detective."

That was how he knew about the rich woman who was killed, and about Mark and Traci having a dog.

"I'm just so grateful we didn't store any financial information for the non-homeless who paid the regular adoption fee. Could you imagine the consequences? My sister had her identity stolen last year, and she's still trying to straighten it out."

"Yeah, it can be devastating," Paul agreed. "We'll need a list of those adopters as well."

"I can get that for you now, if you wouldn't mind waiting a couple of minutes. I had surgery over the summer, and my husband set it up so I can access my work computer from my home computer."

"That would be excellent, thank you."

She hesitated. "I hate to ask, but, would you mind waiting here?"

"That's fine."

"I'll be right back," Mark said, stepping away a few feet and pulling out his cell phone. He took a deep breath and then dialed his sister-in-law's house. Her husband answered.

"Hi, it's Mark," he said.

"Hey! We were just about to send out a search party. You two on your way over?"

"No, something's happened, actually," Mark said, trying hard to keep his voice calm.

"What is it?" the other man asked, sobering instantly.

"Traci was kidnapped a couple of hours ago."

There was silence on the other end for several seconds, and then he heard a door closing. There was a slight echo as his brother-in-law whispered, "What did you just say?"

"She was kidnapped. The entire force is doing everything they can to find her. I just realized I hadn't called—"

"You find her and don't worry about the niceties. I'll tell everyone that you're contagious and staying at home so no one gets the fool notion of bringing dinner to you."

"I would appreciate it."

"If you haven't found her by the morning, then I'll come clean, but it's not going to do anyone any good right now."

"Thank you."

"You call if you need anything. Anything, you hear?"

"I do."

Mark hung up and returned to the doorstep just as the woman returned with the printout. Mark scanned it quickly, and several names jumped out at him, including his own.

"Thank you for your time. If you think of anything else, give us a call," Paul said, handing her his card.

She nodded and went back inside. After a moment they headed toward the car.

"Do you think someone is doing all this to sabotage Animals to the Rescue?" Paul asked.

Mark shook his head. "I think someone is looking for a particular dog, they just don't know which one it is."

"Officers!"

They turned as she ran down the walk toward their car. "I just remembered something else."

"Yes?"

"The tall one had a scar on the back of his neck."

A chill went up Mark's spine. It was the same man who had kidnapped his wife.

"Are you sure?" Paul pressed.

"Yes, I remember seeing it when he walked away. And I'm pretty sure he had some sort of New Testament name."

"New Testament name?"

She flushed. "My father was a preacher, and he used to say he would never name a child of his a New Testament name because every other Christian did that. You know, like after one of the disciples or writers."

"Matthew, Luke, etc.?" Mark asked.

"Yes. My dad said that so many times that whenever I hear someone with a name like that I hear him inside my head and it makes me smile."

"You must smile a lot, then," Mark said.

They got in the car and sat for a moment while she walked back inside. She didn't come back out, and after a minute his partner started the car.

"I think we should go back to the precinct and find out if any of the officers there has a scar on the back of his neck," Mark said quietly.

And talk to dispatch. He wanted to do it in person where he could read facial expressions and no one would overhear the conversation. His phone rang and he glanced down. It was Cindy, probably calling about Joseph. He let it go to voice mail.

Cindy left a message on Mark's cell telling him what she had found. She knew it wouldn't be enough to get Joseph out of trouble, though. If only she could figure out why Clarice had also had the back of her neck shaved as well, then maybe she'd have something.

She glanced at the phone and remembered that she had told Guy she would call him back. She didn't want to, but she had said she would. She took a deep breath and dialed Guy back.

"Hi, it's Cindy," she said when he answered.

"Uh, hello. I'm surprised you called back," he said. "You didn't seem thrilled about the original conversation."

She bit her lip. "I'm really sorry about that. It wasn't the conversation, it was all the chaos. I think I discovered another clue in the murders that have been happening."

"Why don't you tell me all about it?"

"Really?"

"Yeah."

"Wouldn't you rather be having fun with your family?"

"Right now my aunt Beth is explaining in detail to everyone why she's just sure her upcoming sixth marriage is going to work."

Cindy giggled despite herself.

"Yeah. So why don't you regale me with stories of guts and gore? Please?"

"Okay, you got it."

She brought him up to speed on what had happened.

"Wow, seriously?"

"Yeah," she said.

"So what's the new clue?"

"I realized Clarice has a spot shaved on the back of her neck too, even though she wouldn't have been chipped recently."

"Yeah, unless the bad guy was trying to chip her for some other reason."

"What did you say?" Cindy asked, sitting up straighter.

"Unless the bad guy was trying to chip her for some other reason."

"That's it!" Cindy shrieked into the phone. She leapt to her feet and began pacing as she thought. "Is it possible that someone put something on one of the dog's chips, modified it in some way?"

"Like data or blueprints or something?" he asked. "Sure, you could modify a chip and then insert it into one of the dogs in lieu of the standard microchip."

"How would you read it? Could you read it with the scanner they use at the vet's office or the Humane Society?"

"Possible, but unlikely. If someone was going to all the bother of altering the chip, they'd probably rig it so that the information could only be retrieved with a specific device or program."

"Could you hook some kind of scanner up to a laptop?"

"That would be ideal, actually. All you'd need is a USB port. Your scanner could input the data and the laptop could unscramble it."

"Thank you, Guy."

"Go solve the crime and save the day," he said.

"I will. I'll talk to you when you're back in state."

She hung up and tried Mark's cell phone again, but he still wasn't picking up. She dialed Jeremiah next, and she could tell by the sound of his voice that she had awakened him. She quickly filled him in on the latest developments.

"So what if the plot was to steal something, information of some type?" Cindy concluded.

"That would make sense, but there are a lot easier ways to hand off information then embedded in a dog."

"It depends on the dog and where the information has to get to. Joseph's dogs go to dog shows all over the world. If you wanted to smuggle data out, what better way than in the dog?"

"That would make sense," he said.

"What if the vet tech was there not just to chip the puppies, but also to insert the doctored chip last Friday?"

"I'm with you."

"Maybe he was nervous, afraid his partners were going to double-cross him. He embedded the chip, but not in the dog he was supposed to."

"And then Derek or someone else killed him. And then Derek was killed, as well," Jeremiah filled in.

"And Derek's laptop is missing. So the killer has the ability to read the chip, but has no idea which of the dogs present on Friday is actually carrying the correct chip."

"He has to go through all of Joseph's dogs, and when he doesn't find what he's looking for he starts in with the Humane Society's dogs."

"Until he finds the right dog, everyone who adopted is in danger," Cindy said. "What do you think is on that chip?"

"I don't know, but whatever it is, it's worth killing for."

Fear rushed through her, and she turned to look at Buff and Clarice. "I'm safe, though, right? Even though I've got two dogs here. I'm safe because the killer's already checked both of them out."

There was a long silence, and then Jeremiah spoke. "Ordinarily I would say that you were correct, but these are strange times, and I don't think anyone connected to this thing is safe until the killer is killed."

"I'm pretty sure it's a police officer," she said, licking her suddenly dry lips and getting up to double check that the front door was locked securely. It was. So were the windows.

"Do you know which one?"

"No. But Harry said whoever attacked him was wearing Old Spice. I have no idea what that smells like so I tried going by the drugstore, but everywhere was already closed for the holiday. You don't happen to have any Old Spice hanging around, do you?" She realized she was babbling, but she couldn't stop herself. She was afraid.

"Sorry, I don't. I don't know what it smells like either, but even if I did, I'm too congested to be of much assistance," Jeremiah admitted.

"It's okay. I can wait until morning."

"You don't have anything else to go on?"

"No, but judging by Buff's reaction earlier, I would guess it was one who wears a uniform."

"Makes sense to me," he said.

"There have been a lot of different uniformed officers present at the different crime scenes, and I swear that Friday the entire force had to be out there interviewing people."

"That doesn't narrow things down much," he said, breaking into a fit of coughing.

"No," she said with a sigh. "I wish Mark would answer his phone so I could let him know what we found. I'm just worried that while we're waiting for the stores to open in the morning someone else is going to die and it could have been prevented."

"What do you need to do, Cindy?"

The question hung in the air as she pondered its significance. He hadn't asked her what she wanted to do but what she needed to do. It was a powerful difference. "I need to go down to the police station."

"Why?"

"To find Mark or Paul."

"Or the killer."

"Or the killer," she affirmed.

"You don't have to do this, Cindy."

"No, but I need to."

"Do you want me to go with you?" he asked, coughing again.

"Yes, but I think it's a better idea if you stay home and get over the flu. Who knows when I'll need you to rescue me again," she said. She'd said it meaning it as a joke, but it didn't come out that way. She heard the tremor in her own voice and bit her lip.

"I don't think you need anyone to rescue you," Jeremiah said so softly she wasn't sure she had heard him right.

"Thank you," she answered.

"Can I do anything for you?"

She glanced at the dogs and briefly considered dropping them off at his place. That would take time, though, and she had the sinking feeling she was running short on it.

"No, I've got it covered," she said. "But I'll call if I need anything or I get in trouble," she said.

"Do me a favor and call even if you don't."

"I will," she promised before hanging up.

"Buff, Clarice, I'm going out for a little while. Take care of each other," she instructed the dogs.

She grabbed her purse and her keys, took a deep, steadying breath, and headed out the door.

<hr />

When they reached the precinct, Mark hopped out of the car and headed straight to dispatch, Paul trailing behind him. Once there, he waited thirty seconds for the woman manning the line to finish.

"What can I help you with?" she asked finally.

"Did you by any chance send out officers to the Humane Society Monday morning in response to a break-in call?"

"Yes," she said, looking at him strangely. "It turned out a new volunteer forgot to lock up properly."

"Where did you hear that?" Mark demanded.

"From the officers on scene."

"And just who were they?" Mark asked eagerly, leaning forward, ready to find them and tear them apart with his bare hands until they told him where his wife was.

"You."

"What?"

"You and Paul took that call."

17

Mark turned on Paul, who stood, jaw open and face pale.

"*We* took the call?" Mark growled, hand on his gun.

"We're homicide detectives, why would we have taken a robbery call?" Paul asked.

"You radioed it in, said you were close by and that it could be linked to Friday so you'd check it out just in case."

"It was linked to Friday, but we weren't the ones who answered," Paul said, staring Mark dead in the eye. "Someone claimed to be us so that no one would know who actually took the call."

"She said the tall guy had a New Testament name. Paul is a New Testament name," Mark whispered.

"And why would I have been stupid enough to use it if it was actually me connected to all of this?"

He wouldn't have. He knew Paul. The other detective was careful, methodical. He'd been with him when Traci was kidnapped and he had no scar on the back of his neck. There weren't any other Pauls or Marks on the Pine Springs police force. He had to hand it to the killer, the guy was clever, using Paul's name. He had probably hoped Mark would react just as he did. But how had he known the woman from the humane shelter wouldn't remember what he looked like? Probably because she had told an officer the very same thing when he interviewed her at the charity event.

He moved his hand away from his gun and gave Paul an apologetic grimace. The other shrugged his shoulders.

"Thanks for your help," Mark told the dispatcher.

"You're welcome," she said, eyeing the two of them warily.

Mark headed out of the room with Paul right behind.

"Time to start searching for scars?" Paul asked.

"You bet it is."

They called a meeting of every officer in the building to update them on the situation. After getting a good look at the officer manning the front desk, they excused him so he could continue to perform his duty. The rest of the thirty men and women present crowded into the large meeting room, sitting in rows of chairs.

Up front Paul began, "We didn't want a lot of rumors flying around so we figured this was the best way to update everyone at once. As you may or may not have heard by now, our killer has abducted one more dog and this time he's kidnapped a person as well—Traci Walters. Many of you know her, she's Detective Walters's wife."

Gasps went up around the room. Mark struggled not to connect with them, not to feel the horror that others were feeling. Instead he paced slowly around the room, taking a good look at the back of everyone's necks as he did so.

At the front Paul kept talking, giving updates, telling them what to look out for, but keeping quiet about the fact that a cop was involved. Finally Mark finished examining everyone in the room. He nodded to Paul, who wrapped things up.

"No questions at this time. Just remember to report anything even remotely suspicious," Paul said.

The officers filed out of the room, leaving Mark and Paul alone.

"Well?" Paul asked.

"Not a one of them had a scar on the back of their neck. Not unless the scar is a fake or they're trying to cover it up with makeup. I think that's pretty unlikely in both cases. On the face, maybe, but the back of the neck?"

"I agree with you. And we know we've both seen the scar before."

"I jotted down the names of all the officers present. I figure we only were able to check about a third of them."

"It was a long shot that whoever it was would be in the office right now too."

"Agreed."

"We still have to interrogate Joseph," Paul pointed out.

"You're right. Well, he should be sweating it by now."

"If he hasn't already lawyered up."

"I'll go take care of that now."

Paul put a restraining hand on Mark's chest. "I kind of think that I should handle the interrogation on this one."

"You don't trust me to?"

"Frankly, no. And I don't blame you at all, but we can't afford to handle this wrong, and I know your head's not entirely in a right space because of Traci."

Mark wanted to argue, but he knew Paul was right. He sighed and nodded slowly. "I'll be at my desk trying to work a few things out."

"I'll send for you if I get anything."

"Thanks."

Paul headed for the interrogation room, and Mark grabbed himself a cup of coffee and then made his way to his desk. If he could only remember where he had seen that scar, he knew he could save Traci.

When he made it back to his desk, Cindy was waiting for him, sitting in the chair across from his with hands clenched in her lap. He sighed. He had never checked his messages or returned her call. The last thing he wanted was to hear her insist that Joseph had to be innocent and how could he drag him out of her home on Thanksgiving like that.

"Well, well, Miss Preston. What can I do for you this evening?" he asked, unable to keep the sarcasm out of his voice.

She narrowed her eyes, and when she spoke, her voice was tense, clipped, "You weren't answering your phone."

"You noticed? So your response was to traipse down to the police station and try to find me?"

Anger flashed in her eyes, and for a moment he thought she was going to get up and walk out. Instead she took a deep breath and composed herself. "Did you at least get my message?"

He shook his head. "I've been a bit busy. After I visited your house, I had to go home to mine." His throat tightened up, and he fought to maintain control. "It seems the killer kidnapped my wife."

Cindy stared at him, eyes wide in shock. "I'm so sorry," she managed to finally whisper. She tried to put a hand on his arm, but then seemed to think better of it. She bit her lip and tears sparkled in her eyes but did not fall. He was at least grateful for that.

"It happened earlier today apparently. I have my theories as to who did it, but I don't have proof. And without that, I have nothing."

"I think a police officer is involved," Cindy blurted out. The words seemed harsh, judgmental the way she said them, but he knew from the look on her face that she did not mean them to.

"I've come to the same conclusion," Mark said wearily. He had been wrong to jump to conclusions about why she was calling. He took a sip of coffee to calm himself. "Time to swap info?"

Cindy nodded eagerly. "I don't feel good being the only one with the knowledge in my head."

It was funny, but Mark wasn't in the mood to laugh. "You go first."

He listened carefully as she explained everything. When she was finished, he filled her in on what he and Paul had learned. She nodded repeatedly through his telling of events until he came to the end.

"It seems we've gotten to the same place," she said.

"It appears so. Intriguing idea about the chip. It would explain a lot."

"I just can't figure out what would be on it," she said.

Mark scratched his head. "Any number of things, I would guess. It could be business related, you know, corporate espionage."

Cindy shook her head. "Derek was Joseph's personal assistant. Joseph has very little to do with the daily business of his companies, and he has people at his work who handle those details. Derek handled Joseph's private affairs."

"Maybe it was his bank account numbers," Mark suggested.

Cindy hesitated. "That would make more sense."

"But?"

"But why wait six months for that when he probably had that information within one or two? And if he wanted to take the information overseas, Joseph and the dogs have been to several shows in that time period. No, unless he was waiting for a particular country or event, that doesn't click."

"Okay, so what would have happened recently that would have been worth stealing?"

Cindy slipped a deck of cards out of her purse and began shuffling them one-handed. It was a neat trick, and Mark watched her as she thought. "Derek worked with Joseph on his personal finances and his day-to-day activities."

"Which includes dog showing and what else?"

"Charity work."

She stopped shuffling and looked him in the eye. "The charity event Friday: a lot of people donated money for that. Some were organizations, and some were individuals—a few of them very wealthy."

"And Derek would have had access to their information," Mark said. Something the director of the shelter had said earlier came back to him. She had been grateful they didn't keep financial records on the computer because her sister had been a victim of identity theft.

"Identity theft. They were going to steal the identities of a few ultra-rich people," Mark realized. "Not only could they access bank and credit accounts, but they could also make millions opening fraudulent credit accounts."

Cindy's eyes grew wide. "That would make sense. They could steal more money from a dozen than from Joseph. It would make the diamond collar pale in comparison."

"And the diamond collar would be hard to sell, whereas they could take their information out of the country, and then hit one after another without getting caught and make a fortune."

"That has to be it!" Cindy said.

"It would make sense, but the only way we're going to know for sure is if we find the chip. If he was still stealing dogs today, then he can't have found it yet."

"Even if you find the right dog before he does, how will you know without the laptop?"

"I know a couple of tech guys," Mark said. "I'll get them on it. Then I'll track down the rest of the dogs who haven't been stolen."

"Do you need any help?"

He blinked and looked at her. Her eyes were bright, her face was flushed, and she was ready to throw herself in harm's way. It was a far cry from the terrified, mousy little secretary he had met a few months before.

"No, this is a job for the police." He jumped to his feet. "Miss Preston, thank you. Call me if you think of anything else."

＊

Even though she was relieved to have been able to speak to Mark, Cindy returned home sick at heart. She prayed for his wife and that she would be found safe and sound. She couldn't imagine the nightmare he was living, and she was amazed that he was able to function through it. He was an incredible man.

As she finally made it home and parked in her driveway, fear rippled through her. The house was dark, and shadows played around it. She couldn't help but think of Mark's wife, kidnapped from her own home, and in broad daylight. Cindy was angry at herself as she sat in the car and the fear played upon her mind. She should have left a light on in the house, or at least on the porch. She never liked coming home to a dark house, but now the shadows on the porch seemed more ominous than ever.

Did one of the shadows just move to the right of the door? Her heart pounded. *Relax, no one's on your front porch.* She breathed a momentary sigh of relief until she realized that if someone was waiting for her, they were probably already inside.

But wouldn't the dogs be barking if someone was inside? *Not if they're hiding like Buff did earlier. Not if they're hurt or—*

She shook her head violently, trying to dislodge the dark thoughts that threatened to render her powerless and too frightened to move. She might be frightened, but she was not powerless. And she would move even if she were, because she had to, because to give in to fear would mean running for the rest of her life, and she was so tired of being afraid all the time.

The last few months she had been able to lull herself into believing that she was doing better, but it was all a lie. She was jumping at shadows, just as she used to, imagining all kinds of things that just weren't possible and others that, though possible, were extremely unlikely.

She wanted so badly to call Jeremiah. She knew he would come over and inspect her place, walk inside with her and keep her safe from anything dangerous that lurked within. But she couldn't. Jeremiah wouldn't always be there, and then how would Cindy face the dark and the monsters without him if she grew dependent on facing them with him?

She forced herself out of her car and up onto her porch. Shadows seemed to mock her, shifting slightly as though to make way for her passage. She put her key to the lock and heard something move just on the other side of the door.

With a gasp she spun and ran back to her car before remembering that Buff and Clarice were inside, and it was almost certainly them that she had heard. She squared her shoulders and approached the door again.

Once more the shadows seemed to leer and mock her. She slid the key into the lock, turned, pushed through the door as she opened it, and slammed and locked it behind her.

As she reached for the light switch, a wet tongue licked her ankle, and she screamed, even though she knew it was one of the dogs. The lights came on, and Clarice stared at her with a baffled look while Buff ran from the room.

"I'm sorry, I'm so sorry," she told the poodle as she reached down to give her head a quick pat.

She flipped on the outside lights, knowing she would have to take both dogs for a walk before she could barricade herself in her house for the rest of the night. She clipped the leash on Clarice's collar and cautiously eased the door open.

There was no one in sight, and she walked out a few steps, hovering on the porch and forcing Clarice to relieve herself next to the path. As soon as the dog had, Cindy backtracked into the house and slammed the door again.

Buff had reentered the living room, clearly curious about what was going on. She showed him the leash, and he bounded over to her. She repeated the same thing with him.

When she was back inside the house for the third and final time, she threw all of her deadbolts before realizing she hadn't checked the back rooms for any sign of intruders.

Surely the dogs would be acting strangely if there was an intruder, but she couldn't be too careful. Cell phone in hand and at the ready, she walked toward the back of her house, flipping on every light switch she passed.

She checked her bathroom, bedroom, and office and was relieved to find them just as she had left them. Satisfied that they were as safe as they were going to be, Cindy hurriedly got ready for bed.

When she finally slipped between the sheets, she found that her mind was racing a million miles an hour and her heart was still pounding like a jackhammer. She flipped on her side and prayed for sleep, but it seemed elusive.

"God, please let me sleep. I thank You for Your protection. Amen."

It wasn't poetry as prayers went, but it was honest and forthright. They were two qualities she admired, and she believed God must admire them as well. After a minute she felt something jump on her bed and then a second.

She looked up and saw Clarice curling up in a ball by her feet. Buff snuggled into her hip with a contented sigh and gave no signs that he planned to move again, ever.

With a smile on her face, Cindy drifted off to sleep.

Her dreams were plagued by dark creatures that mocked her, laughed at her and whispered the vilest lies she had ever heard. She tossed and turned for a couple of hours, waking every so often to look at her clock.

<hr>

When Black Friday finally came, Cindy was up before the dawn. She fed and walked the dogs and then got in her car and drove to the drugstore. She ended up joining a line of shoppers waiting to get in. She'd had no idea that even the drugstore was offering holiday bargains. She heard rumors going up and down the line that toys were 40 percent off and Christmas decorations were 50 percent off. The excitement was electric, and Cindy couldn't help but feel it.

When the doors ceremonially opened, she bolted for the toiletries section. Her eyes scanned the shelves as she looked for Old Spice deodorant. In dismay she finally saw the shelf where it should have been and realized it was sold out. She checked the body wash and cologne sections as well, with no better luck. She growled deep in her throat and fought back tears. She had to know who she was looking for if she was going to put a stop to the killings.

"What's wrong, sugar?" a large, blonde woman wearing a nametag asked her. "You need help finding something?"

"I was looking for Old Spice. You don't have any in the storeroom, do you?" she asked hopefully.

"Everything is on the shelves today if we have it," she said. "I'm sorry. We should get some more in early next week."

"But that will be too late."

"Then don't tell anyone I said so," the woman said, lowering her voice, "but you might want to get yourself over to Plusmart."

"Thank you."

Cindy turned and rushed from the store. Ten minutes later she was circling the Plusmart parking lot, desperately looking for a parking spot. Several opened up only to be taken by others circling the lot as well. She couldn't help but think that they all must resemble a pack of vultures, waiting to fall upon prey.

Finally she found one within sight of the recycling bins, and she couldn't help but shiver as she thought of Harry.

She rushed into the store, and was no sooner inside than she hit a wall of people. She heard people shouting and screeching around her, calling for friends and loved ones or shouting angrily at others who had hold of what they desired. It was chaos, and Cindy felt fear clutch at her heart as the crowd pushed her forward. She fought her way toward the correct section and finally made it into the shaving aisle.

There she found the Old Spice deodorant, and she pulled off the top and inhaled deeply. She waited a moment, but nothing came to her. Frustrated, she put the lid back on and continued to move. She finally found the body wash and tried it. Still no memories stirred. At last she found the cologne, but it was in a glass cabinet. She fought her way toward the pharmacy, looking for a Plusmart employee who could help her. She finally found one who was already besieged by half a dozen others.

She waited patiently, dogging the employee's steps as he helped first one and then another. Finally it was her turn.

"I need to see the Old Spice cologne, which is locked in a case," she said.

He nodded and waded back in that direction with her following. When he reached the case, she held her breath as he opened it. "I need to smell it," she said.

He handed her the tester bottle, and she sprayed the air and then inhaled. She knew she had smelled it before, but she didn't know where.

"Miss? Miss?"

"Yes?" she asked, opening her eyes again.

"You want it or not?"

"I'll take a small bottle," she said.

He handed her a bottle, and she made her way to the front of the store. Every cash register was open and had a line ten people long. She chose the ten items or less line, hoping that it would at least move fast.

As it turned out, she had chosen poorly. The first person in line had an item without a price tag. The fourth person paid a forty-dollar bill entirely in coins. Cindy looked around, but the other lines had grown even longer at that point, and she was afraid to switch.

Finally it was her turn, and she barely waited for her change before dashing out to the parking lot with her purchase. As soon as she exited the parking lot, she called Jeremiah's home number.

"Hello?" he asked, sounding worse than the night before.

"I am so sorry to wake you," she said. "But you know how you were telling me you could teach me to calm down and focus?"

"Cindy, is that you?" he asked.

"Yes, sorry, it's Cindy. Do you remember telling me that about the focusing exercises?"

"Yes. I can help with that."

"I wouldn't ask if it weren't really important, but I need you to teach me how to do that now."

"What's happened?" he asked, sounding more alert.

"I recognize the smell of the Old Spice cologne, but I can't remember where it is I've smelled it before. I bought a bottle and I have it with me. I just need to be able to calm down and focus so that I can figure it out. If I can do that, then I'm sure we can stop the killer."

"I understand."

"Can I come over to your place?"

"Now?"

"Yes. The sooner I can remember, the sooner we can put an end to this." She took a deep breath. "I didn't want to wake you up again last night, but the killer has kidnapped Mark's wife."

"When?" Jeremiah asked, his voice suddenly hard.

"Yesterday sometime. He took their dog too. He was one of the ones that wasn't adopted on Friday. Mark adopted him Sunday. So, please, I need to come over."

Jeremiah coughed long and hard. "Tell you what, I'll meet you at your house," he offered.

"Awesome. Thank you so much."

"I'll be there just as soon as I can."

"I'll be waiting."

She hung up and considered calling Mark but rejected it since she really had nothing new to tell him. Once she could remember who it was that wore Old Spice, then she would have something to call him over.

A few minutes later she made it home. She deposited the bottle of Old Spice on her kitchen counter before taking both dogs for a quick walk. Finished, she went into the bathroom to wash her hands and face.

"Just calm down," she told her reflection. "You can do this. You just have to remember one little thing. It shouldn't even be that hard. Odors are great memory triggers; you just have to let this one do its job."

Be still and know that I am God.

She took a deep breath and went into the living room. She sat down on the couch to wait for Jeremiah. Both dogs curled up at her feet.

Be still and know that I am God.

She bowed her head and began to pray.

When Jeremiah finally arrived, she was much calmer but seemingly no closer to remembering what she had to. She handed him the bottle of cologne and gave him a frustrated look.

"Still no luck?" he asked.

"None."

"Okay, let's go sit down," he said.

She returned to her seat on the couch and folded her hands in her lap. She felt nervous and a little silly for feeling that way and for asking for help to focus. It should be something she could do naturally.

"Please, help me."

"I will," Jeremiah promised. "But you have to listen to me."

"Okay."

"You need to learn how to calm down and focus. Now, close your eyes and just concentrate on your breathing. Now, slowly, breathe in. Hold it for a count of ten. Then, just as slowly, breathe out. Keep doing that until I tell you to stop."

She did as instructed and was surprised how hard it was to keep her thoughts focused on breathing and not scattering to the four corners of the wind. Gradually it grew easier, but she still struggled.

"Okay. On to the next thing. Keep your eyes closed. When you were a child, did you ever get a puppy or a kitten?"

"Yes, when I was very little, we got a puppy."

"What did he do when it was time for bed the first night?"

"He cried."

"He missed his mother?"

"Yes."

"What did you do?"

"The second night my mother put a clock inside a blanket and let him sleep with that."

"Did it calm him down?"

"Yes," she said.

"Why?"

"Mom said it replicated his mother's heartbeat."

"Exactly. Now, feel your own pulse."

Cindy pressed her fingers against her throat.

"Can you feel it?"

"Yes."

"Now, concentrate on it, on the rhythm, and see if you can feel the blood as it pulses through other parts of your body as well."

She concentrated for a minute, and then suddenly she could feel it everywhere. She jumped and moved her fingers. "Eww," she said, waving her hand.

"It is an unpleasant sensation at first, but it is a quick and easy way to teach yourself to focus."

"You could have warned me," she complained.

"That would not have done you any good. Now, let's try it again. First five breaths."

She took the five deep breaths, holding them and then releasing each slowly.

"Now, tell me when you can feel your pulse through your body."

She lifted her fingers to her throat again until she had the rhythm, and then she felt for it until she found it. She nodded.

"Okay. Now, keep your eyes closed. I am going to let you smell a scent, and I want you to tell me where you smelled it before today."

After a moment she caught the distinct smell of pine. "Camping with my family when I was six."

Next she smelled cinnamon. "Hot cider at Christmastime when I was little," she said with a smile.

And then she smelled something else. She had smelled it earlier that day, but she had smelled it before then. Where?

Suddenly she was in another place. She was in a hall, nervous and uncomfortable. She was sitting at the speed dating table as a tall, handsome police officer sat down across from her, wearing some sort of cologne.

Vince.

18

Iт was Vince!" she gasped. "He wears that cologne."

"Are you sure?" Jeremiah asked.

"Positive. And he was there at the charity event, and he was the first officer to respond to Joseph's alarm going off the night the other puppies were stolen. He took Clarice to the lab where the tests got messed up and said she didn't have any human DNA on her."

"He wasn't there when they arrested Joseph."

"No," Cindy said, tears running down her cheeks. "He was kidnapping Mark's wife when Mark was arresting Joseph."

She stood up and went to get her cell phone. Mark answered on the second ring.

"It was Vince," she said. "I remember that Vince wears Old Spice cologne."

"You're sure?" Mark asked.

"Yes. Have you had any luck finding the other dogs?"

"Turns out a dozen others have been kidnapped from homeless masters who thought the dogs ran away while they were sleeping. They've all been hoping to have word that someone has found them."

"How did you manage to find so many so quickly?"

"This early the day after Thanksgiving? Most of them had dinner at the shelter last night and slept there as well. I'm still looking for a couple of others, including a lady who left with her dog early this morning."

"Bernadette?" Cindy asked, fear welling within her.

"Yeah. You seen her?"

"She was at my house yesterday for Thanksgiving dinner."

"She was there when we arrested Joseph?"

"Yes."

Mark muttered something under his breath. "Okay, I have to go. Hopefully we can find Vince and put an end to all this."

"Good luck," she said.

She hung up and looked at Jeremiah. He was pale and sweating, and she wondered if he'd had a fever that broke. "Are you okay?" she asked.

He shrugged. "I've been worse."

"Do you think you could help me find Bernadette?"

"We can try."

"I know she likes to hang out around the theater some, but I have no idea if she'll be there today."

"Let's go find out."

She put fresh food and water down for the dogs, and then put newspapers down in the kitchen since she didn't know how long they'd be gone. She left the living room light on and turned on the porch light as well. Jeremiah raised an eyebrow but didn't say anything.

They took her car, since she wasn't sure he should be driving. Cindy knew she should let him go home, but she was too afraid to go looking by herself. It didn't take them long to drive to the theater. When they parked, she glanced over at Jeremiah, who somehow looked even worse.

"Should I take you to an emergency room?" she asked.

He shook his head. "It's just the flu, and I haven't really had a chance to rest."

Guilt washed over her. "That's my fault."

"No, it's mine."

She glanced out the window. There were lots of people milling about in the parking lot. The theater was part of a larger complex that had a bookstore and other shops, and the whole area was busy. She should be safe enough with so many witnesses.

"Stay here while I go look for her," she said.

He started to protest, but she held up a hand. "It does no one any good if you pass out and I have to try and carry you back to the car."

He smiled faintly. "If I pass out, you have my permission to call an ambulance to take me to the emergency room."

"I'm going to hold you to that."

"Okay."

"I'll be back in a few minutes."

He reclined the seat back and closed his eyes. "If you're not back in thirty, I'm calling Mark."

"Fair enough."

She locked the car as she exited and then hurried toward the theater. She couldn't help but remember being there on Sunday when the body in the bushes had been found. She got a chill as she walked past the spot. She cast around, looking everywhere, hoping to see the old lady and her dog.

She didn't see them, but she walked all around the building just to make sure. She stood for a moment and thought. Where else might Bernadette be off to so early in the morning on Black Friday?

Around her, shoppers rushed by, intent on heading for the stores. It would be at least another two or three hours before they turned their footsteps toward the theater.

Which meant she shouldn't expect to find Bernadette at the theater. She should expect to find her someplace where the people were. She turned and joined the throng of people heading toward the shops. She bypassed the bookstore and was debating between the others when a sign caught her eye and she veered suddenly to the left.

She found Bernadette and Ginger in front of the Canine Chateau, an upscale store catering to a pet's every whim. Bernadette was stuffing a bill into one pocket and a giant dog bone into another.

"Ginger's getting in on the act too?" Cindy said, unable for a moment to resist the humor of the scene.

"A dog's got to eat. And my Ginger deserves the best," Bernadette said with more dignity than Cindy could have imagined.

"Good choice." Cindy stepped forward. "Bernadette, it's not safe out here. The killer is moving faster, and he's targeting everyone who adopted a dog that was there last week. The detectives are trying to find everyone."

"They wouldn't have to find all of us if they could just find one killer," Bernadette said.

"They're close. They know who it is; they're just trying to catch him. I'd feel a whole lot better if you and Ginger would come home with me so I knew you were safe until this was over."

Bernadette hesitated.

"Please," Cindy said. "I have Jeremiah with me in the car, and Clarice and Buff are at home and would love to play with Ginger. Plus, there's still leftover turkey."

"Okay, you twisted my arm," Bernadette said, scooping up Ginger. "Let's go."

As they walked quickly back to the car, Cindy's heart pounded. Now that she had Bernadette and Ginger with her, she felt like she had a big target painted on her and that something terrible would happen at any moment. She kept swiveling her head from side to side looking for Vince or anyone else who seemed to be looking at them.

By the time they made it back to her car, she thought she was going to scream with the pressure. She unlocked the doors, and Jeremiah brought his seat back upright as Bernadette and Ginger got in the back.

"Hey, there, young fellow," Bernadette said. "Heard you missed my company."

"You heard right," he said with a smile.

"You don't look so good."

"I don't feel so good," he admitted.

"Well, I can make a soup with some of that leftover turkey that will make you forget all about being sick."

"I believe it," he said, closing his eyes as Cindy pulled out of the parking space. Even the drive home strained her nerves. She felt completely exposed and like every car that followed her too closely had a sinister purpose. Once she finally got everyone back inside her house, she gasped in relief.

She sat down at the kitchen table as the three dogs greeted each other. Jeremiah lay down on the couch, and Bernadette busied herself with pulling food out of the refrigerator and finding a pot.

Cindy dialed Mark's number. "I have Bernadette and Ginger here at my house."

"Good. We haven't figured out a way to read the chip yet, if we find it, but we're working on it. Are you okay keeping them there with you for right now?"

"Yes, I've got Jeremiah here as well."

"Again, not surprised," Mark said. "Keep your eyes out, and if you see or hear anything, you give me a call."

"Any luck finding Vince?"

"Not yet," Mark said, anger lacing his voice. "I think he might have gone to ground. We tried calling him, but that didn't go as planned."

"Okay, let me know when you catch him."

"I will."

She hung up the phone and put her head down on the table. She hated this, the waiting and wondering. Every sound outside to her was footsteps. Every time one of the dogs barked, it was because they sensed danger. When Bernadette brushed by her chair, she jumped, and it took all her self-control not to scream out loud.

"You need to relax," Bernadette noted.

"I don't know how," Cindy admitted.

She heard snoring and glanced into the living room, where Jeremiah was passed out on the couch. His left arm trailed down on the floor, and Buff was licking his fingers in a fit of ecstasy. It was all completely surreal to her, and she fought the sudden urge to laugh hysterically.

Noon came, and Bernadette made turkey sandwiches for her and Cindy and fed Jeremiah the promised turkey soup. After eating he immediately fell back asleep. Cindy got up and put a blanket over him and wondered if she should give him anything. She finally decided to ask him the next time he woke up. Sleep was what he needed more than anything else at that point.

She sat down with her deck of cards at the kitchen table and laid out a game of solitaire for herself. Bernadette watched with interest. "You have a second deck?" she asked at last.

"Yes," Cindy said, retrieving it from her office.

The two of them played half a dozen games of double solitaire while Jeremiah slept and the dogs played. Cindy had finally begun to relax when the phone rang.

Mark pounded his fist against the dashboard while Paul stared at him. "What are we going to do now? He knows we're onto him; there's no telling where he's holed up."

They had been searching half the day for him and also for his accomplice, the lab tech who had helped him by faking the blood samples taken from Clarice. It turned out no one knew who the guy was. With local businesses, including vet's offices and laboratories, closed for the day it was making it that much harder to rule out possibilities.

"He must have needed an accomplice to help read the chips," Paul said.

"I know. If we could only figure out where they were taking the dogs, maybe we could find him or the laptop, or Traci."

"Buff's the only dog who escaped that we know of."

"Which means they've either killed the others, or dumped them somewhere, or they still have them."

"If they still have them, they'd need to be someplace where people would ignore a lot of dogs barking," Paul said.

"Like a vet's office," Mark said, "bringing us right back to our original problem."

"Or an animal shelter."

Mark turned to look at him. "I think someone, a volunteer, or something, would have noticed if one of the dogs from Friday's event reappeared at the Humane Society. Even the quarantine rooms are visited every day by a number of people."

"What about a different type of animal shelter?" Paul asked.

"You mean like—"

"Dog pound."

"Paul, I think you might be a genius," Mark said.

"Even though a lot of people in this town turn over lost pets to the Humane Society, there are still plenty who call animal control."

"Let's go."

Half an hour later Paul and Mark stood outside the building in question. Half a dozen hand-picked officers ringed the structure, including Percy Grayhorn, who had not complained to Mark's superior but had insisted on being present if there was a possibility of a hostage situation. The only two members of the force who worked the K-9 unit were also present, but without their furry partners.

"Is everyone in place?" Mark asked Paul, who listened to a radio.

Paul nodded, and Mark took a deep breath. They were all wearing protective vests and had gone over the possible scenarios three times. He nodded, Paul gave the signal, and they all burst into the building.

Mark ran down a corridor filled with dog pens, but stopped short when he recognized Buster. Paul pushed on past him as Mark opened the cage, freeing his dog.

The beagle bayed joyously. Mark had brought one of Traci's camisoles with him and shoved it under the dog's nose. Beagles were known for their tracking skills, and he just prayed this one was a credit to his species.

"Buster, find Mommy."

The dog took a deep whiff, turned around twice, and then headed down the corridor, baying in full, rich tones. The corridor ended in a T. Mark could see Paul running down the left-hand corridor. Buster took the right-hand one. Mark followed the dog.

He heard men shouting behind him, and three shots rang out. He kept running, though. If Traci was here, he needed to find her first and worry about the bad guys second.

Buster veered suddenly to the left into a small room and then turned right into an even smaller one. In the middle of the room was a chair with ropes pooled around it on the floor. Buster leaped onto the chair and bayed as long and loud as he could.

Mark crashed to his knees as he realized that Traci had been held there but was gone. Buster suddenly jumped from the chair and ran to the far side of the room and scratched at a metal door.

Mark crossed to it and flung it open. Buster raced out into a narrow alley and toward the back of the building. There he stopped next to a parking space and cast about on the ground trying to find the scent.

For Mark, though, the stale smell of burnt rubber and the tire tracks on the ground told him all he needed to know. Traci had been moved, probably just minutes before they got there. Buster finally gave up and sat down, looking up at him with great mournful eyes as if to ask him what next.

He reached down and scratched the dog's head. "You did good, boy, it's not your fault," he said, his voice cracking.

Mark turned and walked back into the building, Buster trotting at his side. He retraced his steps cautiously but soon saw one of his officers walking calmly but purposefully toward him.

"What do we have?" Mark asked.

"The phony lab tech. He fired on us, and I winged him. He's alive and talking. Paul sent me to see if you needed help."

Mark shook his head. "Traci was moved before we got here. Still, make sure every room is searched for signs of her, Vince, or anyone else. This whole place is a crime scene. Lock it down."

When Cindy answered the phone, she held her breath when she heard Mark's voice.

"We got his accomplice and we found the dogs alive, but Vince and Traci are still out there, somewhere," Mark said.

Cindy let out her breath, and the momentary joy she had felt over them finding the dogs alive faded as she realized there was still a chance they would find Traci dead. *Or that Vince will find us*, she worried.

"Thanks for keeping us updated," she said and then hung up.

"What is it?" Jeremiah asked, suddenly awake.

"They found the dogs alive, and also captured an accomplice," Cindy explained.

"What about Vince?" he asked.

"He's still out there and so is Mark's wife."

"That's terrible," Bernadette muttered.

It was terrible. One man had caused so much death, so much carnage, and now he held one woman physically captive and dozens of others emotionally captive. It wasn't right. One person shouldn't have the right to cause them all such terror, to tie their hands and make them feel helpless.

She thought of all the times she had seen Vince the past week. How had she not picked up on how evil he was? And why would such a man have hit on her?

Of course, she had only his word that he had actually chosen her during speed dating. His interest in her could easily have sprung not from anything about her but from his assumptions about her relationship with Joseph.

Joseph. She had forgotten to ask if Mark had set him free. She assumed that if he hadn't already he would have by now. That, at least, was good. But it was Joseph Vince had been trying to keep an eye on the whole time, not her. She was sure he had only hit on her because he thought she was Joseph's girlfriend.

And suddenly she knew what she had to do. Vince had given her his number. It was time to use it.

"What do you want?" he growled as he answered the phone.

Her hand shook, but she forced her voice to be rock steady. He had answered, which meant he didn't already have everything he wanted. "The same thing you want . . . lots and lots of money."

"Good luck with that," he sneered.

"I don't need luck," she said. "I have the dog."

There was a pause and then, "So?"

"You have the means to read the chip, and I have the chip. I suggest a partnership."

"Why should I trust you?" he said with a short laugh.

"Do you really think Derek was that clever?" she asked. "Do you really think he was capable of getting the lists from Joseph? No, I was the one who got the lists. I've been working for months to get close enough to Joseph to get access to the things he kept even from Derek."

"I don't believe you," he said, but she heard the hesitation in his voice.

"Then you're a bigger idiot than Derek thought you were," she bluffed. "You see, I, at least, credit you with some brains. After all, you weren't dumb enough to steal the diamond collar from Clarice when you took her in for lab tests. If you had, Joseph would have known in an instant that something was wrong. He might be more trusting than he should, but he's no fool. I've been covering that idiot Derek's tracks for months. The man couldn't even file the paperwork he was given. If it hadn't been for me, his cover would have been blown months ago. You really think anyone would buy him as a personal assistant when he couldn't even keep the simplest things straight?"

She paused, waiting for his response. Jeremiah was looking at her like she'd lost her mind, but she turned away. If she thought about what she was doing, she'd lose her nerve.

"Say I believe you. What do you suggest?"

"I suggest we meet. The cops are no doubt looking for you, so it has to be somewhere discreet. It needs to still be a public place, though."

"There's a dog park on the edge of town, across from the Ono Family Eatery."

"I'm familiar with it."

"Meet me there in one hour and bring the dog. If you don't, I'll know and the deal is off."

"Bring the laptop and get ready to leave the country," she countered.

"I'm one step ahead of you, sister," he said and hung up.

"That's what worries me," she whispered.

"Have you lost your mind?" Jeremiah exploded, standing up from the couch.

"I think maybe."

"What were you thinking?"

"I was thinking that we needed something he wanted to flush him out of hiding. I was thinking that without it, Mark's wife is most likely going to die and a killer's going to walk free."

"You can't just take Ginger into the line of fire, or yourself either."

"I wasn't going to take Ginger, I was going to take Buff and hope he didn't realize until too late that it was a dog he'd already seen."

"Does my Ginger have what everyone's looking for?" Bernadette asked suddenly.

Cindy glanced at the little dog. "At this point, the odds are getting good that she does. She's one of the few who could have it."

"And that detective's wife could die if this man isn't caught?"

"That's right."

"Then you should take Ginger. She and I want to help, for all our friends, and for this woman. Ginger and I wouldn't feel right if anything happened to you or her that we could have prevented."

"I don't think—"

"I insist you take Ginger with you," the woman said.

"And I insist you call Mark right now and tell him where he needs to be when this all happens," Jeremiah said, eyes blazing.

Cindy nodded. She'd meant to have called him already. She dialed the phone, and when he answered, she told him in a rush what she'd done and where Vince wanted to meet.

"You are one crazy lady," he said when she had finished. "You know that, right?"

"It was the only thing I could think of to bring him out of hiding," she said.

"You might be right, but I don't like it."

"I don't see that we have any choice," Cindy said.

Mark paused and then said, "Okay, here's how it's going to go down."

○━◆━○

Half an hour later Cindy was in the car. Ginger was on the seat next to her in a tiny cat carrier that Cindy had borrowed from her neighbor at the last minute. She had left Bernadette inside the house watching over Buff and Clarice.

Jeremiah had been standing in her driveway watching her off when she left. He had volunteered to follow her, but she knew he was too sick. Besides, if Vince caught him doing it, the whole thing would be blown. She would just have to trust that Mark and the others would have thoroughly staked out the dog park and that they would be ready to jump when Vince put in an appearance.

Her cell phone rang, and Cindy jumped and let out a little scream. "Hello?" she asked, picking up. She expected it to be Mark or Jeremiah, calling to see if she was all right. Well, she wasn't. She was completely and totally insane for coming up with the idea. There was nothing remotely safe about any of it. Instead of Mark or Jeremiah, though, it was *him*.

"Change of plan," he growled in her ear.

"What are you talking about?" she stammered.

"We're going to meet at a new location, one the police won't be waiting at for us."

"I didn't—"

"Skip it," he snapped, cutting her off. "Now listen closely. You're going to meet me at Joseph's house in exactly twelve minutes or I'm going to kill Traci here."

Cindy swerved across three lanes of traffic and made a U-turn at a yellow light just as it turned red. "I'm on my way," she said.

"Good, now throw your cell phone out the window."

"What?"

"You heard me. Roll down the window and throw your cell phone out. That way you won't be tempted to call the police. I'm watching you, so I'll know if you do it. Oh, and twelve minutes doesn't give you enough time to stop at any pay phones. It gives you just enough time to get here if you run the red lights. Now toss it."

Cindy hit the power window button and threw her cell out the window of her car, wincing as she did so. Ahead of her the light was yellow. She reflexively put her foot on the brake, then remembered what he had said. With a whispered prayer for safety, she stomped on the gas hard and went sailing through the intersection after the light had turned red. Two cars had to swerve to avoid her, and for a moment she thought for sure it was all over.

When she was finally through, she sent another prayer heavenward that a police officer would stop her, or at least try to. Then maybe they could alert Mark to what was happening.

As long as that officer isn't corrupt too, she realized.

A blue Volkswagen pulled into traffic ahead of her, moving at a crawl. Cindy checked her mirrors, hit the gas harder, and cut off the guy in the lane next to her. He honked and waved his fist at her.

She glanced at the clock on her dashboard. It was seven thirty-four. What time had he called? Why hadn't she checked the clock? As she flew past Central Street, she knew that he was wrong. There was no way she could make it in twelve minutes even with running the red lights.

Traci was going to die, and there was nothing she could do to stop it.

19

Jᴇʀᴇᴍɪᴀʜ ᴡᴀᴛᴄʜᴇᴅ ꜰʀᴏᴍ ʜɪꜱ ᴏᴡɴ ᴄᴀʀ ᴀꜱ Cɪɴᴅʏ ᴄᴜᴛ ᴀᴄʀᴏꜱꜱ ᴛʜʀᴇᴇ lanes of traffic to make a U-turn as the light was changing. He blinked, stunned, and was grateful he was already in the left-hand lane. As he saw her car pass by on the other side of the street, he saw her throw her cell phone out the window.

Something had gone terribly wrong. He passed through the intersection and then turned left into a gas station when there was a gap in the oncoming traffic. He turned around as quickly as possible and was back on her trail.

They were on one of the main thoroughfares, so odds were good wherever she was going, if it was more than a few blocks away, she'd be on the street for a while. He put his foot down hard on the gas and wove in and out of traffic.

He put on his Bluetooth and dialed Mark, leaving his hands free.

"Has something happened?"

"Yes. She just did a U-turn, threw her cell phone out the window, and is driving like a maniac to get somewhere."

"He redirected her, made her toss the cell so she couldn't alert anyone as to where," Mark said, voice trembling.

"It looks as though."

"You're following her?"

"Yeah, I was worried."

"We all are. We're on Third Street, just passed Central."

"Let me know when you have an idea where she's going. I can't alert dispatch to have officers watching for her without risking him hearing."

"Do what you can, and so will I," Jeremiah growled.

He ran a red light and then another. He edged his speed up over fifty and hoped that Vince couldn't actually see Cindy to know that she was being followed.

Her car finally came into view as she was turning right. He managed to make the turn and then dropped back a few cars.

After two more quick turns he realized that they were close to Joseph's home. When Cindy turned up the hill, he parked on the next street over and prepared to hike.

He dialed Mark before he got out of his car. "She just turned up Joseph's hill. I'm turning my cell off."

"Don't do anything reck—"

Jeremiah disconnected him. He bypassed the road up the hill and turned instead into the trees that bordered it on the one side. He began to climb as fast as he could. He had to stop halfway up as a coughing fit drove him to his knees.

Easy, you're no good to her if Vince can hear you coming.

Cindy came to a skidding halt in front of Joseph's front door and flew out of the car with Ginger's carrier in hand. She raced inside the house and then stopped just inside the front door. "Hello?" she called.

The phone on the table to the left rang two short bursts. She picked it up.

"Derek told me the day he died about the intercom system. Figured I'd go ahead and activate it. It ties up the line nicely and is easier than trying to cut the line to the house," Vince said.

"Where are you?"

"Upstairs. Come and find me. I've got a little surprise for you. Suffice it to say that someone here can't wait to see you."

If he wanted to leave the intercom line open, then two could play at that game. She prayed again that someone had seen her racing across town and alerted Mark, or that when she didn't show, he would figure out where she was. She placed the receiver down on the table and then put her finger down on then cradle and then lifted it quickly. He would hopefully think that she had hung up.

She crept toward the stairs as quietly as she could and then walked up them slowly. He hadn't specified which upstairs, so she exited at the second floor landing and made her way toward Joseph's office. She walked inside, but there was no one there.

The curtains were blowing on the far side of the room as they had been the day she found Derek. With her heart in her throat she approached. There was no body this time on the floor behind the desk. She gathered her courage and flung up the curtains, but there was no one on the balcony either.

What am I doing here? I'm going to die and no one's going to know what happened. She clutched Ginger's carrier tighter. *What if it doesn't matter? What if he kills Traci, anyway? Why wouldn't he, he's killed so many others.*

She moved to one of the guest rooms and pushed her way inside. She walked around the bed and even opened the closet door. Nothing.

She kept going. She searched three more rooms. Where could he be? Where did he have Traci? She came to the next room, opened the door, and walked inside. The light from the hallway streamed in, giving vague form to the things in the room. Her fingers felt for the light switch even as she tried to look around. She turned her head and gasped.

There in a corner, arms folded across his chest, his smile gently mocking her, was Joseph.

⚬══╪══⚬

Jeremiah finally made it up the hill and stood a moment, panting, just inside the tree line. He was sick, too sick to be doing this, but he had no options. The police were half an hour away, and Cindy might not have that much time. When he finally stopped wheezing, he darted across the open expanse to the front of the house as fast as he could.

The front door stood open, and after a moment he slipped inside, pressing himself flat against the wall just inside. A sharp gasp came from a couple of feet away. He crouched down before realizing it had come from the receiver of a phone that was off the hook.

He picked it up. It was connected to another phone, and he listened for a moment. Had Cindy left the phone off the hook or had Vince?

⚬══╪══⚬

"No!" Cindy whispered, staring at the image of Joseph in the darkened room. She stood for a moment, struggling to understand what she was seeing. Her fingers found the light switch and flicked it.

The lights flared to life, and she blinked in the sudden brightness. She took half a dozen steps and realized light reflected off of his hair. She froze in her tracks and then she realized what she was seeing. It wasn't Joseph. It was one of the cardboard cutouts of him.

She sagged in momentary relief. Suddenly, she smelled Old Spice cologne. A hand descended on her shoulder and spun her halfway around. The cat carrier banged against her shin, and Ginger yelped. There, standing a hair's breadth from her, was Vince.

"You want to make a deal, huh?"

"Yes," she said, stiffening her spine and forcing herself to look him in the eyes. "I want to make a deal. I want my share of everything. I have the dog you need."

"And what made you think I wouldn't just take the dog from you?"

"Because you're not sure. You're not sure if I brought the right dog, and if you had crashed into my car and stolen him or just took him from me now and he's not the right one, then where would you be? I've got a computer guy who can figure out how to read the chip, so the way I see it, I don't need you nearly as much as you need me."

"Clever girl, but not that clever, I'm guessing."

"Try me," Cindy said, lifting her chin defiantly.

In the carrier Ginger growled low in her throat, and Cindy only hoped she sounded half as fierce as the bit of orange fluff.

"You at least brought a dog I haven't checked yet."

Cindy opened her mouth to respond, but Vince lunged for the carrier. She jerked it away, twisting as she did so, putting her body between him and the dog. He hit her across the cheek and pain exploded behind her eyes. For a moment things went black, and she swayed on her feet.

She felt him grab the carrier, and she struggled to maintain control of it. The dog was the one thing standing between her and death. If he was able to get Ginger and discover that she had the microchip, then Cindy was dead. Inside the carrier Ginger barked and growled and scrambled to keep her footing.

Cindy backed into the cardboard cutout of Joseph with a crash. It fell to the floor, and she nearly tumbled backward after it. While she tried to regain her footing, Vince ripped the carrier from her hand.

She toppled sideways and managed to land on one knee with a grunt. She stared up at him and realized that it was all over. She had gambled, and she had lost. Ginger and Traci would also pay for her arrogance.

"You don't have to do this, Vince," Cindy panted. "You don't have to kill me in Joseph's trophy room. I mean, we're all alone up here. We could just walk down the hall to his office. I know where he keeps his cash. We could be in Mexico in three hours."

"Oh, but I do have to kill you. I've gone to too much trouble, killed too many people not to get this chip. Thank you for your help in that regard. When I'm sitting on a beach in South America, I'll raise a glass to you."

⚬━✦━⚬

Jeremiah had heard enough. He ran toward the stairs. Cindy had given him all he needed to find her. The trophy room was on the same floor as Joseph's office, just a few doors down. Sweat was rolling off his body as he reached the top of the stairs. His stomach clenched, and bile filled his mouth. He forced himself to swallow it and continue on.

As soon as he passed Joseph's office, he could hear Vince's voice. "You know, you should have agreed to go out with me. I could have protected you from all this."

"Kept an eye on me is more like it," Cindy said.

Jeremiah could hear the fear and the pain in her voice, and it took all of his self-control to keep from barreling down the hall and into the room.

"That too. You just had to insist on getting involved, didn't you?"

"It's not my fault," Cindy said. "You're the one killing people and kidnapping innocent women."

"Ah, yes, Traci. I had to admit, I was considering letting her live. That was before you and Mark had to go and figure out what was going on. Why couldn't you have just been content with Joseph as the mastermind? After all, it wouldn't be the first time you had trusted a killer."

"What did you do that made the police think it was Joseph?"

"Mostly that was Derek. He was clever, despite what you think. Clever enough I had to kill him before the end of the deal. You see, he paid all the protestors to be there out of Joseph's accounts. Each and every one of them was a criminal who was absolutely convinced Joseph hired them to stage the protest."

Jeremiah was just outside the room, fighting hard to control his breathing. There was a tickle deep in his throat, and it took all his focus to keep from coughing. He angled himself so that he could glimpse in the room.

Cindy was on the floor, facing in his direction. Standing in front of her with his back to Jeremiah was Vince. He was holding a gun on Cindy with his right hand and carrying the dog carrier in his left.

I'll break his neck, Jeremiah thought. *No, I don't need the detective asking me any more questions.* He paused, hovering as he decided what he was going to do.

"What have you done with Traci?" Cindy asked.

"She's around."

"Tell me where."

"Why, it won't do you any good. You're going to die before she does. But don't worry, she will die too."

"You never saw me driving over here," Cindy said. "You were waiting here with her all along."

"Correct."

"Then how do you know I threw my cell phone out the window?"

"Those few precious moments of very loud road noise followed by a crunch and then silence. I knew there was no way you would risk not throwing it out; you're not a gambler."

"Wanna bet?" Cindy asked softly. "You don't think that the entire police force of Pine Springs is outside waiting for you?"

"No, I don't, actually. You see, I know a lot about the alarm system on this house. I even tripped it on purpose once when my partner couldn't manage to subdue the poodle and lost her. I needed Joseph to come home and find his precious dog for me. So, before you came, I activated the motion sensor, which is across the driveway halfway down the hill. Your car is the only one that has come through."

Jeremiah moved like a shadow, silent as a ghost. He was three steps behind Vince when he felt his chest start to contract with the beginnings of a cough. With no time left, he kicked the side of Vince's right knee.

Vince crashed toward the floor with a shout. Jeremiah followed, grabbing his head, twisting it sideways, and slamming it into the floor as hard as he could.

Vince crumpled and didn't move. The dog carrier crashed to the ground next to him. Jeremiah dropped to a knee, coughed, and then checked to make sure he hadn't actually killed Vince. There was a pulse, and he straightened and turned his attention to Cindy.

She was staring at him in wide-eyed fascination. *Not good.* "Are you hurt?" he asked, trying to redirect her focus.

She blinked slowly as though coming out of a trance. "I don't think so."

"Are you sure? You're bleeding," he said, indicating her cheek.

Her hand flew up, and when she lowered it, she stared at the blood on her fingers. "He hit me," she said.

His first instinct was to take a look, see how bad the damage was, and get the wound cleaned. He took a step forward and then shook himself. *Remember to ignore your first instincts,* he chided himself. He whipped out his cell phone and called 911 for an ambulance.

When he hung up, he found Cindy staring at him in horror. *She knows,* he thought for one panicked moment.

"Is it that bad? Am I going to be scarred?" she burst out, voice edging on hysteria.

He wanted to laugh. She might have been killed, and she had faced that with more calm than she faced the prospect of a scar on her cheek. The cut was shallow and would heal fine. He wanted to tell her that, reassure her. He could tell from ten feet away that she had nothing to worry about. "I don't know, I hope not," he forced himself to say. "The paramedics will be able to tell."

She nodded, lip trembling, as tears filled her eyes.

"Are you hurt anywhere else?" he asked, knowing that she had a badly sprained wrist from the way she was holding it, and seeing the bruises that were already forming on her leg.

"No," she said.

It was the shock. It would wear off soon enough, and then she would start to feel the pain. He didn't envy her that.

He glanced at the man lying on the floor. The headache he would have when he came to was just a foretaste of the pain in store for him. He debated whether to break his arms or to look for some rope to tie him up with. He would have been much happier with Vince dead, but there were fewer questions this way, and hopefully he could help them find Traci if they hadn't already by the time he regained consciousness.

"You don't look good," Cindy said.

"I don't exactly feel good," he said, coughing violently.

He heard two men running, trying to do so quietly. Still he forced himself to act startled when Mark and Paul came into view with weapons drawn.

"What happened here?" Mark asked.

"I got the drop on him," Jeremiah said. "Managed to knock him out."

"I think Traci is somewhere in the house or on the property," Cindy said as she stood shakily.

Paul swooped down and handcuffed Vince while Jeremiah rolled out of the way.

Cindy crossed to Ginger and opened the door of the carrier. She pulled the Pomeranian mix out and looked her over. "Are you hurt, girl?"

The dog was frightened but seemed otherwise unharmed.

"Did you catch any of that?" Jeremiah asked.

"Yeah, and we have an officer on the receiver downstairs who caught a whole lot more than we did," Paul said.

Mark turned and ran from the room. Jeremiah struggled to his feet, coughing. He wanted to follow Mark, but just standing up had made him feel queasy.

He turned to look at Cindy. She looked up from her examination of Ginger with a smile. "She seems all right."

He tried nodding his head, but it felt like a leaden weight on the end of a slender reed. The room started to spin around him.

"Jeremiah? What's wrong?" he heard Cindy ask as he hit the floor.

Mark ran downstairs and to the woods. They had taken a cue from Jeremiah and walked up the hill after they found his car. In the woods he had tied up Buster, who barked when he returned. He untied the beagle and led him into the house. Then he let him smell the camisole again.

"This is it, boy, the big time. Go find Mommy!"

The dog put his nose to the ground and then dashed for the stairs, flying up them.

Mark gave chase as fast as he could. Buster passed the second floor, continuing upward. At the third floor landing he hesitated a moment, sniffing the air, before heading off to the left. The dog slid to a halt in front of a closed door, and Mark opened it to see a small staircase leading up into what looked to be an attic.

Buster ran up the stairs, and Mark took them two at a time. When they came out into the room above, Mark met the frightened eyes of his wife. With a sob he leaped forward and untied the ropes that bound her to the old-fashioned dining chair she sat on.

Buster licked at her fingers as Mark tore the gag away from her mouth. "You found me," she cried.

"Thank Buster for that one."

"Good dog!"

He helped her stand, and then she collapsed against him, crying like he had never seen her cry before.

He heard the stairs creak, and he turned to see Cindy walking up slowly, eyes wide.

"Ssh, it's okay, honey, you're safe now," Mark soothed Traci.

"Safe? Safe? How will I ever feel safe again?" she choked.

Cindy walked forward slowly and put her hand on Traci's shoulder. "You can, but it will take a long time and a lot of courage. You're lucky, though. There are a lot of people who love you who will see you through this."

As Traci continued to cling to him and cry, Mark mouthed a thank you to Cindy.

"I'll help however I can," she whispered.

⚜

Twenty minutes later Cindy watched as Vince was carted off in the back of a police car. She stood beside the stretcher that Jeremiah was lying on. His eyes flickered open. "What happened?" he asked.

"You passed out. Your fever is worse, but the paramedics are working on getting it down. You know, I was supposed to get to call 911 if you passed out on me, but you had already called them."

"Sorry to disappoint you," he whispered.

"I'll forgive you as long as you get better," she said.

"It's a deal."

"Okay, we're good to go," one of the paramedics said to the other. They put the stretcher into the back of the ambulance.

"Is he going to be okay?" she asked.

"I think we got to him in time. He had a fever over 103. I'm not even sure how this man was walking."

"It's a miracle," Cindy said with a small smile. God had sent her own personal knight in shining yarmulke to save her once more.

20

JEREMIAH WOKE UP AND FOR A MOMENT HAD NO IDEA WHERE HE WAS. Then he remembered the ambulance and realized he had to be in the hospital. He turned his head and saw Cindy and Joseph quietly talking in two chairs against the wall. Joseph glanced his way and popped to his feet.

"Look who's awake!"

Cindy came over as well, and he looked up at her. There were worry lines around her eyes that were gradually easing as she watched him.

"What happened?" he asked.

"Pneumonia, apparently," Cindy said. "The doctors said that's what you have. Your fever broke about an hour ago, and you've been looking much better since then."

"When is it?" he asked.

"Saturday afternoon."

"Saturday? Synagogue . . . services."

"Relax, Paul went to the synagogue this morning and let everyone know that you were fine, but sick."

"Oh no."

"He also told them that the doctor had said no visitors until you get home."

"Thank Adonai." He took a deep breath and promptly coughed. When it was over, he asked, "Did everything work out okay?"

"Yes," Joseph answered. "Vince is in jail, and he's going to go away for a long time, so I've been assured. As of this morning all the dogs have been returned to their rightful owners. We also managed to fry the circuits in the chip in Ginger without hurting her at all."

"So Ginger really did have the chip."

"Yes, she did."

"Traci's being released from the hospital this afternoon. Physically she's okay, just a little bruised up," Cindy said.

"Mentally it's going to be a long recovery," Jeremiah predicted.

Cindy nodded. "I'm afraid so, but I've promised to help in any way that I can."

"It's still hard to believe that this was all about identity theft," Joseph said.

"At least they didn't get away with it," Cindy said.

"Well, look who's awake!"

Jeremiah turned his head to the door and saw Mark enter, pushing a tired-looking blonde woman in a wheelchair.

"We're just about to get out of here, but we wanted to stop by and see if you were awake yet," Mark said. "You know, Cindy, Jeremiah, the three of us have got to spend less time hanging out in hospitals."

"Amen," Cindy said fervently. "You know, Harry's getting out today too."

"Fantastic! Where's he going to go?"

"I've offered my house for the next couple of days. Bernadette's got some turkey soup she wants to try out on him to speed his recovery," Cindy said.

"Good news all the way around."

"Thank you all so very much," Traci spoke up. "If it wasn't for all of you, I don't know what would have happened."

"You're welcome," Cindy said.

Jeremiah nodded.

"Well, you kids behave," Mark said, "Because we are out of here."

He and Traci left with a wave.

"I'm going to go check on Harry," Joseph said, slipping out of the room as well.

Cindy took Jeremiah's hand. "You scared me," she admitted.

"I think I scared myself," he said.

"Don't do that again, okay?"

"Which part?" he asked.

"All of it."

"So you don't want me to come to your rescue anymore?" he tried to tease.

"No, that's good. But pneumonia, collapsing, all that's bad."

"I need to take notes so I can keep it all straight."

"If you weren't in a hospital bed, I'd punch you," she said.

"How about you, are you okay?" he asked, looking at the butterfly bandage on her cheek and the elastic bandage wound around her left wrist.

"I'm just fine," she said. "Relieved that a killer is off the street, Joseph's out of jail, and his dogs are back with him, but just fine."

"I forgot!" he said, gripping her hand. "Can you go to my house? I, um, adopted a dog. I didn't want to say anything to anyone until this was all over. He's been all alone there since yesterday morning."

"Inside? That can't be good," she said, wincing. "Where are your keys?"

"Slacks pocket, wherever they are," he said.

Cindy checked the closet. "These keys?"

"Yes. Oh, and please be careful."

"The dog snatcher is in jail, remember?" she said.

"I know, but . . . he's a big dog and probably pretty freaked out."

"I'll be careful," she promised.

He nodded and then felt himself drifting back to sleep. He heard her tiptoe from the room, and then he was lost in his dreams.

Cindy was grateful that the German shepherd with soulful eyes was paper trained. It made the mess much simpler to clean up. She took the dog for a quick walk and then coaxed him into her car with a piece of turkey from Jeremiah's fridge. It meant she would have three dogs still for a while, with the addition of Harry's dog and Ginger still prancing around like the queen of the world, but it was far preferable to leaving him locked up alone.

She took him back to her house and once she was sure he was calm, she left him with Bernadette and went back to the hospital to check Harry out.

When she helped him into the house, he made it to the couch and promptly fell asleep.

The phone rang, and she answered it, relieved to hear Geanie's voice.

"What's going on?"

"Joseph's coming over to pick me up for dinner, and I just wanted to see how you were."

"Wow, you guys aren't wasting any time," Cindy said, walking back to her bedroom for a little privacy.

"If I learned anything this week, it's strike while the iron is hot, or kiss the guy before the police arrest him," Geanie said with a small laugh.

"More power to you."

"What about you?"

"I think I need a vacation," Cindy admitted. Her eyes fell on the trip voucher she had put on her bureau earlier that week. "And I think I know just what I'm going to do."

"What?"

"I've got a voucher for a trip to Hawaii."

"Ooh, you have to use that."

"I'm going to," Cindy promised herself.

"When are you going to go?" Geanie asked.

"I was thinking Memorial Day weekend might be nice; it's already a three-day weekend."

"That will be nice. You can go see Pearl Harbor."

"That is definitely at the top of my list," Cindy admitted. "Seems like a good time to see it."

"Got room for me in your suitcase?"

"No," Cindy said with a laugh. "But I'm sure the next thing you know, Joseph will be taking you on your honeymoon."

"Stop it!" Geanie squealed.

Cindy laughed. "As for me, I'm looking forward to a nice, relaxing trip, no excitement, no killers, just me and a beach."

"Well, make sure to pack a bikini and hope for at least a little excitement," Geanie teased. "I mean, sooner or later you'll find a guy who catches your eye."

Cindy rolled her eyes. Geanie was clearly not going to let the whole dating thing go. "You'll be pleased to know I have a date."

"Ooooh, anyone I know?"

"I don't think so. He's a computer programmer I met at speed dating."

"Going out with a guy you only met for five minutes? That's a big risk, don't you think?"

Cindy thought back on everything that had happened to her in the last few months. "I'm thinking it's more of a medium risk."

"I hope it works out for you."

"Thanks. We'll find out Friday night. And as for your date tonight, good luck," Cindy said.

"What does that mean?" Geanie burst out.

"Exactly what it sounds like. Bye."

❦

On Wednesday Jeremiah stood in a graveyard. He had been discharged from the hospital on Sunday, and it had taken all of his powers of persuasion to convince Cindy that he would be okay at his house by himself. She had returned his dog to him, and he had realized that he did intend to keep him. After much thought he named the dog Captain.

The night before Mark had called to check in on him and to let him know that the funeral for the man who had died on his lawn was Wednesday afternoon. Jeremiah knew it wasn't smart to go to the funeral. Ultimately, he decided to go, not to pay his respects to the dead, but to see who else would.

Mark and Paul stood shoulder to shoulder up front next to the priest, mistakenly believing they had caught the man's killer. He wondered if they were going to all the funerals that were being held for those who had been killed.

Besides them and Jeremiah there were only three others present. Like him they hung back and stood a wide distance apart from each other, although their eyes took in everything.

As tempted as he had been to bring Captain to see if the dog rattled any of their cages, he was glad he had chosen not to. The fewer people who knew that he had the dog, the better for both their sakes.

The funeral was simple and short. Ashes to ashes, dust to dust, and it was all over. It wasn't much to show for a life, particularly his. Jeremiah turned and walked away, anxious to avoid talking to Mark. Out of the corner of his eye he saw the others doing the same.

Mark, however, had different plans and caught up with Jeremiah at his car. "How are you doing?"

"Better," Jeremiah admitted. "How's Traci?"

"Surviving. I wanted to thank you again for all your help. If it hadn't been for you, I don't think we would have found her in time."

"It's okay," Jeremiah said, uncomfortable with the praise. "I just had a bad feeling deep inside when Cindy left, and I followed. Of course, it turned out that bad feeling was pneumonia," he said, trying to deflect with humor.

"Which makes what you did that much more amazing. Look, I don't say this to people, but I'm in your debt. If there's anything I can do for you, just name it."

"I'll keep it in mind," Jeremiah said soberly. In his experience those kinds of favors were invaluable, and he was not about to treat the detective's offer lightly. "Now go home and take care of your wife."

"I am. I had some vacation time coming so I'm taking off through January 2."

"Wow, that's a lot of vacation time."

"Yeah, clearly I need to spend more of it than I do. Plus, it wasn't entirely my idea. Given the trauma of everything that just happened, my superiors strongly suggested that I take the time off."

"Sounds like a wise idea. I wish I could do the same."

"Take care, Jeremiah," Mark said before turning to go.

Jeremiah stared after him for a moment, trying to remember if it was the first time Mark had ever called him by his first name.

⊙━✦━⊙

On Friday morning Cindy was a nervous wreck. It wasn't bad enough that she was worried about her upcoming date with Guy, but Harry had chosen that morning to declare himself fit and well enough to leave her house. She had tried to argue with him, but in the end he was right. He was well enough to leave. She just hated to see him return to the streets.

"Feel free to check up on me whenever you wish," he had told her.

She vowed to herself that she would. Then Bernadette had tried to leave, but Cindy had managed to talk her into staying one more night. She still felt responsible for Bernadette and Ginger. In the end Bernadette agreed, but only if she could make herself useful. She had taken it upon herself to clean the house, and Cindy had let her.

The day had not been going smoothly at work, and Geanie had her head in the clouds for the fifth day in a row. She was completely crazy about Joseph, and Cindy was beginning to wonder if it really might be the real thing.

It was almost lunch when her phone rang, and she answered it to hear Jeremiah's voice on the other end.

"Hey, you got a few minutes?" he asked.

"Are you back at work?"

"Yeah, and Marie is fussing over me like you wouldn't believe."

"Sure, I've got some time, what is it?"

"Can you meet me in the parking lot? I have a surprise for you."

"Is this a bring-my-purse-with-me kind of surprise?"

"Yes."

Three minutes later she walked out to the parking lot. Jeremiah was standing next to his car talking to a woman Cindy's age.

"Okay, what is the big surprise?" Cindy asked.

Jeremiah turned, and so did the woman with him. "Cindy, I'd like you to meet Rosie Stevens. She's been searching for her Aunt Bernadette for three years now."

Cindy reached out and hugged Rosie, surprising the other woman. "I'm so glad to meet you," Cindy said.

"Have you really found my aunt?"

"Yes." Cindy broke away and forced herself to smile despite the lump in her throat. "I'll take you to her right now."

"We can go in my car," Jeremiah said.

A few minutes later they were pulling up outside Cindy's house. Bernadette was outside putting trash in the can. Cindy grabbed Rosie's arm and half-pulled her forward until she heard Rosie gasp and suddenly surge ahead, pulling Cindy forward.

Bernadette looked up as they stopped next to her. The old woman's eyes opened wide in surprise.

"Aunt Bernadette?"

"Rosie, is that you?"

A moment later the two women were hugging and crying. They moved into the house and Ginger jumped excitedly around them, barking and trying to be part of it all. Cindy scooped her up in her arms and backed a couple of feet away to give the two women some privacy. She held the dog while she watched and cried herself.

Jeremiah spoke softly from beside her, and she jumped slightly, having not been aware of his presence until that moment. "It turns out that Rosie left her husband just a couple of weeks after the fight with Bernadette. She's been looking for her ever since. She's in graduate school, doing well, but desperately needs help with her two children."

"A happy ending," Cindy said, crying even harder.

Jeremiah put an arm around her shoulders. "Well, you know what they say. Anything can happen on a Friday."

And the phrase that had always seemed so irreverent to her burst from her lips in a whispered prayer. "Thank God it's Friday."

Discussion Questions

1. Have you ever been in a situation where you were in need and someone helped you out? How did this make you feel?

2. In the story, Joseph manages to use one of his passions (dogs) in his charity work. Is there a way you can do something charitable with one of your hobbies or interests?

3. When was the last time you prayed for a complete stranger, someone that neither you nor anyone around you knew?

4. Has anything precious ever been taken from you? How did you respond? What do you wish you could have done differently?

5. What can you do this year to make Thanksgiving more meaningful?

6. Is there someone you know in need whom you could help? What can you do for that person? What's stopping you?

7. In the course of the first two books, Cindy has learned that there are some risks that are worth taking. Is there something you want or need to do that you've been afraid to do?

8. The book portrays many strong bonds between people and animals. Have you ever experienced this type of bond with an animal? What do you think made it so special?

9. They say that dogs are man's best friend. What traits do dogs have that make them such great friends that might be worth imitating? Do you know of someone in need of this kind of friend?

10. In the story, people make erroneous assumptions about other people. For example, reporters see Joseph hugging Cindy and assume that they are dating. When has someone made an erroneous assumption about you, and what damage did it cause? How do you strive not to do this to others?

An Interview with Author Debbie Viguié

What is your favorite Bible verse and why?

Matthew 6:34, "Take therefore no thought for the morrow: for the morrow shall take thought for the things of itself. Sufficient unto the day is the evil thereof." This verse is both comforting and challenging. It is far easier said than done, yet when we do stop worrying so much, the benefits for our spiritual, physical, and mental health are tremendous.

What inspired the concept for writing the Psalm 23 Mysteries series? How did you choose the setting for your story?

I worked as a secretary in a church for two years. Being there early in the morning when the place is deserted can be a little odd and sometimes downright spooky. A while later when I was thinking of writing a mystery series, this just seemed like a natural choice. The setting of the church pretty much took care of itself as an integral part of the plot.

How closely is I Shall Not Want *based on your real-life experiences? Is any part of* I Shall Not Want *factual?*

No, but although not directly based on my own experiences, it is certainly inspired by them. I like to explore some of the kookiness that is inherent when you work at a church. As far as the more serious aspects of the story, very little is based on my real life. Although when I was in high school, my school did participate in a food drive for needy families where we provided them Thanksgiving dinner.

How long did I Shall Not Want *take you to complete?*

It took me about five months to write it.

What is the symbolism for the title I Shall Not Want?

It symbolizes both the plot of the book and the holiday that occurs during the course of the events. Thanksgiving is a time for celebrating the harvest, for giving thanks for what God has given and for His provision. The book addresses some of the problems facing the homeless who, unlike most people, are in want constantly.

Do you have a favorite character in I Shall Not Want? *Why?*

Jeremiah. I love strong, male leads.

What aspects of being a writer do you enjoy the most?

I love coming up with the initial concept of a story. I find it so exciting! It's the same kind of feeling when I first see the cover. I also really enjoy interacting with fans.

What were your favorite books as a child?

Snow Dog by Jim Kjelgaard, which I've read more than two hundred times, and *The Lone Star Ranger* by Zane Grey, which made me realize I wanted to be a writer.

What is your writing style? Do you outline, write "by the seat of your pants," or somewhere in between?

It's usually somewhere in between although I have gone to both extremes before. Usually I have an idea of what action has to happen in each chapter, just a thumbnail sketch, and then I run with it. Sometimes things change in the actual writing, and that's always exciting.

Do your characters begin to take on lives of their own as you write?

When things are going well they do. Suddenly they are off doing things I had never intended for them to do but which seem perfectly natural and completely in character when looked at objectively.

What new projects do you have on the horizon?

I'm working on the third book in the Psalm 23 Mysteries series: *Lie Down in Green Pastures*. I've got a few other things in the works, but that's the manuscript I've just submitted to my fantastic editor.

Who was the person who influenced your writing the most?

My favorite author, Zane Grey. He was an incredibly prolific Western author who died decades before I was even born. Everything he wrote, though, was very passionate. All his stories were love stories in a way. Sometimes the love was between two people. Other times, it was between a farmer and his land, a pioneer and the forest, even a man and the wild horse that continuously eluded him. And he got inside the heads of both his male and female characters and described feelings and thoughts, replaying scenes from each person's point of view. His writing not only inspired my own but also helped me understand what I was looking for from life and from what kind of man I wanted to marry. My husband, by the way, would have made a fantastic Zane Grey hero!

What message would you like your readers to take from I Shall Not Want?

Judge not lest ye be judged. Avoid making assumptions about other people. It's easy to do, and we've all been guilty of this and all been victims of this. It's never a good thing, and it can cause a lot of harm and build barriers between people that don't need to exist.

What is your greatest achievement?

There are so many achievements that I consider to be profound things in my life that it's hard to choose! Professionally, it's making the New York Times Bestseller List. Personally, it's finding and marrying my soul mate. Spiritually, it's understanding and accepting the work that God has set out for me.

What is your goal or mission as a writer?

To shake people out of their lives and let them escape for a while and feel the strong emotions that aren't always present in everyday life. I want them to escape their problems and come laugh, cry, be delighted, be entertained, and be terrified by the problems facing my characters. And ultimately I want them to feel that if everything can work out in the end for those characters, it can work out in the end for them.

What do you do to get away from it all?

I go to Disney with my husband and have some serious park time. We are huge theme park fans. We're also huge movie fans, and so we get out to the theater as often as we can, sometimes even seeing two or three films the same day.

Lie Down in Green Pastures

—⚬⚬⚬—

1

RABBI JEREMIAH SILVERMAN NEVER QUITE KNEW WHAT TO DO WITH HIMSELF on Thursdays. Thursdays were technically the second day in the week that he had off. Sundays were the first. He hadn't had two consecutive days off since he became rabbi of a synagogue. He had toyed with trying to take off Mondays, but too much seemed to happen on that day. So he took off Thursdays but usually ended up going into work at some point, anyway. His secretary, Marie, had often accused him of being a workaholic. It wasn't true, but there was no telling her that.

It was ten in the morning as he drove down the street toward the synagogue. He slid into the left-hand lane, preparing to turn into the driveway just past First Shepherd, the church next door to the synagogue.

There was no oncoming traffic, and he began to make his turn. The hair on the back of his neck rose suddenly, and he twisted his head around just in time to see the other car as it slammed into him from behind.

Jeremiah's car skidded, sliding in a circle as the sickening crunch of metal filled his ears. He saw the face of the man in the other car, eyes frozen wide, head tilted. *That man is already*

272

dead, he realized as his car twisted and then flipped up onto the lawn outside the church.

In a moment it was over. Jeremiah undid his seatbelt and eased himself onto the ceiling. He kicked the remaining glass out of his side window and then maneuvered himself out with only a small cut to his left leg. He collapsed onto the grass, felt it tickling his cheek, and took several deep breaths. He straightened slowly, checking each bone and muscle as he did so. Everything seemed to be okay despite the fact that he had been in a terrible position when struck.

A shadow fell over him, and he glanced up, squinting.

Cindy Preston stood there, hair flying around her face, out of breath. Her eyes were wide in surprise. "What are you doing here?"

It seemed like such a ridiculous question to him, like the answer should be self-evident.

"Recovering from an accident."

"Are you hurt?"

"I don't think so. What are *you* doing here?"

She blinked rapidly, and then the corners of her mouth turned up. "I guess I'm here to rescue you."

He wanted so badly to laugh. The thought was ludicrous, especially given all the times he had saved her. Still, there was a dead man in the other car, and he thought better of expressing himself. "Thank you," he said instead.

"Ironic, huh?"

"Yes, I guess that is the word," he answered as he struggled to sit up.

She dropped down next to him and put an arm behind his back to help support it.

"The other driver. He's dead."

"Dead?" she said, jerking and turning pale. "How do you know?" She glanced anxiously toward the other car, and for a moment he thought she was going to leave him to go check.

"I saw his face through the windshield right after he hit me. He was dead before it happened, I'm sure of it."

"A dead man crashed into you?"

"Yes."

"A dead man was driving that car?"

"That's what I said."

He realized that she had a cell phone when she hit a button and raised it to her ear.

"Hi, yeah, it's Cindy. There's been an accident in front of the church, and I think the one driver was dead before it happened."

She listened for a moment and then continued. "No, I don't know what killed him."

Another pause. "All right, we'll be here."

She hung up.

"You didn't just call Detective Walters, did you?" Jeremiah asked with a groan.

"I did," she said, raising her chin defiantly. "And what's wrong with that?"

"There hasn't been a murder."

"You don't know that."

"The guy probably had a heart attack while driving. It happens."

"And what if it didn't happen today?" she asked, raising an eyebrow. "Do you want to take the chance that this guy was murdered and the killer wouldn't be caught because it seemed like an accident?"

Actually he would rather a killer walk free than expose himself or his synagogue any more than he needed to to the scrutiny of the police. He squeezed his eyes closed. There was no way he could explain that to Cindy. No easy way, at least. No, whether he liked it or not, he was going to have to play the helpless victim this time and hope that it all went away quickly.

"Can you help me stand up?"

"Not until a paramedic looks you over. Mark was calling an ambulance."

"I'm fine."

"Let's leave that decision to the professionals."

He acquiesced and lay back slowly on the grass, staring up at the blue of the sky. It was March and the weather was starting to get a little warmer. A month before it would have been too cold to lie on the grass waiting. It got colder in Southern California during the winter than it had in Israel.

He heard the sirens of the ambulance, and a moment later he heard Cindy gasp.

"What's wrong?" he asked.

"I know him," she said.

"Who was he?"

"Dr. Tanner, he used to be a church member."

Of course he did, because that's my luck, Jeremiah thought. As the siren grew louder, he began to feel some of the aches and pains caused by the accident. The shock was wearing off, and he could already tell he was going to be stiff in the morning.

I'm getting soft, weak. He closed his eyes.

"You're slipping," a voice said suddenly.

He opened his eyes and saw Detective Mark Walters staring down at him.

"You think so?"

"I do, you're supposed to be the one playing good Samaritan, not her," he said, nodding toward Cindy.

Actually, she's a Gentile, Jeremiah wanted to say, but he was just grateful Mark wasn't calling him that for once. "I must be getting old," he said instead.

Mark snorted derisively, then got down on one knee. "Seriously, you okay?"

"I'll live," Jeremiah said. "I just won't be happy about it in the morning."

He saw a fleeting smile cross the detective's face before he got up and turned to look at the other car. "Let's see what we've got."

<hr/>

Cindy felt strange. She had been so confident that calling Mark was the right thing to do, but now that he was there, she felt a bit foolish. Jeremiah was right. Mel Tanner had probably had a heart attack. The man was in his upper sixties, and it would be the most logical explanation for what had happened. How could a murder victim even be driving in the first place?

Maybe he was poisoned, a small voice inside her head whispered. She bit her lip and wished that her deck of cards wasn't inside the office in her purse. She fidgeted with her fingers while she waited for Mark to look over the body.

While she waited, she watched the paramedics as they checked out Jeremiah. They began to insist on taking him to the hospital for X-rays, and he protested strenuously. To her surprise he lost the argument and with a grimace he climbed into the back of the ambulance before lying down on one of the gurneys.

"Do you want me to come to the hospital?" she asked.

"No! I don't plan on being there more than ten minutes. Besides, with our luck the nurse who thinks we're married will be on duty."

Cindy smirked at the memory of how he had lied to be admitted to see her when she had been attacked by a serial killer. The thought of a little payback appealed to her. "That's precisely why I should come. Otherwise she might be concerned that our marriage is in trouble."

"I'm glad one of us can laugh," he said.

The driver closed the door with an apologetic glance at her, then climbed into the front and drove away. She felt oddly reassured that he drove up the street at a reasonable pace without the use of lights or siren. That had to mean Jeremiah was okay.

She turned to find Mark watching her. She gave him a fleeting smile before asking "Did you find anything?"

He shook his head. "I'll have the coroner examine him, though, nail down actual cause of death."

"Thank you."

He shrugged. "Anything you can tell me about him?"

"His name is Dr. Mel Tanner. He used to go here, but now he goes to another church downtown. He's a retired physician. He's still active in the community, though."

"Thanks, I'll let you know if I need anything else. So you're not heading to the hospital?"

She shook her head.

He made a tsking sound. "Sounds like divorce court time to me."

She shook her head and rolled her eyes before turning to head back into the church.

As Cindy walked into the office and took her seat, Geanie hopped up out of her chair and walked over. "What happened?" she asked.

Cindy filled her in and watched in satisfaction as the other girl registered the same shock she herself was feeling.

"That's terrible!"

"I know. At least Jeremiah wasn't hurt, but poor Dr. Tanner."

"Going in a car crash, that's one of my nightmares," Geanie said with a shiver.

"Jeremiah told the officers that he thought Dr. Tanner was already dead," Cindy said, more to herself than Geanie.

"That's just weird."

"I know, but I guess stuff like that happens. He could have had a heart attack or something."

The front door opened, and the youth pastor walked in. "Wow, did you guys see that accident out front?" Dave asked.

"Cindy did," Geanie answered.

"What a nightmare."

"Dr. Tanner is dead," Cindy said.

Dave turned pale and sat down in one of the chairs reserved for visitors. "Are you kidding?"

"No, why would I kid about something like that?"

He buried his face in his hands, and his shoulders heaved. Geanie gave her a puzzled look as the implication hit Cindy. "He drove the bus to camp every year," she realized.

"Summer camps and winter camps. He was a wonderful man," Dave said. "So good with the kids, so patient. I never knew how he could pay attention to the road with all the noise and chaos around him."

"He was a very nice man," Cindy said, moving forward and awkwardly patting him on the shoulder.

"I'm going to call Joseph and let him know," Geanie said. "I think the two of them sat on a couple of boards together."

"Why don't you go tell him in person?" Cindy suggested. Joseph Coulter was the church's most affluent member. He and Geanie had been dating since Thanksgiving, and she was sure he'd rather hear the news from his girlfriend than from someone else.

"Thanks," Geanie said, grabbing her purse and heading for the door.

"We've almost got a full slate of kids for next weekend," Cindy said after the door had closed. "I'll work on finding you another driver."

"Thanks," Dave said, dragging himself to his feet. "A couple other churches are having retreats at the same time. I'll call around and see if any of them have room on their buses. How are we doing on the sandwiches and cookies?"

"Lunch bags for the drive up will have corned beef sandwiches courtesy of O'Connell's Pub and shamrock cookies courtesy of Safeway."

"You're a genius."

"Hey, the first day of camp is on St. Patrick's Day. It was a no-brainer."

He smiled slightly. "You've been hanging around the kids too long. You're starting to sound like them."

"There are a lot worse things to sound like," she said.

"Amen."